Blossom Gold

And Other Stories

Dan Wallace

Wylisc Press
Silver Spring, MD

Published 2021 by Wylisc Press

Blossom Gold
And Other Stories
Dan Wallace

ISBN 9781733572569 Trade Paperback
ISBN 9781733572576 E-Book
6 x 9
225 pages
Publication Date: January 2021
Cover design by Molly A. Wallace

Wylisc Press
Silver Spring, MD 20901-1205
Inthewallacemanner.com

To George
my brother,
mentor, writer,
and reader

Contents

Blossom Gold

"You're blowin' it, son, you're blowin' it!"

His manager's hawk-nosed face pushed up to his own, it was hard to think with things happening so fast. Breath was hard to catch, yet he was in great shape—the bell rang again.

He hurried out into the middle of the ring to hear at once the sound of wind and the dull "thunt" in his face, again and again. He tried to lever his own arms into their rhythm, but they seemed slowed in jello, hitting often but with never the heavy pop he expected. All arms and elbows and in return "thunt," "thunt," "thunt."

"Thunt," "thunt," "thunt."

All night long that rush of air and that "thunt" sound. Half-sound, really, and half-felt on the sour mash that was his face now, after eight or nine rounds of it. Ten rounds? He'd lost count, but his legs felt like two bars of pig iron stood on end. Roll one forward, then another only to be met by that "thunt." Then smack, and he was down. Smack.

The round was over, there was time, but he didn't have any time, anything left in his pig iron legs and pig iron arms. Sitting there, dazed, amazed by the loss of that good feeling he'd just had just a little while ago, all he could hear was that bell about to ring and that Northerner manager screaming into his head, "You're blowin' it, son, you're blownin' it!"

Sometimes when we run on a summer morning, I look up at the trees and feel like I can see the veins of leaves flicking in the slow air. I see little green dots of chlorophyll marching through them just like the films show at school. It makes me slow down, of course, and my daddy yells back at me then, "C'mon, there, Ellen, c'mon, keep it up, keep up the pace, you'll never be a champ without keepin' up." I run a little faster and he goes on telling me how he woke up last night again after the dream. I look at him like I'm paying attention until he looks ahead at the route. Then, I slow down a little bit to look at the pistils and stamens of the flowers, and the big, old bumblebees inside them, wiggling their fat behinds like an old lady rummaging through a closet. In the fall, I like to listen to the squirrels rustling through the brown leaves. In winter, I look forward to when the creek's iced over, like something out of a peaceful Christmas card. Right now, spring is peeking out just around the corner.

Daddy's dream is never different, so even though I don't listen all the time, I hear him just the same. He sweats it out just like he did twenty years ago, a long time before I was even born. He remembers it every time like he was there right now. Two times, really, whupped by Waban Wilson twice. Daddy can't forget it and here he is, running and jumping rope, sparring, and hitting the bags, heavy and speed. I watch him tap that speed bag around, pitter-patting it back and forth, up and down, whacking it against the wood up top faster than an eye can see. Daddy's good at it, even though he's old now. His red hair's kind of stringy and he has a round belly, too, maybe from beers. His big old legs are white, never getting any sun because of his carpenter's pants. But his face is red like inside a watermelon, and he has lines and bags. Still, his chest and shoulders are big, his arms are big, and he does real damage when he hits the heavy bag, taped all around the middle to cover rips from his body punches. That was his specialty, knocking the stuffing out of guys, Arliss "the Body-Breaker" Truitt.

Except, he could never catch up with Wilson. Wilson ran, Daddy told me, all around the ring backwards, throwing his right jab enough to keep the Body-Breaker away. Later on, when Daddy got tired, Wilson hit him with both hands until the ref called the fight on account of blood. Fights. The two times they fought, Wilson won both by decision. Decisions.

I'm a boxer. Momma had me, then cut out. Daddy took care of me alone, so when I grew big enough, he started to teach me the Sweet Science. That's what people call it, he said. I didn't care one way or the other, we just spent a lot of time together running and training. He got me these little gloves and shorts, and boxing shoes, too. I had so much fun with him, though he used to tell me he was going broke buying me new gear every six months. When I'm in the ring, I'm announced as Ellen "Blossom Gold" Truitt. They say Blossom Gold because of my yellow hair, I suppose.

Some people say Daddy wanted a son, which is why he teaches me how to box. I don't think that's all that true because I'm as good as any boy, though I'm no body-breaker. I just have to punch them a lot of times, keep them off balance so they can't bull rush me. When they get tired, I start pouring it on, one, two, three-shot combinations, and they quit. Of course, after a couple of fights like that, no one wants to box me. Too embarrassing to be beat by a girl, I guess. But I keep training, waiting for another chance, mostly having fun hanging around in the gym with my dad. He says he plans on setting up the old barn out back with a ring and bags, still leaving enough room to park his truck. He hasn't gotten around to it yet.

I like to go outside on my own now and then. It's kind of refreshing and relaxing, no schoolwork, no hassle from boys in the gym where I'm by myself a lot, too. They won't say anything to my face, even after I've tuned them up sparring in the ring. But those boys don't believe I belong. So, I do my workout with Daddy egging me on, I do my homework and get good grades, especially in English and earth science. Then, I head out to the woods down by Mill Creek. It's about a mile from our place, so I do my roadwork out there. I sneak my way through the big oaks, the elms, and the hickories toward the creek. The big trees gives way to tall grass just before I get to the rows of weeping willows on the creek's bank. Crickets fly in every direction leaping this way and that when I push my way through the grass.

I cross over the meadow and wade through the creek to the other bank just at the foot of Green Tree Mountain, which is part of the Monongahela National Forest. On the far side of the creek, I look around for a stump or a log to set on. Then, I keep a look out for water critters, frogs maybe, though they don't show up much except in vernal pools at the beginning of the year. Turtles are pretty common, basking on stones or logs in the water, unless some kind of commotion sends them flapping into the water. Occasionally, you can see their wakes in the water, v-shaped trails as they swim below the surface like little submarines.

Daddy is a pretty darn good cook. He says he likes it, he did all the cooking even when Momma was around. It is true, however, that Momma was not good in the kitchen. I kind of remember when she was still with us, she sat and smoked at the dinner table while Daddy whipped up an omelet or a meatloaf. Momma didn't seem to eat much, just sitting, smoking, and sipping wine out of a jar. Meanwhile, I tucked hard into Daddy's vittles, I always looked forward to his tasty treats. He comes home from work nowadays and whips up something good in no time. We both eat fast and nearly always lick our plates clean. But we wash them anyway, Daddy hunching over the sink, he's so tall. I dry and stack dishes for Daddy to put away.

Mrs. Burkhardt is my teacher, tall and boney, kind of nice brown hair, a pretty face and sharp, blue eyes but no bosom at all. Of course, I'm flat-chested myself, but I'm young and still might grow some. I think the way Mrs. Burkhardt is, though, is the way she's going to be from now on. She's really nice, nice to me and thinks I'm pretty smart. I get good grades and all, but she takes notice of me and spends more time. Once she said I ought to be in junior high, not just the fifth grade. She wants to talk to Daddy about it, but he's so busy working. It don't matter much to me, though. I like school. I think I'd be pretty happy in any classroom. I like Mrs. B a lot, though.

Every Wednesday after work, Arliss headed over to the Mill Creek Country Store for a beer. He went inside and Holden got him one without asking, usually Horlacher Imperial Pilsner. Holden popped off the cap and passed the bottle to Arliss who handed over a dollar. Then, Arliss turned to the barrel on his right, reached in, and extracted two pickles. He shook the cold water off them, pivoted around and walked to the porch outside. Waban sat there in a rocking chair, sipping his beer and taking in the vapors, as he put it. Arliss handed him one of the pickles and plopped down in the rocker next to him, sucking a long swig out of his bottle.

"How be you, Arliss?" Waban asked.

"I am fit," replied Arliss.

"As a fiddle? I think not," said Waban in a jocular tone, his eyes a bit crinkled from laugh lines. Arliss swung his head around and stared at Waban. His hair had gone gray, what was left of it, and his belly covered his legs, testament to his practice of drinking two beers to every one downed by anyone else. Always rolled up, the sleeves of Waban's flannel shirt exposed the frayed edges of his faded long johns barely covering his ham hock forearms and thick wrists. Gray hair dappled his arms, too, while gaps between his shirt buttons underscored his impressive gut, more like that of the silverback gorilla at the Louisville Zoo.

"Look at the pot calling the kettle black," said Arliss dryly, and Waban laughed out loud.

"True, I've added a few pounds, but I am in the pink." Waban took a sip, then said, "So, how is Ellen?"

"Now, she is in the pink," replied Arliss, "and I don't mean girly pink."

"Still beatin' up on the boys, huh?"

"Most of 'em stay away from her now. Sometimes a new feller tries her out and gets a red nose for his trouble."

"I'm sure he does," Waban said. "A chip off the old block."

Arliss frowned at Waban, "Now, you of all people know that ain't true."

"No, no, Arliss, you always had sand. Anybody climb in the ring with you had to run for his life, that for sure." He looked thoughtful for a moment, then uttered, "Excepting Ali, maybe, if he'd been around then. He is for sure big and fast now."

"Excepting you, too. My puss don't look like this for nothing."

Waban scrutinized it and said, "That's true, I guess. Well, we don't need to get into it again now. Just thank God Ellen don't have your good looks."

"Yeah, thank God. Got 'em from her momma, I guess." He paused, thoughts in the past for a moment. "Thank the Lord that's all she got from her."

During earth science, Mrs. Burkhardt told us all about how big the world is, "vast" she called it, with more than four billion people all living different lives from ours. She talked about how each person had their own way of thinking and doing things, that some lived near the highest mountains, Sherpas, she said. Other folks moved around from one low lying island to another paddling canoes in the Pacific Ocean, fishing and eating fruit off of trees. She said that people ate different things— she showed us a picture of one Black man smiling as he held a big worm above his mouth, and all of us kids yelled at how icky it was. Mrs. B said we shouldn't act that way, because people everywhere do different things in different places just to get by.

Some folks don't eat pigs, she said, because of religion. Mrs. Burkhardt explained then how ancient people used to get sick. After a while, they figured it was from eating pork, though they didn't know why. So, their priests told their flocks that pigs were unclean and, to stay right with the Lord, they should stop eating them. What those preachers didn't know, Mrs. Burkhardt explained was that pigs could get some kind of bug living inside them. Eating them caused people to get sick because of the bugs. Trichinosis, she called it, writing it on the chalkboard. That's how I know how to spell it. Nowadays, we know how to keep these bugs out of the hogs, which is why we can eat bacon and chops without getting sick today. Then she told us that even though we know now that pork is safe to eat, billions of people still won't eat it because of their religious beliefs.

That's when the new boy raised his hand to ask a question. He's kind of scrawny, not much bigger than me, with black hair sticking out all over of his head. His skin was pretty light with a few freckles on his face. He wore glasses, too, which didn't help. But he asked a question.

"Do all those folks live in one place, Mrs. Burkhardt? Like, on the other side of the world?"

Mrs. Burkhardt didn't answer right away. Then, she said, "Well, Martin, that's one of the good things about the world. As big as it is, you will find most people who are just alike living together in one faraway place. But you also can see some of them living right next door. America has a lot of different people living here—Orientals, Jews, Negros from Africa, Spanish folks from Mexico, Indians from India, and our own Indians right here in the US of A. Those Indians are different from each other, of course. See, America is a melting pot with folks from all over the world coming here to be free. Almost all of us right here in our classroom aren't from here originally. Our ancestors moved here long ago from everywhere around the world. My family came from England and Germany. How about you, Martin, where did your family come from?"

"Ireland. Me grandparents moved to Newcastle, and me parents came from there to New York. We moved down here for the work."

"Irish," Mrs. Burkhart said, "that's what I would have guessed, Martin, from your last name. Collins is very typically an Irish name."

Then, the new kid said, "Me ma's ma was named Smith." He shrugged, "She was German 'til she married my grandad."

"Well, there you are!" said Mrs. Burkhardt. "Smith is a common name in many countries!"

After lunch, I followed the kids out to the playground. I'm sort of a slow eater, so I'm usually last out at recess. It was a pretty nice outside, just past April Fools Day. The sun was out, and most of us wore our light spring jackets zipped up against the cool air. The playground is pretty nice, with maple trees lined up all around the blacktop, little green buds showing up on the end of their branches. Kids were jumping rope, some were sitting on swings, and a few climbed all over the monkey bars playing tag. A bunch of boys stood over at the far wall in a circle. Still munching on my apple, I moseyed on over to see what they were up to. Boys always seem to have more fun than girls, I don't know why. Maybe it was because they were allowed to wear pants.

When I got there, I heard them shouting, "Mick," "Cat-licker," ""Tater-eater," stuff like that. I peeked between the shoulders of two of them, and sure enough, the new kid stood in the middle, fists closed, his eyes running back and forth from one boy to another. He looked angry and scared at the same time. I looked around the circle of boys and saw just who I thought I would. Jesse Warner, the biggest of them, sneering as usual and doing what he was good at, ganging up on small kids. I didn't like him one bit for that and a lot of other reasons. He was as dumb as a fence post, held back a couple of grades. That was okay, but he was mean, especially to kids littler than him. He kept it up, egging on the other boys, moving them in closer.

I wondered if I should go get a monitor, when the new kid said, "Ye'r a mighty fearful feller with your gang all beside ya'. Why don't ya' try me yerself?"

Jesse's face turned red as a beet. He moved forward, growling, "Why, you little—" and the new boy jumped up and planted one right on his honker. Jesse howled like a stuck pig, covering his beak with both hands while the new kid punched him again and again in his belly. Jesse fell back, but I could see that the body shots weren't hurting him much and I feared what would happen next. Sure enough, Jesse swung a round house that hit the new kid square, sending his eyeglasses flying. Jesse threw his arms around him and flung him to the asphalt. He quickly sat on him and started whaling with both hands.

I didn't have time to get anyone then, so I hopped over, grabbed Jesse's neck with both hands from behind and squeezed. He stopped throwing punches to try and get me while I pulled him off. He turned, yelling what he was going to do, until he saw it was me.

"Cut it out, Jesse, leave him alone," I said as I bounced away.

Up on his feet, now, he kept his distance as he said, "I ought to smack you, Ellen, for what you done."

I nodded, "Sure, Jesse, because I'm little, too, just like the new kid? 'Course, you didn't do so good last time."

"Yeah, but I'm getting' to be a lot more, now, and you ain't grown an inch."

I kind of shook my head sadly, "Think that counts? I got to say, Jesse, you are the sorriest bully I ever seen. We can fight now but if we do, a teacher will probably stop it. I'll get sent home with a note, I suppose. I'm just a skinny little girl, right? But you? They'll keep you after school no matter how bad I bust your puss."

Jesse's big round face got red again, the color of his big, fat sore nose. His eyes, all tiny and slit, showed how much he hated me. He ran his hand back over his mud-colored hair, then said, "You're lucky, Truitt. I been held after school too much already. If I kick your butt this time, they might suspend me. I don't want no beatin' by my pop, so I'm gonna let it go for now. But I'll see you come next Golden Gloves."

I smiled, "See you then, boy."

He and his gang drifted off back toward the building, since the bell was about to ring.

I guessed right that Jesse wouldn't fight. He was bigger, no question, but still slow. I could move around and jab him like I did back in January. But, if he bull-rushed me, it could be a problem. Well, that would be for later, I thought. For now, he left me alone.

"Ta'," said a voice next to me. Surprised, I turned to find the new kid standing next to me smiling. "He's a big boy, I thought I was a goner for a bit. I shoulda stayed away from him, I guess. So, t'anks for bailing me out."

I stared at him. His glasses were twisted some but not broken. Up close, I saw that his eyes were blue-green, different from anyone I knew.

"Do you box?"

"Box? You mean fight? No. Me da' showed me a few t'ings, like always hit 'em in the nose, make their eyes water so they can't see. Hurt's like the devil, too. That was a long time ago when I was little. He's long gone, now. But b'geezus, I can't see well enough myself without my goggles. Sad, too, kids are always teasing me about 'em. You know, four eyes and all. Gets me into a lot of scrapes. Well, if I can't fight, I can always run," he laughed. I laughed too.

"Well, there goes the bell," he said. "See you… what's your name?"

"Ellen. Truitt."

He dropped his chin, "Marty Collins. Nice to meet you, Ellie."

And off he ran.

They performed the cavity search and as usual found nothing on or in him. Robert Redding stepped into the gang shower with spigots all around hanging from blue-green tiled walls, the grout turned black from grime and age. The only one there, Redding crossed to the farthest shower head and twisted the lever to release a stream of cold water. He stood to the side, waiting until the spray turned steaming hot, then stepped in. He grabbed a bar of soap from a shelf beneath the spout and started rubbing it on his hair and face, then quickly moving to his neck and arms. As he scrubbed his arms and chest, one of the two guards called to him, "Five minutes." Redding nodded and worked down to his torso and legs. He lifted his feet to wash them in turn, left first, then right. He placed the soap back on the shelf, rinsed quickly, and shut the water off.

One of the guards tossed him a towel, and he dried himself briskly. The other guard motioned him over outside of the shower. A clean orange jumpsuit lay folded on a chair along with clean shorts, socks, and a white t-shirt. Redding put them, on, slipped on his shoes, and stood up. The beefy red-haired guard named Teddy stooped over and put shackles on his legs. He stood up and cuffed Robert's wrists. "Okay, inmate, march."

They walked down the hallway, Teddy in front, and the other guard

Leroy, a big Black man, trailed behind. As they passed through one gate after another, stopping for another search at each one, Redding wondered why. Tall and lean, with stringy muscles and a concave stomach, he didn't particularly pose a physical threat. True, others might dispute this assessment given his history and especially his recent sins. But Teddy and Leroy were experienced bulls who spent every day handling violent offenders. They weren't fazed by him. So, what was it?

"No one wants anything to happen to you," said Teddy when Redding asked.

"Now, how's anything gonna happen. I'm in lockdown all the time. Even if someone is out for me, which raises another question, 'Who?' there isn't any way they can get to me. How is anyone supposed to get past you and Leroy or anyone else on the job here?"

Teddy said, "It's like this. If you was to off yourself in our custody, that would be bad for the warden, especially considering all the publicity and all."

Robert scrunched up his brows in bewilderment. "How can he be worried about that? I mean, considering what's going to happen to me, my choice."

His mind flew back to the courtroom when the judge asked for his plea, and the utter surprise that crossed the magistrate's face at his reply.

"Really? You sure you don't want to consult with your attorney, Mr. Redding? You realize what you are asking for?"

"I do, your honor. What I have done," he said, pausing to compose himself. "What I have done, I have done terrible things. I should never be allowed to walk free again, ever. But I can't spend another day in jail either, judge, I cannot. So, my only recourse is to request the ultimate penalty for my crimes, for which I am very sorry. I would like it to happen as soon as possible."

His decision created a sensation, of course, which kept growing and growing every step along the way. He refused the ACLU's offer to appeal and resented the many attempts by his brother and mother to have his sentence commuted. The headlines really exploded when instead of lethal injection, he chose execution by firing squad. Considering all this, why would anybody think that he suddenly wanted to commit suicide?

The whole deal dragged on, though, in spite of his wants. He had to go back to court a few times to say his mind was made up. Bottom-feeders showed up, too, reporters wanting exclusive interviews, eager with the questions like, "When you shot those young store clerks on the floor in the back of their heads, how'd you feel Mr. Redding? One of those young men was just twenty-one with a wife and a child. How did you feel when you learned that?"

Robert blew out his breath. The love of his life, Audrey had left him when she found his pistol. She took the kids and left him, and he proved her right by shooting those fellows. After he found her gone with the kids, he started drinking. He knew he was going to do something that night. She was right to go, which was killing him now. Why should he go through it all over again just so some lowlife can brag that he got the goods on Robert Redding?

The requests became more interesting when they started offering money. Suddenly, he needed his lawyer after all, to cut the deals. First, *Look* magazine stepped up, followed by a slicker who wanted the book and movie rights. Sure, he said, if the price was right. It killed time while he was waiting, and now he had something to leave to his mom and brother, and Audrey, too. The attorney got a will written for him, but until bleeding hearts stopped trying to save him, he was sitting upon a boatload of dough and nowhere to spend it.

Then, the letter arrived.

Arliss moved around the roof with a mouthful of tacks. He put a square of tarpaper in place and quickly extracted the tacks one by one, hammering them in a precise pattern until the paper was secured to the plywood. Once he'd finished laying down the tarpaper, he could nail down the wood shingles, overlapping them to ensure that snow and rainwater would run off. The house would be as dry as the desert in all kinds of weather, and he would get paid.

He liked working on rooftops in the springtime. From this vantage point on top of a house built into the side of a hill, he could see the stream and the mountain across the road leading into town. With just about a thousand residents, most of the buildings faced each other on the one main street. He could watch his neighbors strolling up and down the walks on their way to the baker, the bank, the hardware store, or the only car dealer just at the end of the north side. He just as easily could turn to Green Tree Mountain to watch hawks swooping down out of the sky, or buzzards floating above ready to deal with the leftovers. Add the sun and blue sky overhead and a person on a rooftop sometimes might feel like he lived in paradise on earth.

"Yo, Arliss." A voice called from below. The owner Joe McElhenny stood gazing up, his hand in an informal salute to block the sunlight. "Can you come down for a minute?"

Arliss clambered down the roof side onto the ladder. He scooted down, hopping off the third rung from the bottom to face Joe. "What's up?"

"How far you along on the paper?" Joe asked.

"I'll be done before lunch and ready to start shingling this afternoon. Why?"

A long man with a sandy mustache, Joe seemed a bit ill at ease.

"I got some bad news. Amalgamated just laid me off. They're closing the Ripple panel. Don't know how long I'll be out of work. So, I can't pay you no more."

Arliss frowned. "You're kidding me, Joe," he said, even though he knew he wasn't.

Joe swung his head, "I wish I was Arliss. But, I ain't." He stammered slightly, "I'm real sorry 'bout this, Arliss, I really am. I wish I could pay up, but I can't right now, what with Betty and the kids and all. I swear, as soon as I go back, I'll pay you with interest. I swear to

God almighty."

He dipped his head while looking up like he was ready to flinch. Arliss knew that he'd never get paid, never mind interest. With a wife and four kids, no matter when he was called back, Joe would never have the money. He tightened his lips, slightly shaking his head.

"You ain't mad are you, Arliss?" Joe ventured.

"No, Joe. I ain't mad. This stuff happens all the time. Hell, that's why I got out of the mines. Never know when they'd leave us high and dry." Arliss sighed. "I'll finish up the tarpaper. That'll keep your roof dry 'til you can shingle it yourself."

"You got a big heart, Arliss. I'll remember this."

"That's all right, Joe. Lemme get back up the ladder, get this done."

After he finished tacking down the tarpaper, he climbed into his pickup and turned it over again and again a few times until it roared to life. A '57 Ford, he'd bought it back then after his last fight, making his mind up never to go back into the mines or the ring. Rather than do either he decided he'd rather live hand to mouth as a handyman. What he didn't know was that every time the mining companies triggered a layoff, he'd lose work. Now, he might be out of work again if he couldn't find any with the miners being out. Some of them would offer cheaper competition, too. His line of work wasn't rocket science.

That's what finally spurred Millie to leave them. He couldn't blame her, he supposed, she just got worn out by becoming poor again overnight. Though, it was wrong to leave Ellen without a momma, he thought. He'd done the best he could by Ellen, but she was growing up and there was plenty a momma could do to help her along now. And, he had no money coming in.

He pulled up to Waban's store. Before he could go in to get the beer and pickles, Waban waved a bottle and a dill at him to show that he'd already fetched them. Arliss dropped into his rocker.

"You late, boy," Waban said. "What kept you?"

"Oh, Joe McElhenny stiffed me. Amalgamated just closed the Ripple shaft, played out, I guess. Or maybe people ain't buyin' as much coal anymore. No matter, Joe don't have the money. So, I'm stuck."

Waban sat up. "You say Amalgamated called a layoff? You think a lot of boys be out of work, now?"

Arliss raised and dropped his shoulders. "The Ripple shifts, anyways."

"Damn," Waban spat. "That's gonna hurt my trade."

"At least you've got trade," Arliss said sourly. "I'm getting stiffed, and all them boys will be looking for the odd job to keep things together. I'm double screwed. Your store ain't goin' anywhere."

"You don't understand. I'm deep in the red with the store."

Arliss turned to look directly at Waban, his eyebrows knit, puzzled. "How can you be in the red? That store made you a rich man in this town. It is what they call a cash cow. Hell, you even own cows!"

Waban shook his head rapidly, "Not lately. All them big box stores around here now, they're killing me. I've been puttin' back into the store, hoping things will change. But, they ain't and now I'm just about broke. Shit, I had to sell my cows!"

Arliss stared at Waban as though he was a madman. Broke? How could he be broke with his country store the place everyone went to for the past twenty years? Arliss always resented Waban and his store, bought with his winnings beating Arliss the last time. Here, I am, running a twenty-year-old, broke-down truck, he thought, while Waban had managed to screw up an ATM like the store. Just like the man says, who loses money owning a casino? If I'd had that money and opened a store, I wouldn't of lost it no matter what.

Maybe he was being too hard on Waban. Situated right between the brick courthouse and the post office, the big chain store had changed things for sure. Anyone else owning Waban's little convenience setup would have suffered. What really bothered him, Arliss had to admit himself, was dredging up the memory of losing the fight that many years ago.

He shook his head, "I don't know what to tell you, Waban. Times are tough all around."

"It seems they're always tough all around."

"That's the truth, Waban, that it is."

The new boy Marty smiled at me uneasily, sort of like he was guilty of something and didn't want to tell me.

"Me ma and me are moving on," he said.

I was surprised. "You just come here a couple of weeks ago. Why're you moving so soon?"

He smiled in a silly way, "Me ma was let go at the diner. We have folks in Chicago, so we're going there for work."

"Oh."

"Yeah." He smiled again but didn't seem to have anything more to say. I smiled back a little and he said a quick, "Bye, Ellie," and walked back to the classroom.

After recess, I saw him sitting there, looking at Mrs. B. for a while, then out the window. She was talking about mountains, how they were wrinkles in the earth's crust folded so they just about reached the sky. The opposite was true of valleys. One was called an anticline, the other a syncline. Marty seemed to be half-paying attention, and so was I. At the end of the day, he got up and walked out of the room and the school back toward his place down the street.

Waban didn't wait for Arliss to get out of his truck. What now, Arliss thought. He'd been soured on everything since Amalgamated closed the Ripple longwall operation a month ago. The last thing he wanted to hear was Waban flapping his mouth. Of course, Waban had doubled his volume of flapping. While Arliss still sat in his pickup, Waban held a newspaper up to Arliss through his side window. Arliss rolled it down while Waban lifted the paper up folded in half to highlight one short article at the bottom of the page. "Legendary West Virginia Fight Two Decades Old."

Arliss slumped a little back into the seat of his truck. He'd forgotten what day it was. Every year on this date and the other, he skipped Waban's store, opting to fish or hunt instead. The layoff and his own worries distracted him this year, which gave Waban the opportunity to ride him again. Of course, his old foe wouldn't let it go no matter what, not on the twentieth anniversary, not when it was written up in the Herald Dispatch. He'd keep it to wave in Arliss' face as long as it took for him to return to the store. Hell, thought Arliss, if he got tired of waiting, he might even bring it on over to his house. Why not?

"Waban," Arliss sighed, "can't you let it go? It's long over."

"Sure," said Waban, "it's over and done, but, look. We' still famous around here, we' still remembered by folks!"

"And you won."

"Aw, hell, Arliss it could'a gone either way and we did all right, got out of the mines, had ourselves some nice little lives 'til lately. But look at this!"

He pushed the paper closer to Arliss, his finger under the last paragraph.

> The last fight between those two young men born and raised in God's Country will live forever in the memories of those who saw them battle. Their clash evoked the same fervor and commitment as any two brothers who met in mortal combat on opposite sides during the war to preserve the Union. Like those honorable opponents, Waban Wilson and Arliss Truitt shall not be forgotten. In fact, I warrant that many who saw these noble warriors fight then would pay good money this very day to see them reprise their magnificent mêlée.

"You see that?" Waban asked.

"Yeah, we threw down pretty hard," said Arliss.

"No, no, Arliss, the last line. Many would pay good money to see them 'reprise their magnificent mêlée.' You know what that means?

People would come see us fight again, they'd pay!"

"You're crazy, Waban, no one's gonna pay to see a couple of fat hillbillies go at it again? Why they probably be there just to see which one of us falls over first dead from a heart attack."

"No, Arliss, they'd come. Like that computer fight between Ali Clay and Rocky Marciano! Ali's fat and out of shape while waitin' for the judges to decide about his war objection, and Marciano's so old they had to put a wig on his head."

"He was about our age then, Waban."

"Maybe so," Waban replied, "But folks still anted up in droves to see them fight. They'd come see us in Huntington again, Arliss, I bet they would!"

Arliss pressed his lips together in a pained expression. "I don't think so, Waban. Why dig up all that again? It's twenty years past and gone."

"The money, Arliss," Waban said, "We could make some money."

"No," Arliss said, "I don't want to look like a fool out there."

Waban said, "The money, Arliss. We can use that money, Arliss, I need that money or I'm going to lose the store. You need it, too, to take care of Ellen."

Arliss didn't reply, still skeptical, and Waban said, "You won't look bad out there, Arliss. Hell, you been running and sparring all this time. You'll be fine." Waban paused, then said, "Listen, if you're not doing too well, I'll go down for the count."

Arliss suddenly stiffened.

"It don't matter who wins, Arliss, as long as we make a few bucks. You'll need it, too, if they don't open the Ripple panel up again."

Arliss stared at Waban, his eyes steel.

"What do you say, Arliss?" Waban asked again plaintively.

"You set it up," said Arliss, "I'll fight you."

"Well, okay then!" Waban said, smiling broadly. "I think I know a guy in Huntington. Meantime, let's go get us a beer!"

"That's all right, Waban," Arliss said softly, "I gotta go pick up

Ellen at school. We're going to the gym to work out."

With spring full on, school seemed to drag along lately. Most of the kids took turns laying their heads on their desks covering their eyes with their arms, they were so bored. Even Mrs. Burkhardt had trouble keeping everyone's attention. I have to say, even I wasn't listening to her all the time. It was kind of embarrassing when she called on me to say something about what she just said, and I had no clue what it was. She seemed kind of hurt when I stumbled around trying to answer. So, I decided to try harder and I made an effort. But, somehow, learning all that stuff just didn't grab me right then. I don't know why.

"All right, class," she said. "We've talked about how people live in far-off lands, and how we live here in the USA. Still, you really can't learn about these folks or their countries without going there and meeting them. Naturally, that's not possible right now. You all need to stay in school to learn your other subjects. But, there is a way," she said, her eyes looking a bit naughty.

Mrs. Burkhardt stepped to her desk and picked up a pile of papers, which she started handing out as she strolled up and down the aisles.

"This is an information sheet from the International Society of Pen Pals," she said as she walked. "It tells you how you can apply to find a pen pal anywhere in the world."

"What's a pen pal?" one of the kids asked.

"A pen pal is someone you write a letter to, and he or she writes back to you. If you like their letters, you can write to them again. They write back to you, and so on, until you become friends, pals—pen pals! So, if you write to someone in India, you can learn all about what school is like for them, what they eat, what they wear, their favorite things to do, and anything else about how they live. And, you can tell them the same things about yourself here. It's fun and educational."

Some of the kids groaned, but Mrs. B. hushed them up and explained how to fill out the form and write to embassies for pen pal names. Most of us didn't know what an embassy was until she told us.

Kids complained so much about how much it would cost sending letters so far away that she said we could pick people in other states. My guess was that most of us would do that.

I went home after school and wondered about who I would write to. I didn't really know because I didn't really know anyone except my daddy and some of his friends. I liked Mrs. Burkhardt, but I only saw her at school. Daddy wasn't home, so I laid on the couch, thinking. After a while, I figured out that I couldn't think of anyone and I felt kind of lonely about it.

I swung myself up and saw a newspaper on the table that we ate on and where I did my homework. I opened it and paged through, looking for something that might get me going on this pen pal project. The front-page headline warned about something called stagflation, and I had no idea what it meant, maybe a buck breaking wind? I read a little and got lost in percentage forecasts and unemployment rates. The article next to it listed upcoming 4-H contests with a picture of last year's winning hog, a big Yorkshire. I kept on looking, but there really wasn't much there. So, I turned on the TV to see what it had to offer. I saw one of the commercials about the Olympics up in Canada. They showed all these great American athletes, runners, jumpers, and some boxers. Someday I'm going to fight in the Olympics, I thought.

The afternoon news came on, starting with a story about the peanut farmer from Georgia winning some kind of caucus. I remember my dad and Uncle Waban laughing together, talking about how after all these years it looked like a good old boy, one of their own, was gonna be president of these United States. Some more stories went by, not much to interest me, though. Then, halfway through the show, a story came on about a man who killed two other men in a store. He shot them dead and was convicted of murder for it and sentenced to die. I never saw anything like it except on detective shows and the like. I never thought that people really could kill other people like that, and for it that they would be killed themselves. It bothered me so much.

The newsman said that the killer was very sorry and wanted to be executed by firing squad, something of a shocking choice, said the newsman. The show switched then to this fellow, tall and skinny in a gray jumpsuit, his hair a horsetail falling all over his eyes. He pushed it out of the way as he talked, "It is my right to decide whether to live or die for what I've done, and I have made my choice. I am forever sorry for it, I deeply apologize to their families and take full blame for their pain. Therefore, I have determined to leave this Earth, and I object to any and all attempts to delay this happening."

I stared at his long, yellowy tan face, scarred up with pock marks, and his snaggly teeth. Then I noticed his eyes, shiny gray and sharp set in eggshell white all around them. He looked sad to me, lonely.

Waban stopped off at the house, a simple clapboard place, one floor, four rooms, and a bath. Arliss stood inside, the screen door opened a few inches.

"You ain't gonna believe this, Arliss, but it's happening! We're gonna fight on June 10th in the old Huntington Fieldhouse, the main event! They're planning on a few bouts before us, a couple of amateur matches, and one pro fight featuring the town's favorite son. After that, we'll square off. And the money, you ain't gonna believe it, a guaranteed ten grand for the winner, seven for second place, plus three percent of the gate! This could solve a lot of our problems, Arliss."

Arliss said, "Two months. Think you can get in shape in two months, Waban?"

Waban seemed a bit disquieted. "I don't know, who cares? The money's guaranteed."

"That's good," Arliss said, "but you might want to do some training. You never know what might happen in the ring. You know, 'protect yourself at all times.'"

Waban's smile slowly disappeared. "Okay," he said evenly, "that's always good advice."

"I'll be seeing you, Waban," Arliss said.

He examined the envelope, noting that it came from Mill Creek, West Virginia, the writing big and carefully neat. It was addressed to him also in large, fastidious script, Mr. Robert Redding, Utah State Prison, Utah. A simple address, yet it got here.

Usually, he took one look at letters and threw them out without opening the envelope. This time, he tore it open.

> Robert Redding
> Utah State Prison, Utah
>
> Dear Mr. Redding,
>
> I am an 11-year-old girl living in West Virginia. I read about you in the newspaper and I must say I do not understand why you did what you did. Everyone I know says that life is precious and you should not kill. I can understand that when I run down by the creek and see all the animals and birds and how pretty they are. But we kill lots of things to eat. I saw a 4-H pig that won last year and he probably was slaughtered to eat. It is wrong to kill people, but in some places, cannibals eat people who they have killed.
>
> I don't know why you murdered those poor men. You said on TV were sorry and if you really mean it our reverend says Jesus can forgive all sins. You look lonely, too and I know how that feels sometimes. Sometimes I am lonely but my daddy and his friends make me feel better a lot. Maybe you don't have a daddy or other friends to help you. I don't know if that is why you killed those poor men, but I am sorry for them and for you. Please write back if you want to.
>
> Sincerely
> Ellen Truitt
>
> P.S. I am a boxer. I am the only girl boxer but I beat the other

> boy boxers at the junior Golden Gloves. It would be nice to be friends.

Robert read it again, then searched the envelope for an address. He reread the letter once more and put it down. He yelled out for the guard to bring him some paper and a pen.

School years goes by pretty quickly. I'll be in junior high school next year, a big change, I'm guessing. Our schools aren't all that big and they're right next to each other. Still, I look at the older kids and a lot of them seem like grownups. They walk by us little kids like we aren't there. I don't believe they're being mean, just deep in their own thinking. Sometimes I wonder if I'll be like them when I'm older, looking serious all the time. Except for when they're cutting up.

Summer was hiding just around the corner and all of us kids were getting super antsy, ready for school to be over until next year. The weather turned so nice, we could hardly stand being indoors at all. I found myself sighing a lot, wishing I was down by the creek lying on the new meadow grass. Every now and then I wondered how Marty Collins was doing in Chicago. I bet it was still cold there. I didn't think about him all that much, though. I just wondered once in a while.

Mrs. Burkhardt reminded us that our pen pal project was due the next day. The whole class was surprised, how did six weeks go by so fast? Now, we all had to hurry getting copies of our letters together and putting them in order with those we got from our pen pals. Most of the kids had just a few from different states. A couple had only one or two, but they were from foreign countries, which meant that Mrs. B. would be sure to give them 100 percent.

I expected to get 100, too, because Robert had written back to me half a dozen times. I didn't think anyone else would have more letters to show and Mrs. B surely would be amazed. I thought so anyway. Then, I started thinking if handing in letters from a famous murderer was a good idea. People might get the wrong notion. I didn't have much choice though, because if I didn't give them to Mrs. B, I would get a bad grade. Good grades were important to Daddy and they were important to me, too. So, the next day, I handed them in.

Mary Beth Burkhardt looked forward to reading every one of Ellen's writing assignments. For an eleven-year old, she possessed an amazing internal life. Everything Ellen wrote surprised Mary Beth, but it always seemed so natural after she'd finished reading. For the pen pal project, Mary Beth worked her way through the other students' work, saving Ellen's collection for last.

Most of the other students wrote pretty much the same things, simple and mundane— "My name is …," "I am a student at …," "I like to …," "What do you like?" "Please write back." Rudimentary responses followed. The student's next letter, if there was one, covered the basics of life in Mill Creek, West Virginia. "My daddy works at …," "I like to hunt and fish …," "Do you hunt or fish?" and the like. She thought the international exchanges by two of her students might be more fun and read the first overseas reply, "I don't hunt, I live in Dusseldorf."

She sighed, then smiled as she centered Ellen's letters in front of her. After reading Ellen's first letter, her smile faded. It disappeared altogether when she read the return letter from Robert Redding.

> Dear Ellen,
>
> I am glad I read your letter. I get plenty others which I usually toss. Most people write telling how sorry they are for me as if they cared. Then right away they start asking questions about what I did. They all just want to freak out like people gawking at car wrecks. So I stopped reading them. But your letter caught my eye. You didn't make a big deal out of me with all sorts of questions. You just seemed friendly, like a breath of fresh air here.
>
> I was surprised to read you are a boxer. Girls don't usually do that. I was really amazed how you beat eight boys in the

Golden Gloves. You knocked them all out, that is amazing! You must be a very special person.

So, keep up the good work. Try to do good whatever you do. I'll tell you the truth. Truth is always best anyway. I did terrible things and hurt a lot of people. I think about it every day. I had my troubles when I was young but I wasted my life when I should have done better. I have some brains and I could have done other things. But I took the easy way out. I am not a nice person and now I must pay the price. I don't want to cause any more harm. You want to be my pen pal, which is okay. If there is anything to learn from me, it is to choose the opposite direction of how I lived.

Sincerely,
Robert Redding

P.S. You can call me Robert.

Mary Beth sat stunned. Oh my Lord, she said to herself. Horrified by what she had read, she quickly flipped the page to read Ellen's reply.

Dear Mr. Robert,

I am very happy that you now are my pen pal. I thank you for the things you wrote in your letter. I will take to heart your advice, I understand that you did very bad things. But I know that there is good in everyone, our reverend tells us this every Sunday. You are repenting so after your punishment you probably will go to heaven. I hope so.

Also, thank you for your nice words about my fighting career. Because you wish me to be good all the time, I have decided to dedicate all of my fights to you next spring. My daddy is a fighter and he has a big fight coming up in June. It is really special and he has been training hard to win. He lost the last two times. I go running and working out in the gym with him. I run by myself a lot to school, three miles. On weekends I run down by Mill Creek and sometimes up Green Tree Mountain. Last time I saw Mr. Wilson, Uncle Waban to me, running up too, really slow and puffing. I was surprised, he's my Daddy's friend and they drink beer together. He's who my Daddy fights come June. Uncle Waban is the one who beat Daddy twice twenty years ago, way long before I was born.

Last week I sparred with another local kid Jesse Warner who I beat pretty good last spring. He thought he was all that and everything, but I peppered him until he quit back then. So I wasn't worried sparring with him except he barreled in hard and walloped me with a wild haymaker. I fell flat on my bottom first time ever. It was embarrassing. I got up moved in quick and hit him right below his breadbasket. When he dropped his gloves, I hit him one, two, three, and he backed up. He was done, so I quit. I was surprised though when he knocked me on the floor.

That's all I have to write. I will try to think of more next time.

Sincerely,
Ellen Truitt

Mary Beth hurriedly shuffled through the wad of letters until she found the last one sent by Redding.

Dear Blossom Gold,

I loved getting your last letter, baby girl. It's great to know you are the best and I feel like we're growing closer. In your last letter you asked me what my favorite animal is, so see if you can guess.

Tiger, tiger, burning bright,
In the forest of the night.

Neat, huh? It was written by an old poet from long ago, William Blake. He wrote a plenty of cools stuff, mysterious and spiritual, and drew some really cool pictures to go with it. I read him when I was sent to the pen one time and got bored. His poems surprised me, I could see myself in a lot of what he said. Well, it's getting late, honey. I love you Ellen baby and hope you write back right away.

Love,
Robert

"Oh my God, oh my God," Mary Beth uttered, clutching the letters close to her breast. "Oh my God."

Arliss found her sitting on the front steps when he returned from the gym. He felt awkward, standing in front of her his face and body glistening, his old sweatpants and shirt wet with perspiration. He hadn't bothered shaving that morning, either, figuring then what was the point? He also never expected Ellen's favorite teacher to show up on his porch.

He gripped his left bicep and started squeezing as he said, "Mrs. Burkhardt, nice to see you. Sorry I'm kind of a mess, I been working out at the gym. A little surprised to see you here, actually. Ellen up to no good?" he asked with a big grin. It melted away when she didn't smile back, instead her eyes showing alarm.

"What's wrong?" he asked.

Mary Beth stood and held a sheaf of papers out to Arliss. "Mr. Truitt, these are letters Ellen has been writing as part of a class project. The children's assignment was to find a person living far away to become their pen pal. When I read Ellen's letters, I became very concerned."

Arliss took hold of the letters, wondering how in all the world Ellen could be a matter of concern. "All right," he said, "why don't we go inside so I can take a look at these?"

She nodded.

Inside, he apologized for the clutter, sat her down on the couch in front of the TV, then offered her some ice tea. He went into the kitchen and washed his face and hands before pouring the tea. When he returned, she had picked up the letters again.

"Mr. Truitt, please read these, they are so disturbing."

Arliss handed her the glass and sat next to her. He started working his way through the letters, confused at first about what he was reading.

"Who is this," he murmured, "Robert Redding?"

Mary Beth remained silent. She watched him as slowly, painfully, it dawned upon him.

"This is the guy," he said haltingly, "the guy who killed those gas station clerks." He stared up at Mary Beth, "He's going to be shot by a firing squad."

She saw his utter bewilderment turning into agony and she said quickly, "I'm so sorry Mr. Truitt, truly sorry. I had no idea my project would lead to this, I thought it would be fun. Please forgive me!"

"Fuh…," he breathed, looking into the air. He shifted his sight back to Mrs. Burkhardt. "How did she find him? How'd she know where to write him?"

Mary Beth shrugged, "She just sent them care of his prison. And, he wrote back."

Arliss expelled air again. "Holy…, now what?"

Mary Beth drew closer, "You have to stop her, Mr. Arliss. This could be so dangerous. What if he escaped?"

Arliss eyed her skeptically. She looked to be pretty young, skinny, with dull brown hair. The kids called her Mrs. Burkhardt, of course, though everyone knew she was divorced. Maybe she was a mouse, he thought, but she still cared plenty for his little girl. And Ellen cared heaps for her, too.

"I don't think Redding is going to break out of jail anytime soon," he said. "I don't think he's going to be walking anywhere much longer."

"Yes, but his letters are so creepy!" she said. Imploringly, she went on, "You're right, Mr. Truitt, he probably won't get out. But these letters he's sending are bad for her, they might cause permanent damage. She's only eleven!"

Arliss screwed up his face sourly. "I suppose so. She won't like it." He glanced back at Mary Beth. "How you going to handle it in school? Looks like she worked hard on it."

She shook her head, "Always. She always works hard. I'll give her 100, naturally, but I won't return her work. I'll tell all of the students that I want to keep the letters to show other students next year. She won't feel singled out."

"That's great, Mrs. Burkhardt, I appreciate that. And, thank you for bringing all this to my attention."

"Of course, Mr. Truitt. I'm so relieved that you know. She'll understand eventually. She thinks the world of you."

He smiled shyly, "I'd like to think so. But you are her favorite teacher. You do know that, don't you?"

She smiled slightly herself. "It's a mutual admiration society."

Arliss walked her to the door and watched her for a while as she disappeared down the street. Just as she left his sight, Ellen strolled up the walk to the house.

"Hi, Daddy, how'd training go?"

Damn, he said to himself.

Robert Redding paced his cell. Ellen hadn't written him for days and time passed. He asked Teddy every day if there were any letters, but none arrived. He pretended to wonder what had happened to Ellen, but he had it figured out really. Her daddy had found out about their correspondence and forbade her to write him anymore. He did wonder then if she'd been allowed at least to read his last letters. The whole deal maddened him, he thought. It was the only thing he wanted to do now, especially since Audrey didn't come to see him one time since he'd been locked up, never mind bringing the kids. Things here had become an annoying waste of time, with his brother and mother always coming around trying to change his mind. Almost every fucking day, for Christ sake. Through all of this noise, little Ellen was the only one who was pure, sweet little Ellen. All he wanted to do was talk to her, to tell her how he felt. She was the only one who understood.

He did twenty more laps up and down the ten-foot cell, sometimes wringing his hands, sometimes clutching them into fists. He stopped and shook them out, trying to calm himself down. The frustration, though, he thought, and off on another circuit he'd go.

Teddy rapped the cell door bars to get his attention. He stopped and looked at the guard, belly falling out of his shirt and pants. "You got a visitor," Teddy said.

"If it's my brother or my ma, I don't want to see them."

Teddy shook his head, "It ain't them."

Redding perked up. Ellen, maybe?

"It's that Tinsel Town producer agent guy of yours, wanting to talk to you again."

"Fucking ghoul, all of 'em. Tell him to go stick it up his ass."

"I tell him that's what you're gonna say, but he keeps insisting. Says he feels sympathy for you," Teddy muttered sarcastically. "How 'bout that?"

Redding stabbed him with a look. The guard continued in a sheepish voice, "Anyway, he says he can get you a lot more money now for your story. You could leave a helluva lot more behind for your kin, your mama."

Impatient, Redding started to tell Teddy to get lost when he had another thought. "He said he'd get me more money?"

"That's what he said," Teddy nodded.

Redding rubbed the bristles on his chin, a three-day growth. "Let's go see him," he said.

"All right. Lemme get the shackles."

I was pretty embarrassed when Daddy showed me the letters, asking me what was up. To be honest, I was sort of shocked that it was such a big thing. When I read Robert's letters, it was plain to me that he was lonely and that he could use a friend that didn't keep oohing and aahing over him like a monster. He had done awful things and there was no forgiving him on earth. At least, he saw it that way. But he believed that God would forgive him and save him from doing hurtful things again. I felt so sorry for him, I just wanted to make him feel better. I didn't understand why Daddy got all huffed up about how friendly Robert had gotten. Geez, Daddy called me baby girl and honey all the time. True, Robert wasn't my daddy, but he was my friend.

Anyway, I wasn't allowed to write Robert anymore or read his letters. To be honest, I'd hustle back home after school to see if Daddy was around and if the mail had arrived. I couldn't get them all, but I managed to pick off a few letters from Robert before Daddy got them and burned them. In one, he said he'd come into some money and that I should look forward to getting something nice from him before too long. I dared not write him back, though, in case he wrote something about my letter in his reply. If Daddy read Robert's letters before he dumped them, he'd find out about mine and I would really be in Dutch. So, I just waited to see what the surprise was that Robert would be sending me.

Things had gotten tighter in Mill Creek. The Ripple panel had been shut down for more than a month, now, and no end in sight. The whole town worried, those with jobs as much as those without. Everyone wondered if shuttering the Ripple marked just the beginning, that Amalgamated planned on pulling out altogether like in other towns up and down the coal belt. In the meantime Arliss had run out of jobs completely. Even if folks needed work done, they put it off, waiting to see how things played out. He already started dipping into his savings, paltry as they were. He foreswore that he would stay away from Ellen's college fund. Except, how long could he do that if Mill Creek looked to shrink and fade away? He worried his lip nearly raw, looping thoughts over and over again. The fight was still a month and a half off, and he could use that money now. Could they hold out that long?

Rather than waste gas in the truck, he jogged into Mill Creek like every day now. He'd make the rounds up and down the street, hoping to catch on for a day's work. Except a host of laid-off miners stalked the streets, too. Sometimes they annoyed him since they collected unemployment while he and Ellen lived hand to mouth. Then, he'd feel guilty, knowing that most of them had a bunch of kids to feed and a check from the gov didn't go all that far. He ran his hand through his hair again wondering what would happen.

"Hey, Arliss."

He looked up to see Waban opposite him, standing with his hands in his pockets.

"Looking for work?"

"Trying to," said Arliss.

"Yeah, I'm hard up, too. The store's a ghost town these days."

"Sorry to hear that, Waban." Arliss said it somewhat begrudgingly. As bad as it was for everyone in town, Waban had to have it at least a little bit better than the working man.

"I got some more bad news," Waban said. "The fight in Huntington?" Arliss felt a sinking feeling in his stomach as Waban went on. "Well, the prelim between the pros is cancelled. Seems Huntington's favorite son busted his hand while training."

"Oh," said Arliss.

"So, they're only paying us five and three. Plus, no gate."

"Shit," said Arliss, "that sucks."

"Yeah," said Waban. He waited, shifting from one foot to the other. He looked a bit thinner to Arliss, and nervous.

"There's more?"

"Well, I know five grand ain't much right now. I'm not even sure it's worth fighting for at all."

"I'll fight," said Arliss, "no matter how much money."

"Sure," said Waban, "me, too. But I had a thought about how we could sweeten the pot, maybe get a share of the gate back."

"Oh? What you have in mind?"

"Ellen," he said. "Ellen could fight on the undercard."

"What are you talking about?"

"Ellen's amazing," said Waban, "Everyone talks about Blossom Gold around here. Others want to see her, too. Remember that newspaper fellow come around here from Charleston for a story on Ellen? She's a phenom. Folks in Huntington would come out to see her fight, especially after seeing her record, eight wins, no losses, no draws!"

"You're crazy, Waban."

"No, no, I talked to the promoter. He said he'd pay five hundred for her to fight. He'd line up a local boy her age for the match. You make five hundred dollars right off and he'll give back one percent of the gate. It's a good deal, Arliss, five hundred—"

Arliss cut him off, "Win or lose, I get it. What's wrong with you, Waban? I'm not putting my baby girl in a ring with someone I don't even know. Those people come out to see Ellen fight like a freak show. They have no idea how hard she works, of how good she is. If she gets in the ring with some kid outweighs her by a hundred pounds, he'll kill her. The Huntington folks would love that. Forget about it, Waban, forget you ever brought it up."

"But, five hundred bucks, Arliss."

"Forget it! Talk to your promoter friend, tell him we want more or we ain't fighting."

He turned and stalked off back toward home. Son bitch, he thought.

Three days later, he arrived back at the house again without anything to show, and found an oversize carton set on the porch. Puzzled, he glanced at the label: Utah State Penitentiary. Redding. Arliss slowly shook his head back and forth, his lips a flat, tight line, glad that Ellen hadn't seen it first. After opening the carton, he stared down at its contents.

Inside, he found an eight-millimeter camera, a tripod, film, various size lenses, and a complete set of other accessories, all fitted into a leather carrying case. Taped to the case was a note. Arliss opened it, and immediately recognized Robert Redding's handwriting.

> Dear Darling Ellen,
>
> Here's a gift from me to you to help with your boxing. While you're in the ring, your daddy can film you so's you can see yourself and work on your skills. Think of me when you use it. Thank you for being such a sweet girlfriend.
>
> Yours always and forever,
>
> Robert

Such a sweet girlfriend. How much did this get-up cost? Arliss let out a ragged laugh. Maybe he should take a page out of Waban's book, shoot a movie of Ellen in the ring and sell it to some of her fans. He could send copies to promoters who might book her after seeing how good she was. He'd check out all her opponents, of course, to make sure they were okay for her to box. It'd be different than the Junior Gold Gloves for sure. She'd be a professional like her old man. Or a sideshow.

He sighed and shook his head hard. He closed up the box, put it on the floor of his pickup, and drove to a pawn shop he knew about in Charleston. They gave him fifteen hundred for the camera and everything. They'd hold the camera set for 60 days before putting it up for sale, plenty of time for him to retrieve it after the fight.

Daddy told me he didn't want me at the fight. He said those parts of Huntington could be a roughhouse and he didn't have anyone to stay with me while he was in the ring. Of course, I knew the real reason. He didn't want me there in case he lost. I told him he would win, no problem, he'd been training for this chance since before I was born. But a ghost from the past haunted Daddy, losing twice before to Waban Wilson, the Dancing Bear. I wasn't worried, though. I'd seen Uncle Wilson working out on the mountain and he did look a bit trimmer. Still, no way could he catch up with Daddy, who weighed the same he did back then.

Daddy asked Mrs. Burkhardt if I could stay with her while he was in Huntington. She said yes right away. But when I asked her if we could listen to the fight on the radio—a local station decided to broadcast it just like in the old days—she said no, she couldn't listen. The idea of picturing brutal blows described even only in words almost made her sick. Mrs. B must have seen my disappointment and knowing it was Daddy fighting, she said I could listen while she went off to another room. So, that night, I settled in with potato chips and pop to listen to my daddy kick Uncle Wilson's butt.

The big lamps above warmed the ring, countering the air conditioning running full bore to dispel the extreme heat from outside the arena. Arliss looked up at the powerful lights, then around the big amphitheater full of people jawing and yelling to neighbors across the way, joyous about the Rematch of the Century, in West Virginia at least. These days, big crowds like this mostly listened to rock bands or milled around at a car show. He felt a glow at the size of the turnout and the crowd's enthusiasm, how eager they all were to see them back in the ring.

He clambered up between the ropes and stood close in a corner on one side He bounced up and down on the canvas, hitting his gloves together and twisting his head from side to side to loosen up his neck.

They shared the same dressing room, so Arliss had left early to avoid one of Waban's endless yarns. Let him enter last, thought Arliss, Waban owned the bragging rights. By the end of the night, he'd be leaving the ring first.

"Ladies and gentlemen, welcome to Huntington's Veterans Memorial Fieldhouse for a very special engagement, a rematch of the two legendary opponents in West Virginia's bouts of the century." Arliss recognized the announcer's big round face and fake brown hair from when he hosted the big fights up North on TV. Apparently, the promoter had just enough to pay this guy to snazz up everything, then ran out of money. In his nasal New York accent, the announcer shouted out, "In this corner, weighing in at two hundred, thirty-five pounds, with a professional record of 32-7-1, the challenger Arliss 'the Body-Breaker' Truitt!"

The throng roared and Arliss remembered the rumbling noise greeting them in both the other fights fought two decades ago in this arena.

"In the opposite corner, weighing in at two hundred, twenty-five pounds, with a professional record of 25-3-0, including victories in these warriors' two previous encounters, Waban 'the Dancing Bear' Wilson!"

Arliss didn't hear the rest. He met Waban and the referee in the middle of the ring. He didn't hear the referee's instructions, drowned out by the noise in his own head, the dream, the fantasy of a chance to make the past over. The ref directed them to their corners and the bell rang.

"Wilson has come out fast, tattooing Truitt's face with four quick punches, slipping away from a wide hook by Truitt. Wilson slides to the right and pastes Truitt with a left hook, moving out of Truitt's range again. The Dancing Bear is dancing again, twenty years later while Truitt looks befuddled, swinging wildly at the space already left by the slippery Wilson."

"Come on, Daddy," Ellen muttered.

"Truitt's face is red from the constant jabs by Wilson, every now and then sticking in a straight right to keep Truitt off balance. Wilson's a virtuoso out there, orchestrating a boxing exhibition harking back two decades."

"Cut the ring off," Ellen shouted, "move him into the corner!"

"Five rounds in and both boxers look fatigued. Wilson's dancing has slowed somewhat, but his steady blows have tired Truitt as well. We're at the halfway mark, folks, and so far it looks like a shutout."

"You got to move in on him. Get in, grab him, and hit him on the breaks! That's your only chance!"

Arliss spit out the water and gave his corner man a glance. He'd never seen the guy before tonight. Waban's promoter had supplied him and the cut man out of the goodness of his heart.

You're blowin' it, son, you're blown' it. He could hear the little Italian manager's voice screaming at him nose to nose, trying to get him to fight harder, to get him to try to win. Twenty years later and he still was getting his ass handed to him by his best friend.

The bell rang. "Come on, Daddy," Ellen said to herself.

"Truitt's come out of his corner hands high up in front of his head. Wilson's circling, looking for his opening. He throws a left hook, Truitt blocks with his forearm. Wilson steps the other way and throws a right hook. Truitt blocks it, and Wilson shifts low and bounces a left-right into Truitt's midsection. Truitt walks through the body punches, moving forward to back Wilson up. Wilson steps back and to his right, but Truitt cuts him off and into the ropes. Truitt throws two heavy hooks with both hands into Wilson's arms, covers up and presses Wilson against the ropes with his elbows. Truitt steps back and hits Wilson again on the arms. Wilson counters with an uppercut followed by a right hook. Truitt walks through the blows and throws punches to the body again. Wilson covers up! The crowd is roaring on the rampage, finally seeing the fight they expected to see!"

Ellen sighed. That's it, Daddy, she thought, pound Uncle Waban.

"Round seven and Wilson is running. He is exhausted, in deep trouble as Truitt tracks him down slowly, patiently. Truitt feints, Wilson stumbles, and the Body-Breaker has him in the corner! Truitt is unloading all he has, right, left, right, left, hitting Wilson hard. Wilson cannot get out of the corner, his arms are dropping, Truitt's gone to the head! The Dancing Bear dances no more, he's down on one knee!"

"Good job, Daddy."

Arliss pivoted and headed for his corner without looking back. He heard the ref call the TKO and the deafening thunder of the crowd. Facing his corner, Arliss grabbed both ropes and leaned over, his head low. He turned it slightly to peek over at Waban. He looked to be in bad shape, beat up for sure, but mostly exhausted, collapsed on his stool.

The announcer motioned him to come over, but he simply stood up and raised his arm, pirouetting in his corner waving to the bellowing fans. Once around, he split the ropes, climbed through and headed down toward the dressing room.

"Well, did he win?" asked Mrs. B.

"He did," Ellen replied. "Technical knockout in the seventh. I knew he'd win. Uncle Waban's faster, that don't go away."

"Doesn't go away," corrected Mrs. B.

"Doesn't," Ellen repeated. "But Daddy trains hard. I knew he'd wear him down if he just kept at it."

Waban's corner team helped him into the room where he sat down hard on the bench in front of the lockers. "Well, you beat me, Arliss, you got me back."

Arliss remained silent, and Waban went on, "I knew you would. I did a little running the past few weeks to get ready. I'm still pretty quick, too, still pluck a fly straight out of the air. But I knew I couldn't stand up to you for ten rounds. Hell, I couldn't of stood up to you twenty years ago if you'd kept coming. I just wanted to give them a show tonight."

He seemed a bit livelier, noted Arliss.

"And we gave 'em a hell of a show, too. The promoter wants us to do it again. Says he'll double the prize, gate and all."

Arliss stared at him disdainfully.

"It's just an idea." Waban sat quietly for a moment, then shrugged, "Anyway, the promoter made a ton of money and he's going to give us the full amount including the gate. 'Course, I'm not surprised, we did have a contract, and he seen how you can punch."

A wrinkle appeared on Arliss's brow. "I thought you said he'd lowered the prize money."

"Aw, he couldn't do that. We had a contract."

"Then, you told me he was going to lower the payout just to try and get Ellen in the ring."

Waban looked sheepish. "It would'a been a big thing for her is all."

Arliss shook his head at Waban, "You never quit, do you, Waban."

Waban didn't reply, sitting on the bench while Arliss undressed to go into the shower.

Waban hesitated before saying, "You know, Arliss, you might think about Ellen retiring soon. You know, make sure she stays pretty."

Surprised, Arliss stared at Waban. "I don't think that's up to me. She loves boxing."

Waban nodded vigorously, "Sure she does. She loves her daddy, too. If you ask her to, she might be willing to quit."

"I don't think I can do that, Waban. I think it's up to her, understand?"

Waban grimaced for an instant. "Of course, Arliss, but what is she now, ten?"

"Eleven."

"Eleven. And what she weigh, eighty pounds?"

"Sixty-five."

"Eleven years old and sixty-five pounds. So, the boys she whups, she can do that for a while. But they're gonna start getting bigger than Ellen, you know, and some of them might want to exact some revenge, you hear me? It might be best for Blossom Gold to step down, still champion."

"I just don't know, Waban, she talks about going pro all the time someday, about winning a belt someday."

Waban scrunched up his face again. "I don't see how that can happen, Arliss."

"I know," Arliss said, "but that's what she wants."

Jimmy Rose, twenty-five years old out of Provo, read the ad in the paper for marksmen. Angry as hell, he applied, never thinking he'd be picked. Now, here he was, watching the warden and guards and a minister walk Robert Redding into the room. They'd turned an old storage facility at the prison into a makeshift execution chamber. A stout, wooden chair with leather straps rested before a wall of sandbags to stop errant shots. Jimmy and the other four shooters stood behind a thick, drywall screen with five twelve-by-six-inch windows cut out. Gun rests had been positioned behind the apertures, with loaded rifles laying at the ready. Four had live rounds loaded in them, one a blank. Tradition had it that each would take comfort when shooting by persuading himself that his rifle fired the blank. In that way, he could relieve himself of any guilt he might feel for taking a man's life. Jimmy knew better, he knew the odds.

They strapped Redding into the chair. While the warden read the writ condemning Robert Redding to death by firing squad, the guards affixed a small white cloth to Redding's shirt targeting his heart. The minister prayed out loud for Redding's soul and comfort in the life to come. Listening, Jimmy wondered why he had put his name in for this at all. At the time, he'd been furious at Redding for murdering those clerks in cold blood, leaving their wives and children alone on their own. But, staring at this lean man, bent over and grizzled before his time, Jimmy wasn't sure anymore that it was a good idea to take anyone's life. Why not just stick them deep in the pokey and throw the key away?

The warden asked Redding if he had any last words, and Jimmy heard him softly say, "Let's get it over." The warden nodded, a guard put a black hood over Redding's head, and Jimmy and the others shot him dead. Leaving the prison, Jimmy tried to get his mind right about what he'd done. He thought he might, maybe later. But he also knew he'd be living with this in some way for the rest of his life.

When I run down by the creek, I like to watch the blue herons rise up as I go by. They fly lazy in the air like they're sore at me for bothering them and making them have to rise up. Now and then I come up on a deer too fast for it to run. It'll stand there frozen, staring at me until I've passed by, then run. If it's too nervous to wait, it jumps right off and away, its big, fluffy white tail high in the air warning the others. I come across all sorts of critters when I run, box turtles, smooth green snakes, rabbits of course, groundhogs, a surprised fox once in a while, and all kinds of other birds—flickers, cardinals, ducks, geese, and lots of woodpeckers, even the big one called Pileated.

Then, sometimes I dream I'm in a big city, smack in the middle, staring up at the big buildings, my mouth open. I've seen them on TV, big, tall, and gray, looming so far above it makes me wonder why they all don't just lean over and crash into each other. That's when I decide staying at home is best, at least for now.

Red Pump Road

Looking at his reflection in the plate glass front of Maculkey's, Terry MacBride saw that he could afford to lose a few lbs. Further inventory confirmed a rough-shorn, sandy shock of hair with faint snowy accents topping a pale tomato complexion courtesy of the early spring sun. He shrugged and pushed his way through the door. At this hour in the morning, just a few patrons occupied the stools at the bar. Terry beelined over to the booths against the wall and slid into one. He folded his hands and waited for Mary Higgins to arrive carrying the menu.

"The full Irish for me, dear Mary" he said before she could speak. She was a beauty, that Mary, slender and supple as a spring shoot, not fair but full-blooded in her wine olive complexion. He loved looking at her but was more so in love with the razor light of her blue-gray eyes bedazzling with intelligence, verified by every word that passed through her lovely lips. Shame he was a bachelor by confirmation.

"Going to chance both the red and the white pudding, are you? Have you checked with your cardiologist lately?"

"He's given me the go-ahead, Mare, just saw him the other day. No worries, full speed ahead."

She propped the hand holding the menu on her hip, "You're a marvel, Terry. I suppose you want a pint to wash it down."

"Oh, no, Mary, never on a weekday. Coffee will be fine."

She pushed off.

Terry sat forward and pulled out the newspaper from the back pocket of his jeans. He unfolded it and spread it out in front of him, March 1997, the latest edition of *The Gaeilge Glór*. Translated literally as the Irish Cry, he liked to think of it as the Irish Shout Out heard way across the pond. He enjoyed reading about the old country even though he'd been there just once two decades ago. Just 25, he and his best pal Timmy Gleason saved their pennies and flew over on Aer Lingus, drunk as skunks when they hit the tarmac. Terry ran off to the loo while Timmy stood in line to pick up the rental car. They drove here and there, tall Timmy the guide since his mother came directly from the West. They even visited her sister and brothers, digging out spuds one cold morning in June. The two brothers complained loudly about the oppressive heat, which mystified the two American lads, their spring jackets zipped up tight. He remembered they called potatoes *fataí* in the West. More commonly *prátái* in the rest of Ireland, Anglicized into práties. For sure, the West always stood alone, signposts only in Irish, Beamish, Murphy, and O'Toole's on tap, not a Guinness in sight. Quaff a pint just below the ever-present pungent turf cloud clinging to the low ceiling and you live a moment in heaven on earth.

As much as he wanted to, he never made it back. One thing or another got in the way, usually lack of funds despite his good wage as a master plumber. He learned his trade in Philly, and of course during the apprenticeship years, the pickings were pretty slim. Once done with that, though, he earned a good living, but seemed to spend it faster than he made it. He finally decided to return to his hometown, Nottingham, maybe slow down his way of life by slowing down life. Ten years back and his affairs seemed to be in order. Still, he thought, trailing off. So, he moved to Boston.

Mary came back with a heavy stoneware plate, hefty enough to lay low any unruly patron acting out. Eggs, sausage links, Canadian bacon and a grilled tomato crowded the puddings on the dish, corralled by four thick slices of brown bread stacked so as not to teeter-totter too much. She put the plate in front of him along with a thick white mug full of steaming black coffee. Reaching into the shallow front pocket of her apron, she pulled out a handful of butter squares wrapped in foil, depositing them in front of the plate.

Terry wet his lips, putting the paper aside.

"Want a thimble of Jameson in the coffee?"

He frowned, "Now don't encourage me, Mary, I'm being a good schoolboy this morning."

She laughed and turned away as he tucked into the massive meal before him.

It all seemed to be gone in five minutes. Forlorn, he looked up and gazed about as if more would somehow materialize out of thin air. No such luck. He saw Mary far away at the opposite end of the bar, so no quick coffee refill either. Sighing, he slid the bare plate out of the way and retrieved the *Gaeilge Glór.*

He browsed through it idly, enjoying the odd little stories and funky ads with illustrations like those in the Whole Earth Catalog back in the 70s, his salad days. Out on schedule mostly, the monthly's timetable suited Terry, who poured over each issue several times, relishing all of its little idiosyncrasies. Hard for him to recycle the old ones, true enough.

Mary came by again. Instead of standing elbows akimbo, cocksure ready as usual to drop him a peg, she seemed a bit abashed.

"What?" he asked.

Sheepishly, she said, "We got a leak in the kitchen. The overhead sprinkler's dousing the grill."

"Really? And I'm to the rescue once again?"

Mary stooped her shoulders feigning intimidation. "If you will."

He sighed, as he shoved heavily out of the booth. "Maybe I should've had that drop of whiskey after all."

"It'll be there when you're done," she said, brightening.

"That's all right. I have to go to work after all my work is done here." He didn't have the heart to tell her he preferred single malts, a true plastic paddy.

"Quit your grousing," she said over her shoulder on the way to the kitchen. "How else can you get an Irish breakfast so many times for free?"

"Maybe by management honoring a longtime, loyal customer now and then. Or simply out of the kindness in your heart."

"Hey, I only work here, I don't make policy about customer loyalty plans."

"And here all this time I thought you loved me deeply, Mary Higgins."

She stopped at the door and pierced him with the gimlet eye. "If only you knew, Terry MacBride." She gestured to the doorway, "Mike's waiting inside."

On his way to Brookline, he wondered if there was anything to what Mary said last, or if she just polished off the banter. No question, she struck a fine figure just touching 40. And here he was, a fatted calf at 45, ready to be plated for the feast. He shook his head no; a confirmed bachelor, like it or not.

Maybe he should find another breakfast nook. For sure, Mike needed to get his shit together or there'd be no choice in the matter.

"Your sprinkler system's done in," he'd reproved Mike back in the kitchen. "It's so old, I'm surprised to find the pipes aren't made out of lead. You need to replace everything. The next grease fire could totally torch your establishment."

Mike pulled out the index finger propped in his mouth. "You really think so? I always thought the leaks meant that it was working."

Terry sighed, "Not if it's putting out fires that don't exist. Never mind you're likely not passing the next health inspection, you've got a catastrophe looming here. Tell you the truth, Mike, I think your gas fittings look pretty nasty, too. You probably should have the entire set up overhauled."

"How much is that gonna run me?" asked Mike

Terry shrugged, "Four, five grand if nothing else shows up digging into it."

"Five grand? I'll be driven straight out of business!"

"Yeah, well," Terry trailed off.

"Can't you do something, Terry? Give me a price, can't you? We've been friends a long time."

"Aw, I don't know, Mike, I have a lot on my plate right now. It's not so much the money as the time."

"C'mon, Terry, where will you go if I go under? Please."

"Christ, Mike, you're putting me on the spot. I can fix the pinholes you have now, but I can't. I can't take a hit like that either, I'm just treading water myself."

"Terry, I'm begging you," Mike implored, his eyes wild. "Think about it, think of everyone here out of a job, Louis, Mick, Isabella, and Mary. Mary's got her kid, you know, to take care of."

Terry screwed up his face. Mary's daughter Annie was out of the house off to school. How could Mike not know that?

"Please, Terry."

Mother of Christ, he cursed silently wheeling the 450 into Home Depot. Was he really going to be saddled with this God-awful Maculkey's job? A job bestowed upon Job by a ruthless Old-Testament deity, it promised to be an everlasting spiral down a black hole. For sure he would get short-changed big time, he thought, jacking the new hot-water heater into the back of the pickup. No, he shook his head, driving to the Hermann's place, he absolutely could not, would not do it. But, yanking the old heater out of the mansion basement, he sighed. Then where would he go for breakfast?

In quick order, Terry dropped the new water heater in place. He'd tried to persuade the Hermann's to go with a new state-of-the-art electric water heater. Hot water in five minutes with no bulky cylinder corroding away to flood the basement floor not if but when. But, just like the rest of the rich, they balked at the cost, double that of the conventional heater. Never mind amortization over a longer lifespan for the electric unit. They covered their parsimony with phony environmentalism, electric heaters used too much power in an energy deficient world. He shrugged, more work for him down the road. Still, he thought. A new clientele might be nice.

Terry connected the water line quickly, followed by the gas, needing to sweat in a bit more copper pipe to reach the lower height of the new unit. After making sure that everything was tight and right, he cleaned up. He took the trash and his tools out to the pickup. He jockeyed the old heater into the bed, strapping it in place, then threw in the trash and his tools. Once done, he slipped into the cab to have some lunch while waiting for Mrs. Hermann to come home to pay him.

His lunch disappeared fast and still no Mrs. Hermann. She was late, he thought until he looked at the dashboard clock. Nope, he had finished early. He reached into the glove box, pulled out his Irish paper, and settled in. He started reading the ads and started laughing.

> ***The Pet Bistro: Food and Fun for Pets!***
> ***Self-Serve Dog Wash***

Gifted dogs, he thought. Also, appropriate placement right beneath the ad for the Dogwood Café.

> **HARRIET HEMSLEY**
> **Purveyor of the Unnecessary & the Irresistible**

Irresistible what, he wondered.

> ***ASAP Locksmith***
> ***Locks & Keys***
> ***Doors • Cars • Bicycles • Refrigerators***

ASAP? Talk about qualified service, he laughed. And who puts a lock on their fridge?

Then he saw it, a small notice in the personal ad section.

> *Claim your own genuine Irish public house*
> *In the heart of Coyne, Co. Monaghan*

> Pen a poetic description in 50 words or less of your "finest glass of O'Toole's Brown Stout" and send to: Claim Your Own Genuine Irish Public House Competition, c/o O'Toole's Brewery, PMI Station, P.O. Box 4583, Mystic, Conn., 068448-5853. Deadline: March 31, 1997. You must be 21. Five finalists will be flown to Dublin Airport and transported to Coyne, where they will contend in pub games and bartending prowess to determine who will claim Murphy's Pub and Salon.

Terry recognized the ad immediately except for the sponsor. He 'd seen at least three others during the past few years. They'd all been run by Guinness, Ireland's king of stout for centuries to this day, even in the Republic. Of the also-rans, Murphy's and Beamish held their own regionally. But O'Toole's seemed to barely hang on. Like GM over Ford or Microsoft dominating Apple, Guinness regularly overwhelmed local quality with its massive market share and resources. O'Toole's must-see Guinness's win-a-pub promotion as a lethal blow. Hence, their own competing pub contest.

A last-ditch, desperate measure thought Terry. He didn't know a thing about Murphy's Pub and Salon, but he couldn't suppose it rivaled Grafton's in Dublin, considering O'Toole's meager resources. A good chance that Coyne was beyond the back of beyond, too, he imagined. Only five finalists compared to Guinness's ten. Five to fly, feed, and house for a week, half the cost. This all could work to his advantage, he thought.

Terry knew the ins and outs of the contests intimately because he'd entered Guinness's twice before. He missed out both times at the initial essay stage. This didn't surprise him figuring that 30 million out of 30 million Irish Americans had entered as well. They'd all play this year, too, ever dewy-eyed about the Old Sod. They'd go for the Guinness contest again, he figured, while only a few might try the O'Toole's competition. Odds were they never saw the poor O'Toole's ad in the first place. He nodded his head. Definitely he should throw down on O'Toole's. Hell, he even had a couple of essays ready to tweak as needed.

Mrs. Hermann arrived finally, on time. After turning on the water and the gas, Terry nodded with a slight tug of his ethereal forelock to her. Delighted to have running hot water without leaks, Mrs. Hermann handed over his check, accurate to the penny of the agreed upon price. He climbed into his truck and drove off to the next jobsite.

He knew the stories of the past pub winners from articles in the Irish journals. After reading about the winning essays, he learned how he could punch up his own. Then, if he managed to be picked as a finalist, three competitive events remained: throwing darts; pouring the perfect pint with a side serving of craic to the locals; and telling the judges the grandest of Irish stories.

Known locally as the Red Pump Pie Man, he felt sure he had the dart games in the bag. As for the fine Celtic tale, he figured on mining a treasure trove of Irish myths and stories to cobble together one brilliant saga. He felt that he could more than keep up talking craic—known as smack in urban America—to the daughters and sons of Erin. That left just one task to master, he thought, which stymied him. He had never tapped a beer in his life. How could he possibly pour a perfect pint, never mind etching an image of the Sistine Chapel atop its head?

He mulled all the way to his next stop, plumbing three remodeled guest bathrooms before the new owners of the house took possession. While attaching the final Toto toilet, the solution came to him. On the way out of the nouveau manor, he flipped open his phone and made the call.

"Mike, Terry here. I'm willing to fix your kitchen situation, the whole fiasco. Yeah, yeah, I'm glad you feel that way. And yes, I'll give you a price. But there will be strict conditions. Nonnegotiable."

His first night at Maculkey's blurred by. Long, lean Kenny the barkeep did the best he could to help, but the sundown crowd left him little time to mentor. Adding to Terry's stress, Mary stunned him with her cruelty, sending back pint after pint.

"That's a bad pour, I'm not serving it."

"This one's worse, you're starting to put my livelihood at risk."

"For Christ's sake—Kenny! Help me out here, will you?"

Terry stood flat-footed, his face red but feeling blue, too. She took him apart. But Holy Christ in heaven, he blurted silently, how in hell can I win the pub if I'm incapable of doing the simplest thing?

After a lifetime self-conscious for sticking out so tall and gangly, Kenny smiled compassionately as he squeezed by hugging three perfectly poured pints. Mike stepped over to Terry and said, "Why don't you help with the food for now. It's good to get a handle on that, too, Terry. It's a vital cog in the operation."

Terry took burger orders with fries, stabbing the paper squares onto the cook's spike with contained force. After the crowd subsided, he started cleaning up tables and trash. Mike ambled over and said to him in a low voice, "This ain't part of the arrangement. You said you wanted to tend bar, that's it. So, you don't need to be tidying up. I don't want you thinking about reneging, okay?"

"Don't fret, Maculkey, you'll get your new pipes. A deal's a deal, whether I'm up to it or not."

Mike slouched away.

At closing time, Mary wiped down the bar, then went over to Terry and grabbed his shirt sleeve. "Come with me," she said, leading him back behind the bar. She reached beneath it and pulled out four clean Guinness pint glasses. She lined them up next to the taps and turned to face Terry.

"It's crazy to think of putting out a clean pint while you're learning on the run," she said, "and right in the middle of the mad end of workday rush. Mike must be on crack."

"I don't know," Terry mumbled, "I made a dog's dinner out of them no matter what Kenny told me."

'Yeah, well, he's no professor either. It's really simple, you just need to take your time. Watch what I do, then follow suit. I guarantee you'll master in just drawing two glasses."

He squinted, baring his teeth. "I really doubt that."

"Just watch, then repeat." She grinned, picking up the glass, "You know, the same again.

"Position the glass at a 45-degree angle from the tap. Pull the handle making sure the stout hits the side of the glass. Fill'er up to about three-quarters or so. Put the glass aside and leave it to settle for two minutes."

She placed her pint on the bar. "Okay, now you."

Terry picked up the tulip-shaped glass and placed it beneath the tap. "Forty-five degrees," she said.

He carefully pulled the handle towards him, watching the brown stout hit the side, magically turning into beige seafoam.

"That's good. Three quarters full . . . good, now let it rest."

He gingerly put the glass on the opposite side of the spout hoping to dodge comparison to hers.

"All right. Two minutes. Mine should be ready soon."

Leaning against the bar waiting, she said, "When you make the first pour, a trick is to stop at the bottom of the gold harp printed on the side of the glass."

"That's a Guinness Harp. I doubt I'll be using those at O'Toole's."

He piqued her interest. "Really?" she said. "Why's that?"

Before he could hem and haw, she reached over to her pint glass and put it under the tap. "Top it off straight up," she said, stopping the flow perfectly, leaving a half-inch foam head at the rim.

"Now you."

He brought his pint over and started the flow. He pushed the beer lever back, but the head crested and spilled somewhat over the side.

"Shit," he mumbled.

"That's all right, we all do it hurrying," Mary said, cleanly sweeping the excess foam off the pint with a beer comb. "Just go slower."

She moved the pint over to his side and fetched one of the empty glasses. She poured, "Three quarters at forty-five and done," moving it over to settle. "Your turn."

Terry grabbed the remaining glass and held it below the spigot while pulling the handle. He shut it off and set the glass aside.

"Impressive," she said. They waited in silence until she put her glass beneath the tap and filled it, again leaving a perfect foam head. Seeing Terry counting seconds on his watch, she said, "You know the wait for settling is bullshit."

He glanced up, "Really?"

"Yeah, you can pour the whole pint in all at once and it won't be any the worse for it. Guinness added the time-out as a marketing ploy. Keep people hanging and they get thirstier, I guess. Some devotees order two at a time because of it."

"No shit?"

"Yup," she said. "Anyway, there you have it, perfectly poured pints, two apiece. I told you."

"That you did." He looked around and said, "So, what do we do with them now?"

"Down 'em," she said, as she grabbed her two and slipped around the bar to a table. Terry followed with his and sat opposite. They raised their glasses, toasted, and took long draughts perfectly synchronized like a water ballet team.

"You're entering a win-a-pub contest?"

"I am," he answered.

"You really want to run your own saloon in Ireland?"

"I do."

"Oh," she said. After a moment pause, she said, "Jeez, I was just getting used to having you around."

Terry sat back. "I've been coming here for a decade."

"Yeah, well," she murmured, "sometimes things take time, sometimes."

They drank.

"So, this arrangement you struck with Mike, it's all about preparing for the competition."

"It is."

"And pouring a proper pint of Guinness is one of the events."

"Pouring a proper pint of stout," he said, "not Guinness. O'Toole's is running the one I'm going for."

"I get it, smaller sponsor, fewer contenders, better odds."

"Correct. I figure five finalists, half as many as Guinness's."

"Not bad," Mary said. She took a sip, wiped her mouth, and said, "So, what other skills must you master?"

"Well, throwing darts," said Terry.

"You have that covered, Mr. Red Pump Pie Man."

She'd asked about the nickname a long time ago and he'd unreeled his long story about being born on a small farm in a rural part of southeastern Pennsylvania. His parents grew organic produce for upscale restaurants. He came along as a late-life surprise, their only child. Out front of the old farmhouse stood a hand water pump that, just for fun, his parents painted a bright red. Locals began using the red pump as a landmark when giving directions. Eventually, the county named the adjacent two-lane blacktop the Red Pump Road.

"So," Mary said, "born an only child in Red Pumplvania." She leaned over as if to whisper a secret, "I hear only childs don't share."

"Can you call them 'only childs'? Sort of an oxymoron, isn't it? And anyway, how could I share if I was the only one there? I did live a perfect life as a kid, though, with the animals, the woods. My dad took me out hunting for deer every fall, but only during muzzle-loader season. We saw some, but never brought one home. Shooting those muskets was such a pain in the ass, you had to prime the powder with a fuse called a spolette while aiming at the same time. They didn't have much range, either. Makes me think my dad planned on making sure we missed."

She nodded knowingly. "And later you became the Red Pump Pie

Man. Ate a lot of pie, did you?"

"C'mon, you know it's for throwing darts. The board is round, so to mark spaces for scoring points you have to divide it into wedges like a pie."

"Pizza!" she said.

"Yeah, sure. Okay, so everyone knows the object of the game, very simple. Toss a dart and earn points based on where you stick it. The harder the spot is to hit, the more points you get. But what's cool is the inventors figured out early on that shot making is more about human anatomy than target size. Think about how humans can throw compared to monkeys. Physiologically speaking, shoulder construction of monkeys only allows them to throw like a girl"

"Lovely sexist analogy, that," she said.

"Both male and female monkeys throw like girls," Terry continued. "Human beings have physical limitations as well. It's very hard to throw across your body with the same accuracy as straight ahead. The fellows designing the board took this into account by awarding points for nailing such hard-to-hit spots.

"So, a dartboard might look like a numbers crazy quilt, but it's really pretty sophisticated. To be a top-flight dart player, you need to be able to put the darts in any part of any wedge. The bullseyes of course, but also the tiny spaces at the edge for double points, and even tinier spaces in the middle ring for triple points. When you're really good, they say you can slice and dice—"

"The pie," Mary said, "like the Red Pump Pie Man."

"So, you're safe in assuming that you'll skewer all of them with your tiny spears," Mary said, her second pint nearly halfway gone.

"Yup," said Terry, "but I still have to put in the practice religiously. Then, there's engaging the clientele in lively conversation whilst distributing the drink."

"Good craic. No problem, you can talk some shit all night long."

"That would be 'shite,' but true. They also want me to tell a story, sort of like the Mick version of the World's Biggest Liar contest. I'm going to have to think hard on that one."

"Still, another good fit," she said. "Anything else?"

"I don't think," Terry said, squinting concentration. "They might want to see shamrocks carved in the pint heads."

"Not my department," Mary said shaking her head. "See Kenny about that."

She finished off the dregs of her second stout, and he hurried to say, "I'm going Tuesday to Kelly's, toss some darts. Want to come along?"

"I'm working Tuesday."

"When are you off?"

"Mondays."

"How about Monday?"

She shrugged.

Kenny showed him how to manipulate a pint glass beneath the spout to form a good-looking shamrock. It didn't take long for Terry to become adept at carving the garnish into his now perfect pints. Still, he decided he might need to work on a wrinkle of his own to wow O'Toole's judges. In the meantime, he finished the Maculkey's renovation to Mike's great, grateful approval. He continued tending the bar, fine-tuning his convivial stand-up. He also threw darts constantly, harpooning the competition like so many whales. Mary often stood by his side, chiding him hard as much as she could. Otherwise, he waited for the day to arrive when the finalists would be announced.

Alone at home, he often pulled out the verse he'd sent as his entry. After reworking the best of the two that had failed in the Guinness contests, he mailed it in. Now, he reread the final version again and again, wondering if it would even get him in the front door.

Well Again, O'Toole's Again

Pint, plainly,
first love of brown,
thicking the tongue,
sweet bitter down.
Full fed and strong
I wax eloquent,
wane long,
whilst glam glum glories
hair Dingled and storied,
corner my eye.
Do you approve?
The same again, says I,
Roar O'Toole's, O'Toole's rules!

Every time he read it, he worried it to death. Too precious? References too oblique? Would the judges imagine lovely colleens prancing in the Dingle's ancient wood? Or would they be put off by a disgusting image of dingleberries drooping from their hair? After all, the poem had failed already once before. No difference now except the switching out of Guinness for O'Toole's. Maybe all his toil and tears of frustration would amount to a big, fat nothing at the outset. And, he had told Mary all about it. If he didn't make the first cut and she spread the word to everyone at Maculkey's, at Kelly's, his humiliation would verge upon massive! Oh, my fucking God!

Very early the next morning, Terry received the call from Ireland informing him that he had been chosen as one of the five finalists.

Queued up, his old army duffle bag hanging off his shoulder, Terry shifted back and forth more than anxious to deplane. While waiting, he mulled over how odd it seemed to be getting off in Dublin since O'Toole's brewed their stout in a small town west of Cork. Maybe fares to the capital ran cheaper than to Shannon. Finally, the passengers in front of him pulled their carry-ons out of the overheads and shuffled down the aisle. He passed them quickly on the broad walkways to the arrival causeway where he was to meet the O'Toole's representative. When he emerged, he searched left and right for some sort of greeting sign, then above for a banner, perhaps. But no banner. He felt a bit lost for a time, out of touch until he spied an older gent holding a piece of white cardboard, "O'Toole's" hand-lettered on it. Terry headed over.

The fellow holding the sign stood just over five and a half feet, gray-haired with a slight belly out front. He wore brown corduroy trousers, a gray tweed jacket over a dark blue sweater, along with a jaunty patterned tie. Jerry Garcia? Terry wondered. On his head, of course, perched a well-worn newsboy cap.

Before Terry could reach him, though, two other people stepped in front, a tall, broad man and a very tiny woman.

"Hello, sir, I'm Eamon McDowell and this is Nancy Huntzinger. We're both finalists from the United States in the O'Toole's Public House Contest."

Terry held up. Two of his competitors.

"Oh, lovely, lovely," said the man with the sign, "I'm John Smith, your O'Toole's welcome entourage of one, sorry to say. Very nice to meet you, indeed" he said, tucking the sign beneath his left arm to free up his right. He shook each of their hands vigorously up and down twice.

Terry stepped up and said, "Howdy, I'm Terry MacBride, another contestant."

"I know," said Smith, "from the United States, as all the finalists are. Whereabouts there?"

"Boston."

"Ah, Boston, a fine Irish home away from home. And you, young sir?"

"New York City," Eamon McDowell said.

"A Yankee fan I suppose," asked Smith.

"No, the Mets."

"I see. From Long Island, are you?"

"Yes," replied Eamon, brows folded together. Fair-skinned and rosy cheeked, a robust young man, thought Terry, any father's pride and joy. Salad green, too.

"And where do you hale from if I might ask?" he said to Nancy Huntzinger.

"Toledo," she said, "Ohio, not Spain."

"Of course, and welcome to you as well."

"And I'm from Boise," said a deep voice in their rear. Everyone turned to see a heavy-set man with long mustaches. He wore a fedora like Humphrey Bogart's and a long duster raincoat. Terry thought he looked to be the same age as himself.

"I'm George Scanlon, also here for the pub contest."

"Greetings to you, Mr. Scanlon," said Smith, reaching out his hand. They shook, then Smith said, "Well, we're all here now, so we can get on our way. I've a van outside that will accommodate everyone. Do any of you still have some luggage to retrieve from the carousel?"

Everyone shook their heads no, but Nancy spoke up. "Wait, there're only four of us. There's supposed to be five."

"Oh, yes, that's right. I'm sorry, but the fifth finalist, Mr. Sean Miller of San Francisco was forced to withdraw. Contracted a nasty bout of avian influenza it seems. So, it's the four of you who will be competing."

Scanlon leaned over to Terry and whispered in his deep bass, "One down."

"Well then," continued Smith," here's the itinerary. First, we drive to Coyne, 136 klicks from Dublin Airport, that's about 85 miles to you Yanks An hour and forty-five-minute drive, not including loo stops. Once we arrive, you'll all be put up in some very lovely, local B&Bs where you can settle in and rest up this afternoon. In the evening, we will congregate for dinner at the prize, Murphy's Pub and Salon, where you will meet the outgoing proprietor and the judges. Tomorrow morning, after your full Irish breakfast, we'll reassemble at Murphy's to commence the competition. If you have no questions . . .," he trailed off, pausing. "If none, then we'll board the van and be on our way. T'anks, much."

Terry sat next to Nancy Huntzinger, a tiny woman, fortyish, with brittle, curly blond hair, brown eyes, red lipstick, and a calm, businesslike demeanor. He decided to try breaking the ice.

"So, what county does the Huntzinger Clan call home?"

She eyed him for an instance, then said flatly, "Lucas County near Lake Erie."

"Oh," Terry said, feeling sheepish.

After a minute, she said, "My mother's maiden name is Donleavy."

"Right," he said. They lapsed into silence as each looked out their windows watching Ireland pass by. Terry tried to soak in as much as he could, but he soon fell asleep, jet lag catching up to him.

For a town of just under 2,000 residents, Coyne presented a façade of a much larger municipality, complete with a town square hemmed in by an array of buildings erected over several centuries. The finalists stepped off the van dazzled by its silhouette, even though only two blocks deep on the main road. Upon first impression, they had no idea that the rest of the community consisted mostly of single-level, modest homes with truck gardens and small pastures behind them. They found themselves situated in separate bed and breakfasts, each within walking distance of Murphy's Pub and Salon right on the square.

Once at his B&B, Terry called Mary.

"It's so good to hear from you, Terry, but I'm in the middle of it. Can we talk later?"

He could hear the clamor of Maculkey's in the background that caused Mary to shout.

"Yeah, for sure, I'll call you when I can. I've met the other finalists, and it's on already right off the plane. I'm going to have to dig in, Mary, to win this. That's for sure."

"Yeah, well, I'm wishing you all the luck in the world, and so's everyone here at Maculkey's, right boys?"

He heard a loud bellow.

"See? Everyone here's behind you, they all want a free round when they come visit you in Ireland."

"Yeah, I'm sure they do."

"God speed, Terry, and be sure to kiss the blarney stone. It needs a reboot, no question, and you're the man for the job."

"Thanks, Mary, I'll call you again soon, all my love." He hung up, then looked at his phone wondering how he came to say the last thing. Thinking about taking a little walk around Coyne, he fell back on his bed and slept until Smith roused him at twilight.

The four finalists filed into Murphy's Pub and Salon and immediately found themselves behind the bar. Already startled, they froze when met by a furor of calls for pints from the crowd standing three rows thick in front of them.

A silver-haired burly man in a Bohemian Football Club jersey called out, "All right, all right, back off, the bar is now officially closed down." Ruddy faced with thinning orangish hair, he ushered them to the front door, saying "C'mon, you can come back tomorrow when the games begin." Though looking glum, most everyone filed out the front door quietly, many receiving a friendly pat on the back from the bartender as they left.

The man in the football shirt turned back to the bar and said, "I'm Liam Murphy, gentlemen and miss, outgoing proprietor—"

"Outgoing in every way, before, after, and always," chimed in John Smith, followed by chirping agreement of the other remaining patrons.

"Thanks much, Johnny." He continued, "Outgoing proprietor of this establishment and also the transitional host for the duration of the O'Toole's public house contest. Welcome to Coyne, Ireland, soon to be, for one of you, the epicenter of your new enterprise."

Each of the contestants greeted Murphy, reaching over the bar to shake his hand, Terry last in line. He estimated the former pub owner to be in his late fifties, early sixties. Not so old to be retiring, but maybe for him running a pub had just gotten old.

While waiting, Terry gazed around at the bar, dark except for the lamps spaced at five-foot intervals along the wallpapered walls. Grimy from the different kinds of smoke rising in the pub for decades if not centuries, the walls appeared to feature fox hunts on horseback. The riders wore red jackets and jodhpurs, while the horses legs were cut off by a half dozen black wooden booths squeezed in back to back.

"Now," said Murphy, "if you'll all make your way around the bar, we can get on with the preliminary introductions. Here before you are your judges for O'Toole's Win-a-Public-House Contest."

Murphy introduced the judges in turn. Martin Kealy headed O'Toole's marketing team. A slender, handsome young man in his early thirties, his curly brown hair stopped where his Brooks Brother suit took over. Joseph O'Neal, in charge of the brewery's public operations and biergarten, from a long family history of publicans. Fifty years old or so, O'Neal smiled brightly, clearly comfortable in himself and around people.

"We also have two judges from Coyne itself, representing the winner's soon-to-be new patrons. You all know John Smith here, your driver. He also serves as our local rep for the Irish tourist bureau Fáilte Ireland, and on the town council."

John made a motion with his hand, miming a tip of his hat.

"And, the owner of a curio shop in town and another formidable voice on Coyne's council, Maeve McGowan."

She reminded him of Mary, though slighter and a bit taller with burnt red hair. Her eyes were green, not at all like Mary's cobalt specials except for having the same intensity.

They sat across from each other at dinner, a good seafood chowder and brown bread, smoked salmon, greens, and hot, Queens potatoes with plenty of butter. They washed it all washed down with copious pints of O'Toole's genuine national stout.

"Good God, what a spread!" Terry said.

"You mean the butter or the margarine?" Maeve said. He looked puzzled, and she said, "They give you both, you know."

"Why?"

"Coyne sits on the razor's edge of the border, cheek to jowl with the North. Murphy loads his bread dishes with butter for the Green, margarine for the Orange. To make everyone happy."

Terry sat back. Another O'Toole's economy. Real estate must be cheap here.

Maeve started laughing deeply, reaching over to punch his arm playfully. "I'm putting you on," she said, still laughing. "God, are all you Yanks so gullible?"

The next afternoon, Murphy stood in the pub looking at his watch. "All right," he announced "We start at one sharp, fifteen minutes. Everyone in need of a refill, get your glass over to Johnny post haste. There'll be no further commerce while the competition is under way."

A half dozen men piled up in front of the bar where John Smith and another bartender stood ready to serve.

"Time is up, please take your places in the gallery. Judges, to your posts."

The score of Coyne residents sat in four rows of chairs set up in front of the pub's window facing the square. John quickly whipped around the bar and took his seat on a high stool with the other judges opposite the audience.

"Very well. Contestants, please assemble beside me." They joined Murphy at the front of the bar. "Now, we're going to start easy on you. The first challenge will be darts."

Terry expelled his breath in relief.

The crowd roared their approval, and Murphy continued. "None of these fancy aluminium alloy jobs, either. Good, old-fashioned feathers, wood, and steel. You'll compete in pairs, twice, each starting at 501 points, declining by the points you rack up with your darts. First to zero out wins. Seems counter logical but not unexpected of something invented by the Brits. Don't forget, they came up with a ball game where you use only your feet."

The audience started hooting their impatience and Murphy held up his hand. "Tie scores will be decided by sudden-death throws of a single dart each. The winner will receive top points toward the ultimate prize, followed by second, third, and so forth."

Someone in the seats stood up and pointed, yelling, "'So forth,' is it? 'So forth' is fourth!' We see what you said!" and the rest howled and jeered incoherently. Murphy grinned and said, "All right, all right, I'll save the word play for that part of the competition. Ms. Maeve, if you please, pick the order of the pairings from my cap."

Maeve smiled and pulled out two strips of paper from the hat held by Murphy. He read the names, "First pair, Scanlon versus Huntzinger. That means McDowell against MacBride, a bit alphabetical, almost alliterative. Competitors, if you please."

The contestants drew straws to see who would throw first. Terry drew the long one and immediately stepped up to grab a set of darts. He weighed one, which surprised him in having pretty good balance for a wooden bar dart. He scanned the familiar pie wedges dividing the round board, and the narrow rings circling the edge and the middle. Hitting the big spaces between the rings earned the fewest points. Strikes in the outside ring doubled the points while hits in the stingy middle ring awarded triple points. The top space featured the highest single-shot value at 20 points, with just 1 and 5 points earned for hits in its neighboring wedges. Other point values radiated down from there to 12 and 18 respectively, and so on. Terry again marveled at how the seemingly randomly placed point values reflected human physical limitations. Savvy dart throwers knew better and trained relentlessly for decades to defy these structural shortcomings.

Terry was no exception. Without hesitation, he zipped three darts straight and true into the topside middle ring, scoring 180 points. The fans roared as Eamon, clearly stunned, extracted the darts from the board. He stepped back and tossed his first dart into the board for a 9, following with two in the top double ring for a total of 49.

Terry finished the game off in five minutes, checking out at zero with Eamon 150 points behind. The young New Yorker headed over to the bar while Terry sat on a stool, watching Huntzinger versus Scanlon.

To Terry's surprise, little Nancy Huntzinger managed to record a decent score even though lobbing her darts in remarkably high arcs. She held just 110 points when Scanlon zeroed out. That left George Scanlon as his next opponent. They drew straws and Scanlon went first.

The match went sideways for Terry straight off. The spectacular precision at Terry's command in the first match deserted him. Scanlon was good, solid, though not exceptional. But Terry missed his targets. In a long career of throwing darts, droughts occur, he knew. Now, though, ten minutes into the match of his life? J, M, and J! he cried out in his mind. The spectators began to grumble, recognizing his sense of haplessness. And he was running out of time.

Scanlon need just 120 points to check out. At 180 points to go, Terry felt like a dead man walking the way he was throwing. Scanlon tossed his first two darts, leaving him needing only 45 points. Cool and calm, he lifted his dart parallel to his eye and flipped it toward the lower right triple ring, the 45, and nailed it.

Scanlon turned around to bask in front of the cheering masses. Crushed, Terry started to meander toward the bar. Before he got there, though, Murphy called out, "Where're you going? Don't you want to try to match?"

"What?" snapped Scanlon. "It's over, I zeroed out first. I'm the winner of the first stage of the contest."

"I'm afraid not, Mr. Scanlon. If you had been second in the throwing order, you would be correct. But anyone who plays darts knows that opponents receive the same number of chances. Mr. MacBride gets a go at matching your score. Mr. MacBride, if you please."

Terry stopped, frozen. He couldn't believe it, one more chance.

"This is absurd," Scanlon bleated. "I zeroed out; the game is over."

"'Tisn't. However," Murphy said directly at Terry, "you must get exactly 180 points, Mr. MacBride. Any less or more will cost you the match. House rules."

Scanlon folded his arms, smug and satisfied. Staring at Terry, he said, "Go ahead, MacBride, shoot the lights out."

Terry stared at the dark, thick man, wishing he could give him a clout. He stepped up to the line, ready to skewer him, figuratively thinking. Taking a deep breath, he shook himself and fired, one, two, three, straight and true. The three darts buried themselves together in the 60 spot, dropping him 180 points. Everyone gasped. Except for Scanlon.

"Blessed Mother, 180," uttered Murphy reverently. "MacBride did it, he checked out."

The crowd exploded after that until Murphy bellowed, "Sudden death!" which hushed them all.

Scanlon frowned and jerked his head, "Get on with it."

"You first again, Scanlon," Murphy said.

Face hardened, Scanlon toed the line and flung his dart side armed, which caused it to pirouette left to right, careening almost parallel into the middle triple ring, 60 points. He stared at MacBride as he left the line.

Stuck in at an angle, Scanlon's dart left little room for error. Clenching his teeth, Terry threw, barely slicing his dart in a sliver of space just inside the metal edge of the triple ring for 60 points. Noise thundered again throughout the pub.

"Once more, then, second darts," said Murphy.

Scanlon eyed the board. With his first dart at an angle covering most of the 60-point box and Terry's dart crowding the edge, he hesitated. Deciding, he tossed his dart into the lower left-hand triple ring of the 19 point wedge, scoring the second highest possible point total on the entire board, 57. Oh, my sweet Jesus, Terry thought, praying for the first time since he last faced a near fatal catastrophe.

As Scanlon passed by, he smiled saying to Terry, "Knock yourself out, Champ."

Terry mentally wiped his brow as he surveyed the board. He fired directly at Scanlon's dart blocking the 60-point triple ring. His dart hit Scanlon's in the narrow wood at the barrel's neck, splitting it to stick in the spongy board, shuddering.

Amid the sudden silence Murphy uttered, "I've never seen the like."

"Feckin' Robin Hood!" howled a voice from the side.

"Sure enough," cried another, "but through to the board counting for points!"

"Abú!" blasted the locals, raising the roof as Murphy declared in full pitch, "Winner of the first part, Terry MacBride!"

"It was a God-awful mess," Terry said. "I thought for sure I was a goner. But maybe I'm destined for greatness."

"You're destined for something," said Mary. "What is anybody's guess."

He pouted, "I miss you, Mary."

"Yes, well, you're far away," she said. "So, what's up next?"

"Pouring pints. It could be a bit complicated, cranking them out, setting them aside to settle Entertaining the troops while collecting fares, then finishing off the pour with a nicely carved shamrock."

"Sounds like a lot. How do you feel about it?"

"I feel good, confident enough thanks to you and Kenny. I am in first place to start."

"Well, don't get caught from behind. Give it your best."

"I will," he said with false bravado. "And after I win it all, you'll have to come out for a visit, like the queen!"

"Like I'm a queen around here," she said, "fat chance. But I wish you all the luck, Terry. I hope you fill your every dream."

She sounded earnest, he thought. "Thanks, Mary, I'm going to do my absolute best."

"Has anyone ever told you, you look a bit like Brendan Gleeson?"

Squinting at Maeve, Terry said, "Who the heck is Brendan Gleeson?"

"You don't know him? He's a fine Irish actor."

"No. Who's he, a relative of Jackie Gleason?"

"For the love of . . . no! He's been in a bunch of things, he was great on the telly in *Lifeboat* and *The Treaty*. He's made gobs of pictures, too, *The Field, Michael Collins*, all sorts of things."

Seeing that he still looked bewildered, she racked her brain until she came up with it. "*Braveheart*. You saw *Braveheart*, didn't you?"

"Yeah," he said.

"Okay. Mel Gibson's—William Wallace's boyhood friend when he grew up. A big, stout barrel of a fella with a full red beard, red head, too. His name in the film was, . . . I can't remember what his name was. Mel Gibson was always throwing stones at him."

Dawn finally broke over Terry's face. "That guy? He's huge! He's pretty big around, you know."

"Don't look now, Terry, but you're round."

"You really think I look like him?"

"Sure, except for your lack of whiskers. Grow some and you'd be spot on, the spitting image."

He frowned, doubtful. "If you say so. Think I can act, too?"

"We'll find out soon enough," Maeve said. "Murphy's summoning the players. Let's see if you can light us all up again with your pint pouring palaver."

The order of the straws placed Eamon McDowell first, followed by George Scanlon, with Terry up third, and Nancy Huntzinger last.

Earnest though he was, Eamon soon showed himself not up to the event. He poured beautiful pints with workmanlike shamrocks carved in their heads. When it came to collecting payment, however, he faltered in making change. The wild card that stymied him came from his boyish good looks. Word of the movie-star Yank in the contest attracted a host of young Coyne women, most of them ordering a half-pint of O'Toole's instead of a full glass. At 90 pence each, the half-pint math befuddled Eamon. In consideration of his American roots, the town patrons didn't hold this against him. But his ultimate downfall came from his conversational skills.

"Did you hear about the tour guide saying, 'We're now passing O'Toole's, the finest brewery in Ireland.' And John Smith jumped off the bus yelling, 'I'm damned if we are!'"

Blank stares bore into him and red-faced, he continued. "Then there was the notice outside an Irish dance hall which proclaimed that 'Ladies and gentlemen are welcome regardless of sex.'"

He blushed saying it, and a few giggles ensued. Eamon gave it one last try. "A notorious piker comes into the pub and says, 'Why are you giving me a dirty look, Murphy?' And Murphy says, 'I didn't give you a dirty look. You had it when you came in.'"

Murphy immediately stepped in and patted Eamon on the back "Thanks much, Mr. McDowell, well done. Our next contestant is George Scanlon. Mr. Scanlon?"

Scanlon took over and immediately said, "Ta', Mr. Murphy. Okay, step up lads and lasses for your drinks. First, new rule; I will require exact change."

The swell of spectators laughed, causing Terry to glance over to see Eamon shrink even more. Nancy Huntzinger put her hand on his shoulder while whispering in his ear.

"You should know that I am a picky man," Scanlon said. "In fact, I'm close on to being full bore obsessive compulsive. You've heard the one about the Irishman grabbing hold of the fly landing on his pint and squeezing the littler bugger while saying 'Spit it out! Spit it out!' Well, I tell you now, anyone who spills a drop on this floor will immediately receive a mop and a bucket of suds courtesy of the new management."

Again, the customers laughed as they handed over their notes and coin. All the while, Scanlon poured pint after pint fluidly, each one inscribed with a shamrock so precise it seemed he'd used some kind of a stamp. Holy shit, marveled Terry, the guy's a machine.

"The only doubt I've had about my obsessive compulsion disorder is whether I'm obsessive compulsive enough. My mother used to say to me, 'George, you're always contradicting me. And I'd say, 'Mom, I never do,' and she'd immediately say, 'There you go again.'"

All barked laughter, and Scanlon held out his hands like an icon of Christ as he said, "Everyone have a drink? Thanks so much."

Murphy marched to Scanlon, shaking his hand, saying warmly, "Well done, Mr. Scanlon, well done."

Scanlon bowed and swept away to the wings.

"Next up, Mr. Terry MacBride."

Son of a bitch thought Terry.

"Well," he said, standing at the taps, "tough act to follow. Props to you, Scanlon."

Scanlon grinned, nodding his head.

"Okay, then." He hunted around for something to say, searching the faces of the men and women before him for some kind of encouragement. He plunged in.

"Let's start on a positive note. Who can I get a pint?"

He began drawing pints while he talked rapid fire, "It's great to be vying for this fine tavern, though I'm sure you'll miss Mr. Murphy. They say he's leaving 'cause his best girl spurned him. But when one of his lads told him to forget her, he said, 'How can I forget a girl with a name like *Gobnait ni Mathghamhna*?"

Groans of laughter trickled through the crowd as one disembodied voice rose above, "Did you ever hear such massacred pronunciation?"

Not missing a beat, Terry said, "How about the Yank at market who picked up a melon and cracked wise saying 'Is this the biggest apple you grow around here?' And Maggie minding the stand said, 'Buy that grape or put it down.'"

Again, the reception was mixed, another voice shouting out, "For the love of God, have mercy!"

"How about the terrible storm last week? One farmer said his hen had the wind at her back and laid the same egg five times."

Terry cringed waiting, one beat, two beats, three—the room exploded with laughter.

"Jesus Christ, how many duds do you fire to get a live one?"

Terry replied, "Well, as my dear cousin Henny O'Youngman once told me, 'A thousand gags is worth getting one laugh.'"

Another man stepped up and said, "What's this in me glass?"

Terry looked down, then answered, "That, sir, is a four-leaf clover. I applied it to the head of your pint to bring you extra special luck."

"Huh," said the man, while another said, "There's none on mine, just a shamrock, nicely done though it is."

"True, sir," said Terry. "However, I'm in the competition of my life and when preparing, I had to make a decision. Should I embellish tradition or stick to it? How will the judges react? So, back in the states I conferred with my beloved godfather Remo O'Gaggi. You might know him for his role in our other countryman Martin McScorcese's film *Casino*. I asked him what I should do, and Remo said, 'It's a brilliant idea . . . but look, why take a chance?' So, I did both. Half the pints I drew have four-leaf clovers, half shamrocks. Let's hope the luck spreads generally throughout this pub and all of Ireland."

The audience generally laughed while doing their best single-handed clapping.

Nancy Huntzinger took her turn with what looked like little enthusiasm. She did a commendable job pouring and embellishing stout, also handling every transaction without a hitch. Unfortunately, her engagement with the customers seemed tame at this point. Except for one stunning moment when without warning, she started singing *Jimmy Mó Mhíle Stór*. She sang the plaintive ballad of her boyo gone off to sea beautifully, yearningly, in perfect Irish.

The milling imbibers stopped moving as though frozen in place deep in outer space. She finished, but still, no one budged for a full beat of the heart. As one they all cried to the rooftop in a joyous uproar. Nancy smiled humbly and retired from behind the bar.

"After long, painful deliberation, the judges have come to a consensus on the winner of this day's challenge," Murphy announced. "The order of accomplishment—and all of our contestants are very well accomplished," he continued, "are Mr. Eamon McDowell, fourth, Ms. Nancy Huntzinger, third, Mr. Terry MacBride, second, and first, today's champion, is Mr. George Scanlon. Congratulations, Mr. Scanlon."

The shout went up and Terry joined the applause with everyone else, smiling grimly.

"What this means, ladies and gentlemen, is that the victor of O'Toole's Brewery's first ever win-a-public house contest will be decided tomorrow in the final event. I cannot think of a more fitting conclusion to this heated competition."

"I've made it to the last round, Mary," Terry spoke into the receiver, "but I'm facing a formidable foe tomorrow."

"Just one?" Mary said. "I thought there were four finalists."

Terry shook his head as if she could see him, "No, the others are too far behind. The woman, Nancy Huntzinger, told me that she and the young fellow McDowell decided to leave in the morning. They have no chance, so they're packing up to tour the country together for a week or two before heading home. Nice lady, she is, turns out."

"I thought you said she was a bit older than the kid."

"She is," said Terry, "lucky for both of them."

Mary laughed.

"Anyway, it's dead even between me and Scanlon now, though he might have the advantage. He won the pint pouring leg, a lot of back and forth with the patrons. He knocked them dead and tomorrow we tell stories to the judges."

"Well, how did you do?"

"I came in second."

"That's good, Terry, I'm sure you'll do fine. Just rally your inner smart-ass self and get on the job. I have faith in you, MacBride, so step up and stand in."

Surprised, he said, "Ah, Mary, you're the best. I'll give it my all."

"Swear?" she said.

"Swear."

"All right then, go to bed now and wake up roaring."

Scanlon began. "Dr. Samuel Johnson pretty much hit the head of the nail when he said 'the Irish are a truthful race. They never speak well of one another.' This to be expected from a Brit who lived when most thought we hung from trees by our tails, though they would've preferred by our necks. But Johnson also appreciated certain Irishmen, one being Oliver Goldsmith, author of *She Stoops to Conquer*. Before that, Goldsmith earned notoriety for his other wicked satires, often at the expense of the English. True to form, Goldsmith also liked a taste more often than not, which more often than not created a gaping hole in his purse. Upon more than one occasion he supplicated Johnson for a few pounds for rent to keep the sheriff at bay. And, upon many of those occasions, Johnson would send the money to Goldsmith who would immediately drink it up. Frustrated when asked again, Johnson marched over to Goldsmith and asked him if he had anything he could sell. Goldsmith gave him a sheath of papers which Johnson took to Newberry and sold for 60 pounds. The haphazard wad of papers was published as the *Vicar of Wakefield*.

"Johnson gave the coin to the landlady, then later said in exasperation, 'For God's sake, Goldsmith, why didn't you sell the manuscript yourself and pay the rent?' And Goldsmith said, 'I didn't think of it.'

"'But, if you don't write for money, why do you write?' asked Johnson.

"With his nose in the air, Goldsmith said, 'My dear friend, I certainly do not write for moneygrubbing landladies. I write for, . . . I write for, . . . now why in hell's name do I write?'

"And that sums up, good people of Coyne, both the genius of Ireland and its madness. I am proud to be a relative, even if but a synthetic one."

Scanlon bowed to a warm round of applause. Murphy shook his hand in passing, then addressed the audience."

"Thank you, Mr. Scanlon, for your entertaining and enlightening trip down memory lane. We will now adjourn for some lunch, after which Mr. MacBride will regale us as well, we hope, with his take upon the Irish condition."

"Of course," Terry began, "as Mr. Scanlon so nicely pointed out, the Irish command the language. But, there's more to be told, some quite mystifying.

"More than a century ago, the great showman P.T. Barnum decided he needed new blood in his sideshows of unusual people and odd curiosities. He told all of his scouts to search out the world for new acts. One of them came into his office and said, 'Sir, there are rumors coming out of Ireland of an exceptionally powerful man there.'

"'Oh? Did you offer him a tryout?'

"'We telegrammed him, but he declined.'

"'Really? So, do you think these claims of his strength are true or just folderol?'

"The aide shrugged, 'I don't know, sir, no one here has ever seen him.'

"'What's his name?'

"'He's known as Strongman McCarthy.'

"Interest piqued, Barnum decided to go to Ireland to see for himself. He booked the fastest liner across the ocean, rode the express train to Drummin, and hired a car to drive him to the village of Bohola, where the prodigious McCarthy was rumored to be. Outside Bohola, they passed a field where Barnum spied a man behind a plow churning up a great earthen furrow like a spoon through chocolate batter. To Barnum's amazement, the man pushed the plow without oxen or donkeys anywhere in sight.

"'You must be Strongman McCarthy!' cried out Barnum.

"'Ah, you flatter me, sir,' said the stout farmer, wiping his brow with a kerchief. 'I'm no way near the man.' He then picked up the plow with one hand and pointed down the road, 'He's in Bohola right now, performing for the locals.'

"Stunned, Barnum thanked him and urged his driver to the village with all deliberate speed. In no time they arrived at the outskirts of Bohola where Barnum shouted at the driver to halt. In a blacksmith shop next to them, a smith stood shoeing a draft horse. Barnum watched slack jawed as the blacksmith held the horse's leg over his shoulder while pounding a nail into the shoe with his bare fist.

"'I've found you, Strongman McCarthy!' Barnum bellowed.

"Startled, the brawny smithy looked at him and red with embarrassment, said, 'Bless you, you're generous with your compliments, but I'm hardly the physical phenomenon of the likes of McCarthy.' He dropped the horse off his shoulders, picked up his anvil with one hand and pointed, saying, 'You'll find him dead center in town putting on a show for the local folks.'

"Flabbergasted, Barnum jumped into the car and headed into the village. In no time, the car couldn't move, swallowed up by the crush of people around the square. Barnum exited the car and started walking toward the nexus of the packed crowd. As he pushed and wheedled his way forward, he looked up and saw a large banner hanging across the street. A great cheering roar went up as he read the letters on the banner: 'Strongman McCarthy, World's Strongest Man.'

"Barnum shoved and thrust his way finally to the front as another shout of approbation split the air. He looked up and saw a tiny stage in the square upon which stood a spare man of average-height wearing dull, beige boxer tights on skinny pins, a faded lavender silk sash around his waist, and a canned-pea green colored undershirt on his inverted chest with three whiskers peeking out of the middle. The slight man sported a large proboscis with two enormous black mustaches hanging like buggy fenders down his dour mouth. Using one large hand to push back his thickly pomaded black hair, he barked, 'And, now for my next feat of improbable strength—'

"Dumbfounded, Barnum said to himself, 'this is Strongman McCarthy?'

"'—I will pick myself up by the seat of me pants and hold myself out at arm's length.'"

Terry paused.

"And he did."

He waited for it, he waited.

The judges began a measured, rolling laugh, slowly doubling over. The local onlookers watched, eyes popped, befuddled. Then, the dam burst roaring through the small pub.

"I won," Terry said. Telling her, he felt like he was seven years old again, cozy and comfortable buried in warm bedcovers, waking up stretching on a new spring day. He felt like he could kiss the wind.

"My God, Terry, that's wonderful!" Mary said, "I thought you didn't have a chance, really."

"Not a tinker's chance, huh?" he said wryly. "Neither did I, I guess. But I won and it was wonderful."

"My God, it's just hard to believe. I've never known anyone who won anything, never mind myself."

"Yeah," he said. "So, when you coming over?"

A pause, then "When am I coming over? I don't know, never."

"Oh, come on, Mary, you have to see my new concern. It's a dream come true, and just wait until I fix it up."

"I can wait, Terry," She said. "Christ sake, it's your dream, not mine. I've been working in a bar all my life it seems, nowhere near a romantic notion for me."

"Sure," Terry said quietly, "I just thought you'd like a nice holiday in the old country. I'd pick up your airfare, of course, put you up in a decent B&B."

"Well, that's really nice of you, Terry," she said sweetly, "but I'm just up to my neck, here. Annie's coming home for spring break and I plan on doing something with her, so . . .."

"Sure, sure. Listen, just think of it as an open invitation. I'd love to show you around, you know?"

"Thanks, Terry, that'd be great. One of these days . . .."

A bit sad, Terry turned his attention to his new acquisition. After surviving the maelstrom of winning the prize, he had to admit to himself that in the broad light of day, it was a dump. Whoever laid out the interior created a mini-rabbit warren of ever darkening nooks and crannies crammed everywhere possible into a narrow scalene footprint.

A door wedged in at the back opened to reveal a steep stairway. Upstairs led to a stifling loft with two filthy opaque windows likely dating to the 18th century. Broken bar stools, tables, and other trash filled the room. Downstairs he found a cramped cellar where the furnace stood, emitting heat that rose through old cast-iron gratings up to the floors above.

He worked his way around a labyrinth of stout kegs, full and empty, and other abandoned equipment. To his surprise, he discovered that the pipes from the loos upstairs were still connected to an old septic tank. Others led from the tank to the outside wall, but to what drain field? Buildings on all sides took up any past open ground. Curious, he traced the line from the tank elbow to the wall until he noticed an old decal on the pipe, "Co. Monahgan Water Services." It hit him then. The old septic tank had been joined to the town's sewer system. Why in the world keep an old septic tank going?

Terry leaned over the tank to see better. Jesus Christ, he mouthed, sucking in his breath at the odor. No matter why it was coupled up with the sewer line, it seriously needed basic maintenance. He'd have to deal with that sooner rather than later.

First, though, he addressed the pub front door, stripping and painting its stout wood Fisherman Green with gold trim. Then, he washed clean the small windowpanes set in two rows at the top of the door. He surveyed the crazy accessway that regularly deposited unwary customers behind the bar instead of in front. Someday, he'd have to redesign the entire setup. For now, though, it would have to wait until he started earning some cash.

After finishing the door, he bleached the wooden floors followed with a polyurethane application. He also scrubbed down all of the tables, the stools, and the bar top. He rubbed them all in with Murphy's oil soap, laughing as he wondered if the former proprietor owned shares in the company. Just as he finished this task, the lighting lads came in with the new fixtures to brighten up the place. On the back wall past the bar, he installed a 36-inch TV for Irish hurling and football games to be viewed at his discretion, of course. He felt a small pang of yearning for the Red Sox and the Phillies games underway now. He would no longer see them anymore unless one or both teams made it to the World Series. Unlikely.

While he awaited the final touch, Terry cleared out all the refuse upstairs, setting it curbside. He mopped and scrubbed the loft clean, including the windows. Then, he painted the walls a bright yellow, and the window frames eggshell white. In the corner next to the wall facing the square, he built a tiny bathroom above the loos on the first floor. He fitted pipes below for a shower, sink, and commode, closing it off with a folding door. This left room for a single bed, a small dresser, and a very small armoire, though no chair. He compensated by ordering one of those big upright pillows with arms sticking out for reading in bed or watching the telly. Next to it on the dresser, he place a little boom box to listen to tunes on the radio or diskettes. A few lights and he felt at home, rent free. He would need a throw rug or two, though. Maybe he'd find one at Maeve McGowan's curiosity shop.

Terry put off dealing with the cellar for as long as he could, but he knew that it loomed above him somehow below him. It annoyed the hell out of him that he'd have to get into it. He thought he'd put plumbing behind him and now he had to deal with this mess, and for no good reason. He'd run into Murphy in the square a week back and asked him directly, "Murphy, why the heck did you keep that crazy septic sewer set-up in the cellar?"

Murphy said, "Save water. They charge for it in Ireland these days, can you imagine? With water coming out of our ears?"

"You save that much on water?" Terry said.

"Takes a lot of water to push shite through a pipe. But, it's the principle, mostly."

"Yeah, but you still have to clean sludge out of the tank regularly. The gas build-up could get dicey."

"So, I hire a couple of strong gossoons to dig it out for a few punts. It's still cheaper."

"Yeah, well, you might've hired them one last time before you handed it over to me."

"Yeah," said Murphy, "I thought about it, but . . .," and smiling, said, "you know, I was retiring and such."

"Okay," said Terry, "thanks."

Thanks a lot, he said to himself. He took a deep mental breath and began assembling the tools he thought he might need to go after it, including some Wellingtons. Before he started in, though, the final embellishment arrived at the door.

Terry stood watching as the men on the scaffolding carefully laid in the letters, red with green and white trim stretching across the length of the storefront façade. They finished surprisingly fast, and he beamed when he read it:

The Red Pump Road
Public House
Terrence P. MacBride, Proprietor

Wiping away a few stray tears, Terry said silently, thanks Mom, Dad. He rubbed his eyes and tipped the workers before walking down the street. Time to buy some rugs.

"So, when's the official grand opening?"

Maeve asked him the question while rolling up the rugs he bought, a bit too small to cover the loft's entire floor, but a start. With practiced hands, she wrapped them in brown paper and tied them tight with twine.

"In a week or two," he said. "I have to deal with some waste management matters in the cellar."

"I see how that could be a priority," she said. "The place smelled pretty ripe oft times in the warm months."

"Yeah, it goes deeper than that. Could be some safety issues about it, too."

She pursed her lips, dipping her head slightly, knowingly. "Well, I hope it all falls into place for you. I'll be over to see how it goes, having a vested interest in your success and all. Given that I and me fellow judges gave you the nod, you better come through."

"Sure," Terry said. "I'll do my best not to disappoint."

Slightly distracted, he surveilled the trinkets and knick-knacks around the shop. Counters full of miniature harps and Irish crosses stood next to racks full of Spice Girls and U2 CDs. Knitted linen doilies hung from the walls adjacent to shelves of coffee table books on Irish mansions and stone beehive huts. It would take him days to inventory everything here, he thought. He glanced up above Maeve and saw a bright red, yellow, and orange paper tunnel a foot in diameter undulating from one end of the ceiling to the other.

"What's that?" he asked, pointing above.

Maeve craned her neck around and up. "Oh, that's the trunk of a dragon." She looked back at Terry and grinned, "For a Chinese New Year's party. The tail and head are around here somewhere."

"A Chinese New Year's party? You have a large population in Coyne, do you?"

She smiled, a bit abashed, "I suppose not. I bought it on a whim three years ago. No one's shown much interest since then."

"Huh," he said, still staring at it. "You say you still have the head and the tail?"

"Yeah, sure."

"In good shape?"

"Yes."

"When is the Chinese New Year?" Terry asked.

"It's lunar, so sometime around the beginning of the year, January or February."

"So, it's past," he said.

"This year," said Maeve, "but they celebrate it every year."

He dropped his sight to hers. "How much?"

"At this point, five pounds."

"I'll take it," he said, reaching into his wallet. "I'm short. Can you put it on layaway?"

"Sure," she said, "but the vig will be 50%."

"Reading a lot of Elmore Leonard, huh?"

"Yeah," she said, "but I'm not kidding."

"I'm sure you aren't. I'll come get it later, if that's okay."

"I don't know, after three years there's always a mad rush for dragons around here. Don't wait too long."

Smiling, he grabbed the bundled rugs and left the shop.

On his way back, he thought about Maeve McGowan. Skinnier than Mary, almost bony, she still caught his eye. Such a vibrant person, full sure of herself no matter what. So, now he was teeter-tottering between two women? God knew he was better off single.

Two weeks later, the Red Pump finally opened. Terry felt more relief than pride of ownership. Focused on being ready, he'd dug a sizeable hole in his finances, including taking John Smith and a couple of other neighbors on as his staff. Coin coming in helped him to reestablish his equilibrium. Indeed, the town people jammed the place, their chatter nearly drowning out the Irish music echoing throughout.

Without question, the new public house in Coyne proved to be a spanking success to all in attendance. Word of mouth spread the news repeated to Terry by well lubricated patrons: "You're the man, MacBride, you're the man!"

Terry breathed his relief that night, and better yet, every night afterwards for the next two weeks. The success of the Red Pump, as the locals soon called it, had legs and Terry was in the black.

Terry paid off Maeve first thing. She attended the opening night but hadn't shown up since. Aside from nipping the 50% interest right off, he wanted to see her.

"You had a good turnout for the opening," she said.

"We did, and it's kept up well since."

"Feeling flush, now, are you?"

Terry backed off, "Well, I'm able to pay off some of my bills. I'm hopeful this age of prosperity will continue for some time."

"Yes," she said, "that's certainly everyone's wish."

"So," Terry said, leaning his elbows on the counter, "when can I get my dragon?"

"In a hurry, are you? We're a good eight or more months off from New Year's, you know."

"True that, but I thought what the hell. Why not sponsor a celebration now? A special event. Who'll be the wiser in Coyne?"

She snickered, "Quit the enterpriser you are, Mr. MacBride." She thought for a moment, then said, "How about I deliver it to you this Sunday morning?"

"You don't want me to fetch it now?"

"No, I still have to dig up the head and tail. You surprised me by settling your debt so soon."

"Yeah, well, I couldn't afford not to. Anyway, Sunday's fine, though you know I can't serve alcoholic beverages 'til 12:30. I could lose my license if someone were to rat me out." He smiled at his own joke.

"Tea will be fine," Maeve said.

"You sure you don't need help bringing it over? It'll be pretty unwieldy with the head and all."

"I'll manage," she said. "I can get a lad to help me if I need to."

"I imagine so. So, 10:00 am? Great, see you then."

On Sunday, Terry awoke early to his alarm. He jumped out of bed, pulled off his t-shirt and drawers, and stepped up to the sink to shave. Afterwards, he hopped into the shower for a thorough cleansing. After drying off, he climbed into fresh drawers and donned out of armoire his best casual weekend shirt and khakis. Socks and shoes, comb hair, and down the stairs.

He looked at his watch, 9:50, not bad. Enough time to get the kettle going and warm up a few biscuits in the microwave. He'd already told John Smith not to set up this morning. So, he had the place all to himself and his guest Maeve, at least until half past noon. Everything looked to be in place, he thought, smiling as he pushed open the door to the first floor.

The lights were on. Surprised, he started toward the bar but stopped cold in his tracks. Draped in twisted loops across the counter lay the Chinese dragon grinning at him, fangs, horns, and barbed tail complete. Terry hesitated, then started to tur around.

"Good morning, Terry," said Maeve, sitting in the middle booth behind him. Opposite her sat two young men, black haired, dark red lips, ivory white skin, deep blue eyes staring dully at him.

"We let ourselves in," she said, "hope you don't mind."

"No," said Terry carefully, "that's okay, I guess. Who are these guys?"

"A couple of friends of mine from Omeath. They helped me bring the dragon, thank God. You should've seen me, tripping all over it before they arrived. It's a miracle I didn't tear the paper. Anyway, there it is."

"Sure, thanks." He shifted weight. "So, what can I do for you? Can I get you some tea, maybe?"

Maeve lifted her cup, "Already served ourselves. Cheeky, no? We got here pretty early, didn't want to wake you. I guess you're still on Boston time."

He bayed a single brittle laugh.

"Why don't you get yourself some tea and sit with us, have a nice chat."

Terry moved around the bar and poured himself a pint glass of water and returned to sit at the table.

"Great," said Maeve. She paused. "Introductions are in order. This is Declan Dougherty and his cousin Tommy White just here for the weekend. They visit now and then to help me with some heavy lifting."

The two men grumbled greetings and slid into silence.

Maeve said, "Terry, we're very happy to see your brilliant success with the pub. You've really made quite a go of it, beyond all expectations. You've revived its fortunes, turning it once again into a great asset for Coyne. For all of Ireland."

"I appreciate your compliments," said Terry flatly.

"Yes," Maeve said, looking down at the tabletop, "but there's more you can do." She raised her eyes to fix them on his, "More you must do. An obligation."

Terry sat back.

"As a son of Ireland, you're well aware of the struggle we've been in with the Brit oppressors for almost a millennium. They have soaked our nation with its people's blood without compunction or contrition. And they insist upon occupying our land to continue exploiting our fellow countrymen and women to this day. The fight goes on, Terry."

"Wait a minute," he said, "I thought things are supposed to be changing. At least, that's what all the papers are saying. Both the Ulster guys and the IRA sent out signals about ceasefires. Jesus, you think I'd be here otherwise?"

Maeve sneered, "The UDA and the UVA are all murderers and drug dealers. They'll never stop. And neither will we until we free all of Ireland. Oh, some weak sisters in the organization might dither about peace, but the true freedom fighters will fight on 'til we win." Her eyes seemed to smolder, "and we will need everyone's help to prevail, including you, MacBride."

He took inventory around the table before replying. "What do you need?"

"A tithe to fund the cause."

"A tithe. How much?"

"Twenty-five percent rendered each month."

Terry sat quietly, looking around the table. "I don't suppose this had anything to do with Murphy selling his pub."

Dougherty raised halfway up, huge fist curled, until Maeve touched him lightly. He sat down, stone-faced.

"Murphy's out, true enough. He has no heart for it anymore. This is about you now, MacBride. What, you thought we'd keep Ireland all quaint and rustic just for your benefit? Welcome to the real world. Step up, MacBride, like your heroic ancestor did. Earn your keep."

Terry nodded. "So, it's stone soup for me from here on in."

Maeve rose up. "I don't care what you call it. Just be ready by the end of the month."

The three of them left the pub, filing by John Smith as he strolled in to set up for the post-Mass crowd. He gave them a backward look, then stopped at the edge of the bar.

"What's this?" he asked.

"A Chinese dragon," said Terry morosely. "I bought it from Maeve last week. She and her friends brought it over."

"Oh. What do you plan on doing with it?" John asked.

"A special event. Chinese New Year's."

"Hah." He thought a moment, then said, "Didn't they already celebrate that back in February?"

"I guess," Terry muttered. "But May Day's coming up, we could do it then. Most don't know what day Chinese New Year's on, and for those that do, we can tell them it's a Commie Chinese New Year's Celebration."

"Now that's crackling genius thinking," said John. "Any excuse to raise a pint, right?"

"Sure." Terry stood up and walked over. "Let me get it off the bar. I'll stick it in the cellar for now."

After closing up, John turned off the lights. Terry sat in the dark, wondering what would be next. Kneecapping, maybe? Or a perp walk to the poor house. He could go home with his tail between his legs, but how could he face that at Maculkey's? How could he face Mary? Lord, he missed Mary.

He sighed and lifted himself up to leave. Outside, he pulled the door shut, locked it, then gave the doorknob another yank to be sure.

He called Mary, but she didn't answer. Alone, he considered his options. He decided to go see Murphy.

Liam Murphy answered the front door of his house just a block off the square. As soon as he saw who stood in front of him, he stepped aside. Terry walked in.

"When did it happen?"

"Yesterday morning. She and two strongarms were sitting at a table when I came downstairs. They let themselves in so as not to disturb me, she said."

"Shite. And how much was she asking?"

They sat in the front parlor, tea and biscuits before them. Terry could hear Murphy's wife rattling around in the kitchen, letting them talk in private. The house looked nice, he thought, well kept but also well lived in. Irish lace framed on the wall, family pictures when the kids were young, gone off now like wild geese. A briquette of turf lying in the hearth for a special occasion. Evidence of a life he'd never lived.

"Twenty-five percent. Monthly."

"Mother of God, what a feckin' leech! Trying to drain you like that, she's a regular Vampirella."

"How much did you have to pay?" Terry asked.

"Fifteen percent between the two of 'em," he said, staring off, muttering, "That was plenty enough."

"Two of them?" Terry said, "What do you mean 'two of them?'"

Murphy turned his attention back to Terry. "There's IRA Lieutenant Maeve McGowan running the Provos here. She's batshit crazy, a disciple of Michael McKevitt, a real feckin' thug if ever there was one. Then, there's the UDA—" Seeing Terry's blank expression, he said, "The Ulster Defence Association, formerly in cahoots with the Ulster Freedom Fighters. The UDA declared a ceasefire in '94, but some of the UFF psychos are still at it. I'm surprised that lot haven't come at you as well yet. Anyway, I paid them both, 15% split down the middle. Still, the burden of it chased me out of the business over time. The O'Toole's contest was a godsend. I jumped at it."

Terry rubbed his jaw, processing everything. "So, you're telling me I can look forward to another holdup by some Ulster whack jobs?"

Murphy nodded his head, "For sure. I mean, their man is right in there with you."

Confounded, Terry said, "Who?"

"John Smith," Murphy said, as though Terry should have known. "He's been a Union agent for decades, just as long as McGowan with the IRA." Terry sat utterly befuddled while Murphy went on, "It's funny, you know, Maeve McGowan's a Protestant while Smith's a Catholic. Yet, here she is a diehard nationalist whilst he's defending Northern Ireland's political status. Just goes to show . . ..

"Anyway, the balance of power in Coyne has been equal, leading to an informal truce between the parties, thank God. When I told them I planned on retiring, that's when they struck the deal over the contest for the bar. O'Toole's was only too glad to accommodate."

Terry swung his head like a bull in an arena stuck by the matador. "You mean, I'm the ultimate patsy?"

Murphy scrunched his face sympathetically, "No, Terry. You're the winner."

"Cold comfort, Mr. Murphy."

"I can see your point of view. Anyway, John will be after you, no question. He's not mad like McGowan, but he will show muscle if he must. When he first talked to me, I waffled a bit. Next thing you know, I'm walking home one night when two bully boys sandwich me, knock me down to the pavement. One leans in and says, 'We aren't feckin' around here, Murphy. I swear to God, if you don't do what Smith wants, I'll pop a pea in your pod myself,' poking his index finger into my temple with every syllable. I paid them both.

"But it looks like the Maude Gonne of Coyne wants it all, now. This could lead to a new level of complication."

Murphy stood up, "I'd tread carefully if I were you, Terry."

All the way back to the Red Pump, Terry brooded about the whole thing. Cut and run, sure, but he wouldn't escape his bitterness. They had ruined his dream come true. They should be paying him, not winning.

He sat up in bed all night until he decided what to do.

When John Smith walked into the pub, before he could begin his routine, Terry stepped up to him at the bar.

"I did some research," he said, "and I learned that you'll be wanting considerations concerning the Red Pump."

John halted. Terry watched a series of rapid-fire expressions cross his face, finally settling into a calm firmness, waiting.

"And?" Smith said.

"And, I don't seem to have much choice, do I?"

Smith softened a bit. "No, Terry, I'm sorry, but you don't."

"All right," Terry said, "but, here's the thing. Your IRA doppelganger has already spoken to me. She's made clear what she wants. Twenty-five percent. All of it."

Smith suddenly seemed less composed. "Why that's untenable, completely out of the question, highway rob—"

"I know. If anyone takes that much, we can change the name from Red Pump to the Golden Goose Grill."

"I'm going to have to have a word with her," Smith said, his mouth clenched.

"No, you're not. Not alone. I'm not going to help you yahoos fire up a brand-new bloodbath. I'll be long gone before that. Instead, we will meet, the two of you and any associates you both would like to invite, sans hardware, here at the Red Pump. And we will sort this out starting with the framework of the old arrangement, percentage to be determined. If you agree, say yes or no."

Irritated, Smith didn't respond.

"Yes or no."

Finally, the gray-haired Irishman said, "Yes."

"Very well. Sunday morning, 10:00 am. I'll invite Maeve and make sure she understands the conditions."

He started to leave, then said, "Oh, one other thing. Your services here are no longer needed. You can go now, I'll give you your final check on Sunday."

Smith slid past the bar and went out the door.

Later that night when fully dark, Terry slipped a letter about the meeting into Maeve's curios shop postal slot. As instructed, she called the next morning with a single-word answer, "Yes."

He said "Okay" and hung up. Now, he could get to work.

After closing Saturday night, Terry headed down into the cellar with his toolbox and walked over to the old septic tank. Next to the access lid on top, he found the small cap used to bleed excess gas. He set the box town and put on a mask, then loosened the cap using penetrating oil and a heavy-duty wrench. A rush of foul-smelling fumes began to exude which he measured with a portable methane detector. He allowed it to escape slowly, taking timed readings. Once the gas content dropped to a certain level, he twisted the cap tightly back on.

He got to his feet and positioned a step ladder near the tank just beneath a heating grate above. He climbed the ladder and twisted hanger wire hooks to the grate spaced in a measured circle. He stepped down and retrieved the trunk of the Chinese dragon, its head already removed, and one end sealed shut by the tail paper and duct tape. He carried the closed end of the dragon up the ladder and carefully taped it tight to the grate and the hanging wire hooks. Then, he gently released the body, which stretched out down to touch the septic tank top.

Terry descended and moved the ladder to the side. He cut long stripes of tape and arrayed them in a circle just outside of the tank's lid. He taped half of the dragon tube around the access lid and carefully affixed tape lengths to the other half. Then, he quickly popped and propped open the lid and taped the rest of the tube around the opening with the lid up inside as fast as he could, airtight.

The dragon trunk billowed around as gas filled it until it reached the top at the grating. A precarious arrangement for sure that he would have been forced to attend to before, thought Terry, now would serve another purpose.

Maeve and her men arrived first, raising their arms and twirling to show they were unarmed. Terry directed them back to a table near the loos, the only one with chairs upright. The others rested upside down on the tables in preparation for mopping the floors, Terry told them.

John Smith came in a few minutes later, also with two loose-limbed companions. When Terry asked about armament, exasperated, John answered, "Not my style."

"All right," Terry said, "Take your seats with the others. I'm going to jack up the heat a bit downstairs, then I'll be back to talk. Don't assassinate each other while I'm gone."

He headed downstairs to quickly stoop by the bloated dragon tube. Using an ice pick, he poked a hole in the lower part of the dragon cylinder and quickly stuck the methane detector tube in for a reading. Pulling it out, he rapidly slapped a stamp of duct tape on the hole. He checked the reading and nodded his head, satisfied. He tossed the detector aside and reached for the spolette he'd made last week. Set to burn for fifteen minutes, the black powder fuse reminded him of childhood days hunting deer with his dad using muzzle loaders. Thanks again, Dad, he thought.

Terry slipped one end of the fuse an inch into the small hole and taped it off. He lit the other end and left for the stairs.

"O'Toole's, anyone? Tea?" he said, standing behind the bar. They all looked at him like a fugitive from a looney bin.

"I'll have a cupper, then," he said, searching beneath the counter. He barked, "Feck!" Standing up, he said, "No cream. I'll pop over and borrow some next door, just be a sec," he rattled off, stepping out.

Murphy waited by the curb in his car. Terry hopped in, and they took off. One block from The Red Pump, they heard the sound of a deep thump. Terry levered around to see a billow of smoke puff above the pub.

"Did you kill them all?" asked Murphy.

"Of course not," Terry said facing front. "You think I'm a murderer like that lot? I checked the methane level half a dozen times, just enough to blow through the grate, that's all. They all should smell pretty much the way they always do, stinking up the place."

"True enough." Murphy glanced over at Terry and said wryly, "Now you know why I had to save on the water tax."

He drove straight to Shannon. Terry jumped out and grabbed his bag. "Good luck, Murphy, and thanks for the ride. Hope you don't get in trouble for this."

"No problem, peace is on its way. Those hooligans are on their way out."

"Good to know. Well, take care, Liam."

"You as well, Terry."

Waiting in the airport, he called Mary. "Listen, I'm coming home, Aer Lingus Flight 420, into Logan around 9:00 pm. When I'm back, I'll come see you."

She met him at the airport.

Kenny left Maculkey's, and Terry took his place. Six months later, he and Mary moved in together, with her daughter Annie's full approval.

On April 10th, 1998, the Irish Republic and Northern Ireland struck the Good Friday Agreement, ending the Troubles after three decades.

A few weeks later, Mary called out, "Terry, answer the phone."

He screwed up his face, "Why? You're right there."

"Because it's for you, buddy! Overseas."

Terry headed over to grab the phone, which Mary hit him with lightly on the arm. He leaned over and gave her a peck on the cheek as he took the receiver.

"Terry MacBride here."

"Terry," a distant voice said, "it's Liam Murphy, from Coyne, Ireland."

"Liam Murphy!" said Terry. "How the hell are you? Still kicking? No repercussions?"

"No, no, that's done. They signed the peace; things are on the rise."

"Well, that's great Murphy, congratulations. So, retirement's good, yes?"

"Well, no, not exactly," he said. "I've come out of retirement a bit. After you left, O'Toole's asked me to take over the pub. It's still called the Red Pump, by the way."

"Oh," said Terry, feeling a pang of remorse. "That's great, Liam, I'm glad for you. I hope the damage wasn't too great after the, uh, incident."

"No, not so bad," said Murphy, "aside from shite being all over the place."

"Really? I must've miscalculated the amount of methane after all. No one was hurt, were they?"

"No, not at all, outside of their egos and the steep dry-cleaning bills. They all cleared out except for Smith. He's still touring people around. McGowan left for Belfast, I think. You're a feckin' hero around these parts now."

"No way! Maybe I should return."

Murphy remained quiet for a moment. "That's why I called, Terry. Things are better around here, business is booming. People come to the pub just to hear your story over and over again."

"Well, that's great, Murphy, but I'm pretty much settled—"

"Yeah, I was thinking, Terry. I'd like to buy the place back."

"Really?"

"Yeah. Officially, the place is yours, your name is still on the title and all. But expenses have accrued, plus taxes, so you couldn't just walk in and take over. I thought I could relieve you of the burden—"

"And the water tax," Terry said.

"Yeah. Well, they got rid of that this year, so, no. But, anyway—"

"How much?" Terry said.

"Oh. Well, there are expenses . . . ."

"C'mon, spit it out."

"35,000 Irish."

Terry crunched the math rapid fire. "Hold on," he said. He covered the receiver and yelled out to Maculkey at the end of the bar, "Mike, I'll buy you out, $50,000 cash down payment."

"Done!" yelled Maculkey.

Terry held the phone to his ear, "40,000 pounds and you get it back. On condition that you don't change the name."

"Done," said Murphy.

They all partied wildly at the grand opening of The Red Pump Pub West, four-leaf clovers neatly carved into every pint of Murphy's Stout.

Mary threw her arm around Terry's shoulder and said, "So, what's next, *acushla*?"

Terry rubbed his chin. "A special event. Chinese New Year, maybe." He turned his head to look at her. "What do you think?"

"They celebrated that a couple months back, no? We'd have to wait a year."

He shrugged, "We could do it next month." She pulled back, smiling but doubtful.

"Who the hell would know?" he said, grabbing her close in to plant a kiss on her cheek. He said, "Who the hell cares?"

John Hall

That morning, John Hall woke up and decided to start drinking again. He hadn't had a drop for twenty-one years for obvious reasons and there was no obvious reason why he started again that morning. He simply opened his eyes, sat up, pulled his green baseball cap off the bed post and put it on. Without waking his wife, he climbed out of bed and left the room to search the breakfront for a bottle.

John stooped down to open one of the scarred, maple doors and began rooting around, pulling out the bottles by their necks to see what was there. He found a dusty one, with just a finger left of peach brandy. He also found a third of a bottle of Amaretto, an unopened Dry Sack, some Piña Colada mix, and various other odds and ends kept around for friends who might want a drink. Not many did, though, either because they didn't drink much or didn't want to, around him. He didn't care, it had nothing to do with his drinking. The left-over stuff told the story of what he didn't like when he was drinking. Before he quit drinking the last time, he finished off the good stuff. All that was left now had piled up over decades after different parties and celebrations. Well, he wouldn't let it pile up anymore.

After wading through everything in the liquor cabinet at home, John went out and bought his old favorite, Cutty Sark, in pint bottles easy to hide. In the old days, he used to call it Cutty Shark, joking with his boys that the Shark had taken a chomp out of him again, that the old Shark had hold of his leg and wouldn't let go, kept gnawing away. But it was okay, fellas, he'd say, it was okay because that dumb, fuckin' Shark was chewing on his hollow leg. So, it didn't hurt. The fellas all would laugh, phlegmy with booze and cigarette junk.

He slowly began to mess up. He started missing work a day here and there. The days he made it in, he was late and high. Before going inside, he'd drink a little peppermint schnapps to cover his breath. But Pete, the floor foreman, didn't take too long to figure it out anyway.

"Yo, John," he yelled, "what the fuck?"

He smiled sheepishly and got to work.

For years, John operated a forklift, ever so deftly slipping the bars under the skids and maneuvering them over to the vans. He never lost one sheet of the stack of newly printed fliers or letters, brochures, mini-catalogs, broadsides, whatever they'd run off the press that day or the night before. The aroma of fresh ink evoked mimeographed tests handed out by their old teachers, each student bringing them to their noses for one strong sniff before plowing into the problems.

For a while he managed to keep it all together, which kept Pete at bay. Then, on a day of reckoning, John drove a corner of the skid into one side of the loading dock door. A flutter of newly printed sales sheets wafted to the floor.

"Oops, sorry Pete," John said, already hurrying around the bar of the forklift to retrieve the fallen promos. "It's okay, Pete, none of 'em even got dirty. Woo, lucky me!"

He stayed out the next three days.

On Friday morning, he came in sober though a bit slow. But the Shark in a Mountain Dew bottle gave him a lift at lunch time, and he roared through the afternoon, showing Pete that he was back on top of it.

The owner, Rob, called him into his office. In his mid-forties, slightly paunchy and with thinning blond hair, Rob didn't allow his appearance to hide his amiable, Southern Maryland working-class roots. After a hitch in the army, Rob had started as a pressman on the night shift. His unfailingly friendly manner caused a longtime rep to bring him down to try sales. Twenty years later, he bought the company from the retiring owner. Rob ran a union shop, and everyone loved him except for the strippers, of course, who loved no one. He was almost glad when the new, direct-to-press technology forced him to close the stripping department, though he did give all those laid off more than healthy severance checks.

He gazed at John in genuine bewilderment. "John, what the hell's going on? You haven't had a drink in twenty years."

"Twenty-one," said John involuntarily. Still wearing his fixture green baseball cap, he sat uncomfortably in the leather-covered chair in front of Rob's desk.

"Okay, twenty-one. Why are you fucking up now?"

John stared at his shoes.

"Jesus, what about Mary, your kids?"

"The kids are moved out."

"Okay, what about Mary, what about yourself?"

"Mary's okay. I'm okay."

"John, you're screwing up," Rob said, shaking his head. "Pete doesn't know when you're coming in, if you're coming in, or what shape you're gonna be in when you do show up."

"I came in fine this morning."

"And what did you have for lunch? Shit, John, I can smell it from here."

Guys working for Rob screwed up all the time, like the one who borrowed a hundred dollars. Then, a week later the guy called Rob at home at three in the morning, demanding that he bail him out. Rob gave them all second and third chances. At some point, though, he had to protect the business for everyone else, for all those guys who always showed up ready to work.

"John, I'm sorry, but you're just too undependable. You're out of control, so I'm going to have to let you go. I'll tell George to cut you a severance check. If you straighten yourself out, come back and see me."

The severance didn't last long, which meant he soon had to give up his beloved Shark. Mary had ten fits when he told her he'd lost his job. She'd known before then that he'd gone back to drinking. She nagged him at first and threw him out of the bedroom when he was let go. When he started selling stuff to get drinking money, she threw him of out the house. He was kind of glad that he'd sold the silver candlesticks they'd gotten at their wedding. She might have tried to hit him with those.

He didn't care all that much about living outside. The weather was warm and would turn warmer before the winter wind sent the chill into him. "The Hawk" they called it in Chi Town. For now, there were plenty of trees and bushes to sleep under. During the day he'd hook up with Kennedy's Labor to earn enough to get his load on that night. Things got a little out of hand, though, whenever he forgot to take a piss before he went to sleep. That tipped off Kennedy that he hadn't changed his clothes for a while, for as long as he'd been on the street in fact. Eventually, they stopped giving him work. So, he took up panhandling.

"The best new places," Albert told him, "are the median strips on big streets in and out of the city. Three lanes each way with stop lights, you can go walk up and down the strip 'til the light changes. Get yourself a sign that says, 'Homeless, Hungry, Vietnam Vet, God Bless You.' Them guilty motherfuckers can't resist that shit. You can clear twenty bucks an hour."

"Get the hell out!"

The three of them stood on a corner in Southeast, long, lanky Albert, bulky Larry, and John, the smallest at five-six. Larry whined, "I can't say I was a Vietnam vet, I was twelve when that shit went down."

"Then say you're a Gulf War vet, it don't matter. They still give you the money."

"Sounds like a great gig," said John.

"Yeah, but you gotta be careful where you go. It gets crowded at some places, like Connecticut Avenue. Some of those motherfuckers get there early, don't appreciate latecomers or the competition."

"That's not a problem, we can sleep there. Hell, we got to sleep somewhere, right?"

Albert spread a slow smile. "Now you're starting to think right, John. One other thing, though. You got to stay away from spots where there're the spic flower sellers. They can really jam a strip up and there's no chasing them away. Too many of them, they work in teams. Same with the cripples. Man, they got some fucked-up dudes on them strips, legs bent every which way. Can't chase them off 'cause they don't run fast enough."

They all laughed.

"I seen like three or a dozen of them messed up in some way," Larry said.

"It's like a club," John said.

"A club-foot club," Albert said, and they all broke up again.

"How'd they get that way?" Larry asked. "The same, I mean."

Albert said, "In olden days they'd do that to people, Gypsies and shit. They'd buy kids from poor people, too many mouths to feed, then fuck them up on purpose, break their legs, burn their face, cripple them. Then they'd put them out on the street to beg, the sympathy vibe and shit."

"They all Vietnam vets, huh," John said.

Albert glared at him and continued. "The bosses come around now and then, take all the money."

"You shittin' us!" Larry said. "They do that?"

Albert answered in a matter of fact voice, "It's just a different kind of pimping."

"Damn, that's cold," Larry murmured. "You think they still do that shit now?" he said, looking creeped out.

Albert shrugged, "Who knows? Maybe so, you never know what those Latin motherfuckers up to. Look at them Hispanic drug dudes. Back in the day, you cross them, they cut your throat, pull out you tongue through the slit. Call it a Columbian necktie. That's when they ran everything."

"Oh, man," said Larry.

John squinted and said, "How you know all this shit?"

Albert blinked implacably. "I was a high school teacher before."

And they all nodded their heads.

In December, money grew tight. People at the median strips didn't want to open their windows to keep the cold out. Every aluminum can in town seemed to have been vacuumed up. Everyone was thirsty and cranky.

John tried to get one of those jobs handing out promotional fliers near the Metro stop at Dupont Circle. But his clothes were too tattered and dirty, and the gang foreman picked another guy new to the streets. John hadn't seen Mary for months, but he didn't even bother going over to the house. She'd changed the locks a few weeks after tossing him out. And, anyway, she'd already thrown out or given away any other clothes he'd left there.

Late one afternoon, he thought about heading over to the shelter on D Street for a meal. But that was a good ways away and he was thirsty, not hungry. He sighed and started over anyway. He walked no more than a few blocks when he saw it: President Jackson dressed in green staring up at him from the concrete.

"Good golly, Miss Molly!" John said, staring down at the crumpled bill. He whipped his head around, back and forth to be sure no one else had seen it. Quickly, he bent at the knees and groped on the ground while keeping his eyes up on the lookout for anyone else on the make. He grabbed the twenty and stuffed it into his jacket, making sure that it wouldn't fall out of the hole in the pocket.

Rising up, he almost pranced down the sidewalk to Metro Liquor. He bounced inside past the security guard directly to the counter, twirling his twenty above his head like a girl with a parasol.

"Two pints of the Shark—Cutty, my man, right away."

The clerk, a round-faced man tipping the scales at 250–300, smiled smugly as he turned to the glass cabinet behind him. He brought down two bottles of Cutty Sark and inserted them each into a separate, small brown bag He handed them over with one hand while plucking the twenty with the other as he said, "Enjoy." He turned to the cash register, which dinged open while John stuffed the slim bottles into his coat side pockets. The clerk handed over a few singles, and John pushed them in on top of one of the bottles. He left the store and skipped down the sidewalk until he reached the corner, out of sight of the liquor store front window. John quickly unscrewed one of the bottles of Cutty Sark and held it above his head, draining half of it in seconds. He screwed the cap back on and tucked the bottle into his side pocket. Smacking his lips, he started up the street toward where they all hung out to drink more.

Funny that way, you could walk on the hill among narrow, tall red-brick row houses dating back a couple hundred years. Gay couples lived in them now, or young lawyer families with their kids' Target tricycles left outside on their sides in their mini front yards. Then, just two blocks over, you could watch the young colts dash back and forth clanging a ball on rims hanging down from iron backboards. The boards were full of rows of holes, the way they used to make them back then for some forgotten reason. Ten-foot high hurricane fences stuck out of rust-stained concrete walls surrounding the playground. The broken-down blacktop court itself ran just 50 feet long. At either end of the park, wide-open entranceways marked the absence of long-gone gates. Old rundown, wooden row houses two stories high flanked the little park on all sides.

The fellas liked coming to the court early in the morning when the boys sat stuck in school, or at twilight when they ran to get home, dinner at six sharp or get hit up side the head for being late. December cold kept most kids off the court, though a few roundball addicts came out after school. But darkness fell fast in the winter, leaving the playground barren at twilight.

During early morning hours, John and the others drank whatever remained from last night, necessary to calm the daily shakes of the winos. In the evening, they came back with what they'd found during the day to share while sitting on a corner of the wall where the fencing had been bent out.

When John neared the playground, he saw Albert and Larry sitting there opposite a couple of other guys standing on either side, passing around a crumpled brown bag with a bottleneck peeking out. John didn't know the others, which didn't matter much. People came and went. One of them took a swig from the bottle straight up above his head. He lowered the bag, shook it, then flipped it between the wall and the bent fencing out of the playground.

John bounced over to Albert and Larry, feeling high enough almost to jam a ball through one of the hoops.

"Hey, man, what up?" he said, almost gushing.

"What up with you?" Albert said, drawing back just a bit from John's good cheer.

"This, my man!" John said, pulling the half-full bottle of Cutty Sark out of the right pocket in his jacket. He passed it to Albert and hopped onto the wall next to him. Albert drank long, then handed the bottle over to Larry.

"That's good." Albert twisted his head around, eyeing John. "I see you got a good taste before you got here."

John nodded, "I had my share," he said, pushing back the nearly empty bottle offered to him by Larry. Larry didn't know what to do with it, and offered the bottle to Albert, who ignored it.

"How you come to get so lucky in the first place?" Albert asked.

John grinned, "I came across some cash flow on the sidewalk, a five-spot. Bought the pint, drank half, and came by right after."

"A five-spot, huh," said Albert, "not a sawbuck?" He watched John's face go somber and said more loudly, "A Jackson? What the fuck, man!"

Albert hopped down from the wall. Face-to-face with John, he reached over to grab him with one hand by his shirt collar. He pulled, bending John at the waist close to him while searching each of his jacket pockets.

"What the hell, man?" John shouted until Albert suddenly let him sit back while he held the unopened pint of scotch up in his face.

"What the hell is this, man?" Albert yelled.

“Gimme it back, it’s mine,” John said, grabbing at the bottle. Albert yanked back; the pint bottle fell to the macadam and shattered, Cutty Sark spraying in every direction.

“You dumb motherfucker! Look what you done!” bellowed Albert.

“Me? I’m the motherfucker? You fucking stole it from—”

Before John could finish, Albert threw a roundhouse left at John’s head, which he ducked by twisting on his side. He lost his balance and fell headfirst on the pavement, hitting it with an audible crack.

Albert froze above him. The other four men stood motionless, dumbfounded. Larry stooped and stared closely at John lying crumpled on the blacktop, quiet.

“His eyes open,” Larry said. He glanced up, his own eyes wide with shock. “I think he’s dead!”

Without waiting, he jumped up and ran pall mall through the gate out of the playground. The other three men followed quickly.

“Damn!” Albert said in a whisper. “Good Lord Almighty.”

He stooped down and look closely. John’s green cap lay next to him, his head surprisingly bald. His eyes were half-open, the whites dulled to yellow. Albert put his hand on John’s chest and felt no movement. He leaned over, his ear close to John’s mouth. Nothing.

Albert straightened up. He was dead, dammit. Fuck!

He stood up and peered around the playground. The dim light made it hard to see very far, but it looked like no one was around. Albert bent over at the waist, grabbed John by his clothing and hoisted his slight body on top of his shoulder. He saw the hat down below and squatted gingerly to grab it with his free left hand. He slowly rose and walked quickly through the open playground gateway.

Careful to hew to the backdrop, Albert made his way up northeast through the labyrinth of alleys dividing rowhouse blocks throughout the District. Almost all of them lacked street signs and lights, which meant travelers had to know their ways. Born and bred in the city, Albert knew his way by heart, reinforced by familiarity with many of the back lanes used for drinking sessions.

An hour put him close to where he wanted to be, just off 12th NE and Rhode Island. He paused in the shadow of one dark home to catch his breath. John might tip the scales at bantamweight, thought Albert. But after lugging him around on his shoulder for an hour, the scrawny sucker seemed to gain a pound every five minutes. Sweat drenched Albert despite the cutting frigid air. He was almost there, however, just a half a block away from his uncle's place.

The stately clapboard loomed darkly above on a slope adjacent to the sidewalk, so close that a six-foot stone retaining wall kept the yard intact. As long as he could remember, his Uncle Henry Jones had lived in the old house, keeping it spic and span, painted every five years the same pale green. He replaced the roof every fifteen years, never mind the thirty-year warranty, and washed every window in the house, all three stories, re-caulking any gaps before switching out screens with storm windows in autumn.

He kept his yard the same way. Perennials around the foundation, with outer beds planted each spring full of peonies, begonias, and vinca, first nurtured by Aunt Mabel, long gone herself. No matter, Uncle Henry saw to them every year, all part of the order of things. He manicured the entire yard, which made Albert scarce as a kid, ducking out on helping whenever he could. Never mind the few bucks his uncle gave him at day's end. No amount of money was worth that much work.

One particular feature of Henry's set-up attracted Albert this night. Built on a high hill with a steep slope to the street, the property did not have a driveway. Instead, the original owners cut a space out of the stone retaining wall into the hill for a single-car garage. Closed in by padlocked double doors flush to the edge of the sidewalk, the wooden structure featured a slanted roof that peaked perfectly parallel to the grassy lawn above. Two single-pane windows at the top of each door allowed the only natural light into the narrow cubicle, which turned darker each year as grime gradually coated the glass.

Uncle Henry never used the garage to park a car. “Pain in the ass pullin’ in and out of it, dodgin’ all the cars comin’ and goin’ up and down the street. Besides, who need a car in the city?” He’d jerk his thumb back over his shoulder, “Bus stop right there on the corner.” Henry never owned a car, which didn’t stop him from joyfully sharing his criticism of the garage more than once. The garage became a limbo for dried paint cans, out-of-service appliances, a few sticks of broken furniture including an old chest of drawers, and some worn-out rakes and shovels half covered by some tattered tarps. Uncle Henry kept his valued tools, his riding mower and his snow-blower in an immaculate shed erected near the back door of the house. The old garage stood forgotten mostly, the exact state that attracted Albert right off.

At the back of the house, he lowered John down in the dark corner between the wall and the stairs. He crept up the steps hunched over to look into the kitchen. No sign of Uncle Henry, asleep of course at this late hour. Albert turned and lifted a plant pot to fetch the keys to the backdoor. He silently opened it and slipped inside. Not risking a light, he groped on the side of the wall near the door until he found the key hooks. At the bottom on the far side of the row, he found the one he wanted. He then worked his way over to the kitchen sink and reached down to the bottom drawer on the right. He smiled to himself as he pulled out the flashlight. Good old Uncle Henry, everything in its proper place.

Albert went out the back door, locking it behind him, then hopped down the steps leaving John Hall where he was. He trotted down the steps near the house to the street sidewalk and jogged toward the inset garage 30 yards away. Glancing around back and forth to be sure no one else was about, he inserted the key into the padlock. As he suspected, it refused to open easily, almost rusted completely shut. After working the key in and out and around, he finally managed to yank the lock off of its loop. He pulled one of the dull-green pine doors open, scraping it over the raised sidewalk, and held the flashlight high inside to take a look. Once he knew the lay of the land, he worked his way in and cleared a passage through the pile of junk to the back of the dark chamber. Satisfied, he left, closing the door behind him, and headed back to fetch John's mortal remains.

Inside the garage, Albert shifted forward to drop John off of his shoulder into a broken captain's chair propped against the back wall. John's mouth hung open now, which along with his open eyes made him look like he sat silently screaming. Albert pulled back quick and tried to close John's mouth and eyes. He couldn't do it, rictus now set in like concrete.

Fuck this, he said to himself, turning away to look around for a tarp. He snatched the nearest one and draped it over John.

"So long, John," he said with a nod, "Good luck in the next world. Maybe one where you share you liquor."

He flipped the tarp over John's head and left the garage. After securing the padlock, he strolled up the sidewalk to return the flashlight and the hidden house key. When he reached the steps, though, he saw through the backdoor window a light in the kitchen.

Damn, Uncle Henry up with the chickens, he thought, even though he didn't raise chickens anymore. Now what? Thinking about it, Albert decided that his uncle wasn't likely to miss the flashlight or the garage key right off. He couldn't do anything about it now, the sun was starting to peek out in the east. He'd have to wait until nighttime again.

Just then, he smelled bacon. And coffee. He rubbed his chin stubble. Maybe Uncle Henry would enjoy some company, put on some more eggs. Sooner or later he'd have to go to the loo after that.

Albert continued up the back steps to knock on the back door.

In the dark, John Hall sat dead in the chair. But he didn't feel dead. He didn't feel anything. He wasn't sure he could see anything. He remembered what happened, how he ducked, lost his balance, and cracked his skull on the blacktop, blinding, white-lightning pain that he remembered but couldn't feel now. He recalled Albert picking him up over his shoulder, blood rushing down to his head, he knew but couldn't feel.

He couldn't see, either. What happened? Where the fuck was he?

In a garage, John knew, though he couldn't see or feel. Albert's Uncle's old garage now used as a shed to dump old stuff no one used anymore. In the dead of winter, cold as shit outside, ice on the side of the windowpanes filthy with years of dirt. Icey inside, too, though no breath showed in the dim moonlight, which he also could not see.

So, his eyes didn't work. Can't see, can't feel, so what did it all mean? A senseless, seeping chill shocked him awake; he was dead.

What else could he be? Unless he was in some kind of ultra-coma, like that French dude he'd seen on deep cable on the crazy shit medical show. Frozen stiff by a killer stroke, all the guy could do was breathe and see. Communicated by blinking his eyes, John remembered, wrote a book that way, died a couple months later.

Locked-in syndrome, they called it, immediately wondering how the fuck he could remember that as Shark saturated as he was. Never mind that, maybe that's me, thought John. Except he didn't see and he didn't breathe.

What now? Nothing about him worked, so was he dying or was he dead? Considering everything, particularly the last things he remembered happening, he was forced to conclude that he was dead. Dead and gone; dead as a doornail; dead to me; dead to the world; dead, not proud; dead, dead, dead. And stuck in a crusty old garage. He pictured Albert dumping him in a heap, tossing a dusty old tarp halfway over him, and padlocking the garage door shut. Albert, sneaking over to the backdoor, replacing the key beneath the pot, and announcing himself to his uncle like he'd just arrived, "What's for breakfast?"

Meantime, John sat there waiting for putrefaction, the worms crawl in, the worms crawl out, fungi, really. First, though, he'd shit the bed, pooping and peeing in his pants. Sighing in his head, he girded himself for the rest, bloating, bacterial critters eating his guts, blood pooling turning him red, his body stiff, then going limp, stiffening again, finally relaxing for good, stinking up the place, all that and more. Topside, he'd be gone in a month. Buried six-foot deep, it could take as long as 12 years. In sunlight or someplace arid, he might simply shrink into a leathery stick figure. Then again, temps below 4 degrees Celsius could slow the process down, off and on maybe until spring. Still and all, talk about being long in tooth.

John stopped short. What the hell? Where was all this coming from? Squinting, he concentrated hard, calling up decomposition stuff he'd seen on *Dr. G Medical Examiner*. Okay, but how could he remember all that so clearly?

He hadn't had a drink for a few hours. That could be it, except it didn't make any sense, considering how pickled he was from recent, acute boozing. Maybe that's why he could think at all, an out-of-body experience within his body, like transplanting his brain into some kind of Frankenstein creature. But his swiss cheese gray matter should work more like Abby Normal's in the Mel Brooks movie. How could he be having all these notions, departed as he was?

He smelled bacon cooking, wafting down to the garage from the kitchen in the back of the house. Shit.

Time passed.

Fixed in time, he remembered everything. Memories ran through his mind, boyhood, throwing sticks at cars and running like hell when a driver jerked over to the curb, leaping out to chase them. Lying to his momma about doing it while the red-faced guy said he'd take us straight down to the police. After the guy left, Momma looking down at him, elbows akimbo, confronting him demanding the truth; he stood crying, confessing.

Going to his first party wearing his Sunday suit, dancing and drinking coke madly, seeing girls for the first time. Leaving late at night, walking the two blocks home over packed snow in the middle of the empty street, gazing at the dark, clear sky full of stars and an endless future.

Bragging about how good he was at sports, tough until Jerry Kunkle pushed him down and sat on his chest. Trying to breathe while saying he'd only been kidding. Getting thumped in practice as the littlest guy on the football squad. Becoming a shadow in the halls.

Daddy getting drunk and mad. Momma stepping in, but not all of the time. Spending more time out of the house. Smoking his first smoke, having his first drink. Joy-riding Daddy's car and getting ass-kicked for it. Meeting Mary.

Spring and summer rolled by and nothing much changed. Body fluids seeped away, some bugs feasted, but few other scavengers appeared, warded off by stray cats.

He felt bad about Mary. Off and on his girlfriend in school, later she seemed to dig him despite his bad habits. She picked up a few of them herself, smoking mostly, though not much for the drink. He loved her for her natural beauty and nice coloring, full-blooded, sort of lightly tan all the time. Her clear blue eyes reflected her inner being, straight without rancor or meanness of any kind. Considering all the dumbass shit he always did, he wondered how she kept putting up with it all. Not easy on him, but never calling it quits until the last time. He always felt bad about Mary, how he paid her no attention most of the time.

Same with the kids, Junie and Johnny Jr. He never hurt them; he wasn't a nasty drunk. He just forgot them a lot, missing ball games and birthdays. He did go to their graduations and always celebrated Christmas with them, though usually he was lit up a bit. Took its toll, Junie knocked up and married at 17, Johnny Jr. off to the military at the same age. Both seemed happy, though, as far as he knew. They never came home, but they talked to their mom on the phone. She'd tell him after.

One time they'd gone down to visit some relatives of hers in El Paso. Sitting around the modern hacienda, the folks passed around some local Mexican cigarettes, Delicados Ovalados. Funny looking, they weren't round, instead regular cigs sort of flattened into ovals with delicate blue pinstripes circling them at regular spaces. When smoked, they lasted as long the extralong cigarettes in those days called 100s, like Silva Thins or Virginia Slims. No filters and guaranteed to cause a smoking cough within a few weeks, the Mexican ovals seemed imbued with sugar. Rumor had it that poor urchins scoured the streets of Mexico City for half-used cigarette butts to take to the plants for repackaging into Delicados Ovalados. Hence, the hacking cough. He remembered Mary laughing while puffing on one without inhaling, the scent of her favorite perfume mingling with the smell of the acrid smoke. Delicados and Shalamar, smoke and perfume.

Fall and winter slipped in again. Lots of cold rain and its attendant erosion. The tarp draped over him seemed to be flattening on top of his diminishing shape. Dropping temperatures slowed the process, though.

He relived the old times again, the down times, the distractions. Work tasked him. He trimmed trees for a while, falling out now and then, happy to collect Workers Comp to drink up. Sometimes he abstained when Mary weighed in. Pretty soon, though, the tree company gave him the boot. Then construction, fired; moving company, fired; garbage truck, fired. Mary kept them fed and sheltered, though she wasn't crazy about the situation. When he got let go by Kennedy Labor, she raised the roof. One more drink and she'd toss him out.

He quit on the spot. Her brother fixed him up with Rob Johnson at C-Print and for twenty years he rose at six, ate breakfast, put on his green cap, and took the A-7 bus to the warehouse. The first year, he stacked printed material. A year later, he took over a forklift and loaded the deliveries. Twenty-one years later, he woke up and started drinking. Mary gave him a couple of months to try and straighten out until he sold the dining room table for drinking money. She changed the locks that day.

He missed Mary now, too late as it was.

Five years gone and for some reason he'd mummified. Memories kept recurring, more detailed each time, so much so that he figured he must be using 80% of his brain like offhanded bragging by the guy in *Defending My Life.* An afterlife supernumerary played by Rip Torn in the movie, his lowkey boast riffed on the conventional wisdom that most living people used only 10% of their mental capabilities. Now considered an old wives tale, John recognized, yet here he was after life, using his mind at a level far higher than ever before in his entire previous existence. In this time, he dwelled upon his past like in *Groundhog Day*, again and again, but every time in greater detail.

I know I repeat myself a lot, he exclaimed to himself, but heck, it's a new day every day!

Ten years through, things changed. Uncle Henry died and Albert inherited the house. The first day after moving in, he ordered a pile of dirt and some rolls of sod. He wheelbarrowed the dirt over and filled in the sides and back of the garage, tamping the dirt down, adding more, and tamping again. When the dirt reached the rooftop, he shoveled more dirt on it until he had a seamless layer across from one side of the garage to the other. After that, he unrolled the sod over the dirt, tamped it down, and watered it. Albert watered the sod during the next few weeks until it had meshed perfectly with the rest of the grass growing in the yard. In ensuing days, he brought in a stone mason to close up the gap in the wall to cover up the garage doors.

There, Albert said to himself, that shit's done for good.

Damn, John thought to himself.

As dark and black as Albert cloaked the garage, John still knew what was up. Along with recalling all of the events in his life, he could project things happening around him. He couldn't be sure if what he knew was real and true, except he just knew it was so. Mary moved on, Albert drank, Larry cleaned up, Rob sold C-Print, the kids on the playground bickered and balled, seasons changed, time marched and life went on.

Mostly, John didn't dwell on all that. Too busy looking at his own shit, decades gathering every iota—baby teeth in a box, picking at the plaster in the wall, Daddy strapping him good, lying about drop-kicking the football through the front window, Daddy strapping him good. Lying to some sweet thing to get to third base, shouting at Junie and Johnny Jr. for no reason at all except for the Shark. Selling his blood to get more. Going over all those days, nights, hours, and minutes that he couldn't account for, despite seeing them like in a mirror image over and over again.

He mulled, too, whether this made up his Judgment Day. He stayed away from thinking about Jesus and heaven, lashed to the ill-at-ease feeling that his last stop would be the other place considering his bad behavior. In his head he expected to see all these angels, saints, and saved souls standing on clouds around a huge, encrusted gold throne with God enormously looking down on him, big, gray beard and fierce eyes. That seemed all out of a childhood dream. Maybe what he saw made up the real Judgment Day, going through every crappy thing he'd ever seen and done in his entire life. Why not? Who could feel worse about the worst things someone had ever done than the person who had done them? Who could condemn someone for bad things more than that same person? Okay, so he sold some of his blood to get more hooch. Suppose he tracked where each pint went, see which lives were saved, wouldn't that count for something? Except for the lives that weren't saved. Maybe this explained why he kept thinking about all this shit all this time shriveling away in his corrupt, desiccated body in a makeshift car tomb instead of inside the Pearly Gates. He felt bad enough, but really, what the fuck?

Twenty years in, something changed. After going over it all over and over again, he drifted. He drowsed, dreaming a waking dream of things he'd never seen before. Subtle at first, walking down some street in Williamstown, PA, eating funnel cake. Drinking home brew outside a cellar on some farm in Iowa. Seeing younger versions of people he knew, having conversations with them that he'd never had. More aware of the shift, he found himself in places he'd never been to, walking on causeways near windmills in Holland. He pounded poi in Hawaii, and drank aqvavit in Norway, pulling a face while yearning for Cutty.

So, now what? After exhausting what might have been thinking about his past, had he moved on to what could have been? Does this mean that the things he sees going on around him are not what is, but what could be? Is this what you do when you're dead; work on seeing, feeling until you find yourself shaping the world's existence in a different way? John suddenly blinked to a show he'd seen on *Discovery* about quantum mechanics and alternate realities. Not just one universe exists, but endless numbers of them, so many that anything imagined under any sun existed as another reality. When he saw things happening around him that he couldn't see and saw things he'd never seen before, could this be quantum thinking? Living is limited to seeing only what you see; death is wide open.

High living caught up with Albert, forcing him into an assisted-living home. To pay for it, he needed to sell Uncle Henry's house, though most of the money went to back taxes. The Pepperdines, a young couple with a toddler, delighted in purchasing the property, which needed a lot of work. In town and not too far from a Metro stop, they were happy to pay top dollar for it and invest almost the same amount in renovations. They put on a badly needed new roof, knocked down a wall to create a large living/dining space, and punched a hole in the wall to the kitchen for a counter looking into both spaces. They also expanded the back of the kitchen with a vast sunroom, even though it faced a northern exposure. They also bulldozed a driveway from the street up past the kitchen to a new carport that replaced Uncle

Henry's shed.

The trouble came when they decided to install a playground apparatus on top of the lawn right above the garage. In the winter, a heavy snowfall combined with the weight of the playset to collapse the roof of the garage. Dismayed, the young man of the house decided to fence it off temporarily and deal with it in the spring.

When warm weather arrived, the working crew periodically reported progress to the Pepperdines. They gingerly removed the playset without incident and started to excavate the site to install a concrete base. At that point they informed the owners about finding old shingles and broken wooden two-by-fours. Later on, they let the Pepperdines know that in pulling out all the shingles and cross boards, they'd discovered the ruins of an old building, maybe a one-car garage. They also informed them that full demolition and removal would require considerably more work, which would mean greater expense. Rather than risk having sort of a man-made sinkhole in his backyard, Jason Pepperdine decided to bite the bullet and go ahead with the dig.

Two days later the foreman came to the back door.

"We gotta problem."

Jason stood at the head of the rectangular hole while the foreman pulled back the rotten tarp. Jason flinched when he saw the dark brown, shrunken leathery cadaver lying there, head straight up, jaw hanging open in eternal rictus. My God, thought Jason, he looks like he's 5,000 years old lifted straight out of a bog somewhere in Germany or Ireland. Something out of National Geographic.

Jason suspended the project and called the authorities. No one had any idea of who the John Doe was. They extracted DNA to see if they could find any relatives. They also attempted to interview Albert Jones, too, but left with no information due to the former owner's dementia.

"I called the Medical Examiner's office," Jason said to his wife Elsa. He rattled the ice in his tumbler, now just a quarter full of Caol Ila after his first swallow. "They're willing to obtain the remains and hold them until an identity is established. If none's found, he'll be buried in the unknown section of the city's public cemetery."

"You mean a pauper's grave?" Elsa said, her voice rising. "That's so cruel."

"No, Babe, it'll be okay, they do this with a proper amount of dignity for sure."

"I don't know, Jason. He's been here so long, he's like family in this place."

"Oh, for …" he rolled his eyes, saw his wife's shoulders beginning to slump, and quickly spoke to stave off the waterworks. "Look. I'll pop for a coffin. We'll give him a good sendoff, believe me. Don't cry, it'll be all right," he said, patting her shoulder, thinking to himself, a nice, cheap metal casket for sure.

Across the universe, John found his relocation to be an annoying distraction. Unearthing him revealed that he had become a shrunken, leather bound carcass. Maybe he was a living mummy like in *The Mummy*, but no hot evil Egyptian chick was coming around to save him. At least the bugs hadn't fricasseed him.

What about bugs? If birds can think, can bugs? There seems to be no correlation to brain function and physical size. In fact, the idea that butterflies have complete circulatory systems—tiny little veins, arteries, and hearts—blew his mind. And look at how bees handle themselves, knowing where they are, where they've been, and telling all the other bees how to get there. Maybe bugs think just as much as he does dead. If so, do they make decisions about whose remains to munch on? Do maggots admire someone's nose and therefore rule it as off limits for lunch? Is this really how King Tut's proboscis survived? Or didn't?

He sighed. He really needn't stay for the trip to the cemetery and all that. On the other hand, where would he go while his new neighbors laid his mortal remains to rest? The change of venue didn't matter to him.

The Pepperdines crumbled dirt on his metal coffin, then slowly turned away, careful to avoid another freshly filled grave next to John's.

Once gone, the cemetery caretaker pushed the pile of earth into the hole.

John wondered why people buried other people alone. Even married couples in graves next to each other occupied separate coffins. In Pompeii, bodies hugged close together in death. Sooner or later, everyone runs out of life. Life is too short to make other lives shorter, lonelier. Better to leave obsessive, compulsive successes behind.

Quiet.

John wondered, do other dead people create realities to talk to other dead people? He remembered then that you always find something you've lost in the last place you look.

He searched around the other fresh gravesite.

"That you, Albert?"

Quiet.

Then, "God-damn me to hell. You still here?"

John smiled, then laughed.

Artsy Fartsy

Steel work in Xavier, PA, had begun to fade long ago, finally disappearing altogether by the end of the eighties. Management followed the unemployed workers who migrated out of the neighboring bedroom community of Williamstown. The City of New York happily filled the vacancies by giving bus money and Pennsylvania welfare forms to Latinos on its rolls, who moved west drawn by the beckoning of a charismatic priest preaching the promise of new opportunity. Thus, Williamstown's financial crunch caused by an ever-shrinking tax base was compounded by the added burden of picking up the tabs for all of those out-of-work aliens. Spanish-speaking and Catholic, they'd sit all day on row house stoops bickering with the old, Lutheran Pennsylvania Deutsche women who were scrubbing their front concrete steps on their hands and knees with bristle brushes and buckets of suds. So, the locals told it, anyway.

What this meant for the Williamstown Art Museum for FY93, Dylan lamented, was no budget to do anything, making it just one more stark monument in the dead landscape of the city.

"It's like ancient Roman buildings after the Visigoths ravaged them," he said in the soft rhythms of his voice, "followed by the vengeful Christians carrying off the pagans' stones to build their sacred cathedrals. Or the Turks storing gunpowder in the Parthenon only to have a stray cannonball set the magazine off. Later on, Lord Elgin placed the capstone on the catastrophe by smuggling to England what temple reliefs had been left intact on the premise of protecting them from further barbaric indifference. The irony, of course, and in only the way the British can work it," he laughed, "is that their long, passionate romance with ancient things Greek also compelled them to bully the Turks into giving Greece her freedom. Yet, to this day, the

Brits refuse to return the Elgin marbles to the Greeks, who've been wailing for their stolen stone legacy ever since."

"So, is that what they call statuary rape?" Ben said.

Dylan rejoined, "Indeed, pillar pilfering or maybe Acropolis Now," and they both laughed.

He had walked into the house to find it quiet except for the bare hint of music drifting down the stairs. He dropped his briefcase on the dining room table, walked up the stairway to the bedroom in the rear, and without a word lay down flat on his back to the settling sounds of Barbara Cook singing Cry Me a River. Dylan dangled his hand idly in the air, his arm propped up on his elbow, and Ben casually lifted his to twine their fingers together. They waited for Barbara to finish before talking about the day.

"Yes," Dylan said in a drawn-out sigh, "soon the new Christians will be mining the Williamstown Art Museum for stones to build their holy edifices. I wonder what form they'll take?"

"Balloons," said Ben, "balloons of stone that will float by displacing the air, the same way concrete ships bob in the water."

"Is that possible?" Dylan asked.

"Lord, I haven't a guess. The only concrete ship I ever saw was sunk near Cape May, New Jersey. Though, I don't think it sank because it was too heavy."

"Perhaps it foundered under the weight of disbelief," Dylan suggested, "faulty suspension."

"Could be. Anyway, you don't have to worry about the Museum. It's going through tough times, true, but there are enough scions of past robber barons left to keep it going. Where else would they go for grand openings?"

"You have to have something opening for it to be grand," Dylan said.

"Well, you're doing that, you're being innovative on no budget," Ben said. "What about the Area Artists of the Avant-Garde? That's an event."

Dylan frowned, shrugging, "I had to dredge up some kind of show for the summer. It's the cheapest thing I could think of, though God knows what we'll get. The Board is acting as the selection panel. My lord, Ben, Dottie Schaeffer is going to judge art. Can you imagine?"

"Yes, well, Dottie will be Dottie. But, don't fret, Dyl, maybe this time two negatives will work a positive. It's that way in all the Romance languages."

"I can only hope and pray."

"And cajole? When does the final selection take place?"

"Two weeks from Friday. That gives us enough time to notify the artists who've been accepted and get the space ready to mount the show. The gala follows, when the winners are announced, then the show stays open to the public for two weeks after that."

"Well, then, there's time to insinuate your way into getting what you want, my wily young fellow."

Dylan nodded to the ceiling, "Yes, I might be able to avoid utter embarrassment if I'm lucky. But I don't see how matters can continue like this. I might as well be a sideshow huckster."

Ben turned on his side to him, "We can always go back to Carolina, open up a gallery there. Then you can bring in the pieces you like."

Dylan glanced at him out of the corner of his eye. Ben had always been happier back home. Who could blame him?

"Where, in Belhaven? Who'd buy any of it in Belhaven?"

"All right, how about Greensboro? And don't forget the Internet. Belhaven is transformed into an entirely different community online."

"Yes," murmured Dylan, "that's a notion." He returned to staring at the ceiling. "But it would be nicer if something good could happen here, to give us other options.

"You know," he said after a minute's thought, "we do have such nice things to see at the Museum, a number of just beautiful things."

Tanya enjoyed the ramshackle state of this little town, called a city by the natives of course, but really, it was a small town with numbers. She loved the low profile of it, two or three stories high except for the giant headquarters of the local power company, the PSP. Built in the twenties, the monolith soared twenty-two floors high with big sash windows on each floor. Every year during the holidays, the big windows were lit up in a tall, Christmas-tree pattern, red, green, and white.

Next to the PSP building stood the Look Steakhouse, run by an 86-year-old Greek. After living in Williamstown for 60 years, he finally traveled for the first time back to his home village this past summer. His nephew went along, lugging with him 13 valises full of butter, hams, cheeses, and cash—you couldn't return from America empty-handed, so pronounced his uncle. Tanya just loved these small-town stories to death.

She also luxuriated in the town's sprawling park system that shaded the Macungie River's major tributary, the Little Macungie. The stream coursed through gentle wooded slopes, grassy banks, and even an old farmhouse taken over and spruced up by the Park Service to store maintenance equipment. You could follow the Little Macungie all the way to Cana, a petite village founded by the Moravians in the early 1800s, five miles outside of Williamstown. Tanya liked to walk through the old cemetery near the church, marveling sadly at the number of long biblical names on tiny flat stones dated life spans of only months or even weeks, so many babies dying in those days, and mothers.

In contrast, you could travel across the bridge from Williamstown to view stately Old Xavier, that part of the decrepit steel town occupied by the exquisite stone structures of the town's first buildings: a mill, a church, and communal living quarters constructed with precise masonry to rival any found in Europe. It made sense, since they'd been put up around the same time the burghers in the old countries were erecting their guild houses. Now, Old Xavier was the seat of a small college notable for hosting annual music festivals.

Of course, Tanya liked best the pizza joint they always sat in, nothing but linoleum floors, phony paneling, a few round Formica tables for two, cheap chairs, and the counter festooned with signs that said "No checks;" "Minimum Order 1 Slice 1 Drink to Occupy a Table;" "The Proprietor Reserves the Right to Refuse Service;" and the age-old standard, "No Shoes, No Shirt, No Service." Far from fitting the Disney stereotype of a happy-go-lucky Italian cafe host, the owner here, of indistinct ethnic background, was squat and stony featured. He uttered not one word, friendly or otherwise, as he unceremoniously slapped down like so many dead flounders single paper plates laden with wedges of his admittedly delicious pizza. If he was indifferent to the average customer, he openly despised the gang, dubbed "the Colony" by Hitchcock. Each of them would buy one slice of pizza and one drink, then sit for hours monopolizing four of the six tables, picking off a pepperoni now and then, nursing their drinks watery from melted ice, and talking endlessly, with those who smoked taking turns outside while the others saved their seats.

The owner tried to refuse them service once, but they raised such a stink, threatening to call the cops and chasing the other customers away with their outburst, that he caved in and gave them their food and beverage. After that, an uneasy truce was reached, in that Tanya and the others really didn't want the cops brought in, thinking that it was a fifty-fifty proposition of whether or not the local law would uphold their constitutional rights, low-income earners that they were. Apparently, the pizza guy wasn't sure either, probably fallout from his unsweetened disposition universally known around town.

So, he served them and glared, saving his best burning-eyes expression for Hitchcock, of course, easily singled out as the ringleader because he was the loudest and also the oldest. Tanya didn't care, she enjoyed John's bounding energy and his goofy irreverence. He was damn good looking, too, tall and boney muscled, with sharp features and one of those short beards popular among the male model set a few years ago. Of course, his was gray, now, but he could have been a model himself, she thought, back when his whiskers were brown or black, or whatever.

He liked her, too, which was good since he usually disdained those he called young artist wannabes, even though he himself hadn't had much success during the twenty years he'd been at it. "Things will change," he said, "or they'll stay the same. I might get lucky, hit the right psycho-demographic curve ball, and sell a shitload of stuff. Or, like so many artistes before me, I might not be discovered until long after I'm worm poop."

The gang, this afternoon made up of Mitch, Davy, his girlfriend Louise, and Mitch's side man, Joe Bob, listened happily, ready for any kind of rap from Hitchcock that might relieve the midday doldrums.

He shook his head, "Doesn't bother me, I'm not in it for that kind of stuff."

"Then what are you in it for, Hitchcock?" Tanya asked, grin slightly canted.

"Why, the money, of course."

The group hooted and he followed, sotto voce, with a forlorn, "You don't believe me." He had just rolled in from busing the kids home from day camp. Most people drove school buses to supplement their income, but Hitchcock depended upon it as his sole means of support to free time for his work.

"You can't give me a straight answer?" Tanya persisted. "Too scary for you, too serious? What is it for you? The work?"

"I hate work."

"Well, then, what? What really rings your chimes?"

He reached over and clasped both of her hands in his. She smiled knowingly, ready for the come on. It was something she was used to, given her black-haired, ivory-skinned good looks. She always tried and failed to disguise it with severe dress, usually black denims, belt, and boots topped by a white t-shirt.

"You really want to know? My innermost secret obsession, forcing me, driving me to create art that nobody likes, nobody wants, and that keeps me a pauper in what otherwise would be my highest earning years? This, you really must know?"

"Sure," she said flatly, smiling, waiting for it.

"Okay," he said, pausing. "I do it," he said, hesitantly, "I do it for, for . . .," lowering his eyes demurely, "for you—and the other groupies."

She cuffed him hard across the top of his head as everyone else all roared laughter. "You asshole, I'm no groupie," she said pulling away.

"No, but you could be if only you'd try. Give up your futile pursuit of the muse, Tanya, give it up and follow me."

"Screw yourself, Hitchcock."

"Been there, done that."

"I'm not surprised," she said dryly.

"You would be if you saw the videotape."

"Better than your etchings, I'm sure," she said.

Hitchcock drew back. "My etchings are swell. All of my stuff is great and it's just a matter of time before everything comes together and takes off. When that happens, so do I, straight to San Francisco. But I'll still call."

"Oh yeah," Mitch said, "and when does all of this happen, Johnny Boy?" He was a dark, morose-looking local who dreamed of being the next Keith Jarrett. Along with his nighttime security job at the Art Museum, he played weddings to keep his hand in. "You've been at it a long time now, you know?"

"True, but things are opening up all over the place, locally. Seriously, I'm in talks with the Sellersville Arts Place about guest curating a group show for the Collective, which of course would feature my devastating studies center stage," he turned to Tanya, "and Tanya's immediately to my right."

"Thank you so much," she said.

"Listen, be grateful I don't suggest you for the Gallery in the Alley. And there's the Take the Art Off the Wall exhibit in the Old Xavier Mill; people pay $100 and get their choice of the pieces, taking turns by lottery. I could walk away with a C-note and some decent PR if I get into that."

"Did they tell you if you're in, yet?" Mitch asked.

"They haven't told me," Hitchcock said, "but they haven't finished lining up the exhibitors, either. So, I'm hopeful. And, if worse comes to worse, I can always count on the Museum's Area Artists of the Avant-Garde exhibit. No money, but exposure," he admitted.

Tanya and the others laughed, "Oh yeah? Who's going to see it? The Bach Society after the high school concert?"

"Don't knock it. They're the people in this burg with money, remember. And you should laugh, Tanya, considering the odds of anything you have to offer being selected. Allow me to reintroduce you to Mr. Slim and Mrs. None."

"Hey, up yours, Hitchcock, I've got just as good a shot as you do. Maybe even better, given the wide swathe you've cut around here with your crap over the last twenty years."

Hitchcock yawned an angry grin, "That's why you left New York, your work is so cutting edge."

"It's as good as anything you've done," she said.

"Unhuh. Time will tell."

An uncomfortable silence settled over the table, Louise leaning to whisper into Tanya's ear while Mitch and the others traded furtive glances, their shoulders hunched as though waiting for another series of blows.

"Well, anyway," Hitchcock said quietly, "that's what's out there right now. And it's a hell of a lot more than was ever happening here twenty years ago, believe me."

He stood up. "And, if I'm going to make some hay out any of this, I need to get at it."

No one said anything as he turned to go. He made it the three steps to the front door, then whirled around.

"You coming?"

When he said it, his eyes burning straight into hers, Tanya flushed with a wave of fury that subsided as fast as it had come upon her. She sighed as she got up and preceded him out the door wondering why. He could be such an asshole sometimes.

Dylan arrived at the Museum early, but not before Charlie Kunkle, the senior security guard. A huge, meaty pillar, Charlie enjoyed looking down at Dylan, both literally and figuratively. He'd been guarding the Museum for more than three decades, whereas Dylan had just arrived four years ago, fresh from curating and teaching at Johnson Union College in Wicklow, N.C. Dylan had cringed mentally the first few times he'd encountered Kunkle, sensing immediately that the man despised him for his size, his Southernness, his occupation, and his living arrangement. He had to wonder though how the big jerk could possibly know about that part of his life just by looking at him. Of course, Kunkle had no idea. Dylan could kick himself for bringing his own paranoia to what he later observed to be a general disparagement of all other people by the private bull dick, as he'd described him to Ben. Kunkle simply liked to find something he could consider despicable about everyone so that he could feel superior to them. After he'd achieved that to his own satisfaction, he was pretty easygoing.

"Hello, Charlie, how's the crime wave going?"

"About usual. Somebody spit dye on the Homer, is all."

Dylan stiffened, then relaxed, quickly chiding himself for flinching at Kunkle's lame joke. He probably had read in the paper about the art student in Canada throwing up on a Mondrian as his own act of performance art. The Williamstown Art Museum didn't have any Mondrians, of course, so Kunkle had substituted the Winslow Homer, the pride and joy of the collection and sure to raise the hair on Dylan's neck at the thought of its defacement.

"Yeah, since it matched the color in the painting," Kunkle said, "we didn't arrest him. We just took him down to the cafeteria and spilled grape juice on his shirt."

"You did the right thing," Dylan said evenly, "he'll never get the stain out."

"Yeah," Kunkle grinned as he passed by, "I thought you'd approve."

Bonehead, Dylan thought as he headed toward the front doors. Then again, Kunkle had known about the Mondrian travesty, which in its own way was impressive. Apparently, the big lug could read the paper—unless he'd seen it on the local news.

The Williamstown art aficionados had established the Museum in 1957 by buying and renovating an old convent, knocking out the walls between the bedroom cubicles and constructing a concrete slab and pillar facade as the entrance. A new wing had been built in 1964 by the Schaeffer family, owners of a large department store that had closed after the suburban malls had gone up. Luther Schaeffer also had contributed the largest part of the permanent collection, mostly pieces by minor artists from the Renaissance, a few oriental porcelain objects, a study by Henry Varnum Poor for the Land Grant Frescos up at Penn State, some unfinished pencil sketches by Whistler, and the Museum's two prizes, the Eakins and the Homer. After the museum had opened, a few other nice and unusual things had come its way, like the living room set by Frank Lloyd Wright and the blue felt typewriter by Beuys. Mostly, though, the Schaeffer Collection defined the Williamstown Art Museum and old Luther had been smart enough to provide it on indefinite loan. This meant that his widow Dottie held sway over the Museum, one reason why she was the head judge at the upcoming competition.

Dylan liked to walk through the museum in the morning on the premise of checking for anomalies, but in fact, he just liked to look. He loved fine things of any kind from any time, the reason why he was suited perfectly to his work.

As he strolled across the broad vestibule, with its slate tile floor and display counter doubling as the museum store, he sensed the wave building within him again. He walked through the new addition on the right, a clear, white modern space with the best lighting in the entire structure, shining first on Wright's blond furniture, so deliciously modern in the 1930s, nowadays knocked off so badly by any number of Scandinavian furniture makers. Further on, the tracks illuminated stark pottery from the 70s, and the gripping, bleak minimalist paintings and sculptures of the 50s and 60s, until he reached the broad stairway that would take him up into the old nunnery to see Schaeffer's still life paintings from Paloma, 1478, 1532, and so on.

The old oils relentlessly displayed rough-hewn gray tables piled with dead-eyed fish and fowl. Scales and feathers glistening from the egg tempura next to clumps of berries so failed in their naturalistic rendering as to be presciently and weirdly impressionistic. Truly third-rate work, he thought, and he loved them all, all familiar friends to him after four years of gazing. Sometimes, after being seen so often, things once thought ugly become beautiful.

The lighting in the old wing was hideous, though, he rued again as he did every day. And so little was known about these minor artists that the spare descriptions below their life works were completely understandable, but still, unacceptable.

He came to another one of his favorites, the wooden sculpture of St. Bartholomew, flayed alive according to tradition. In this manifestation as in most, he held his skin rolled up like a diploma proudly received for martyrdom. The carving was a good one, but sometime during the intervening centuries termites had eaten half of Bartholomew's face away. This natural catastrophe rendered a more realistic grotesque atrocity purportedly suffered by the saint compared to the fastidiously sanitized epidermal cylinder grasped in his hand.

Dylan naturally saved the best and his favorite for last, the American Arts Tradition gallery, also on the first floor in the north wing. There, a handsome work by Cecilia Beaux hung and next to it, Poor's fresco studies. Beneath, a card quoted Forbes Watson in a 1940 issue of the Magazine of Art on the sensation, "Out of purely American subject matter of a particularly significant kind, certainly one of the greatest works of art produced in this country."

The quote made Dylan frown when he thought of the recent book he'd just read about the Surrealists escaping fascism by coming to New York. From there they went on to influence the burgeoning Expressionist movement. The author suggested that artists like de Kooning, Pollack, Rothko, and Newman, who had come of age during the Depression, were trying to find an alternative to the pictures of hillbillies and downtrodden workers then passing as serious art. They appreciated the side of Surrealism devoted to "psychic automatism," wrote Watson, and other techniques for spontaneous artmaking to elevate their work beyond the cornball style of social realism.

Shaking his head, Dylan wondered if Watson had asked any of the Expressionists about this. Or had they all conveniently been dead by the time she'd postulated her critique? He doubted that she'd ever seen Poor's frescos and he could only imagine what she thought of Thomas Eakins' ultra-realism or the different fires brewing beneath the stories in Winslow Homer's work.

He sidled over to the Eakins, another signature anatomy class painting. Light sharply demarcated an examination table, with students and professor standing half in, half out of stark illumination and shadowy blurring falling into pure darkness. The bloodless naked corpse on the table conflicted severely with the ruddy skin tones of the upright observers in their starched shirts, dark suits, and ties. The contrast portrayed a plain parable of clear, pure death poured over by the massed confusion of the living. Dylan constantly saw new issues here and he questioned whether the Surrealist author ever could.

He moved to the Homer, "The Day's Catch." Inside a bowed wooden boat two men exerted themselves pulling up a net full of fish that churned the seawater into multiple, minute dramas of green and white froth as they struggled to escape. Dylan loved to marvel at these muscular men, with fibers of their brown arms calling to mind the striations of tree trunks, their thick dark shirts barely able to contain their power. A far cry from his own slight self, he saw them akin to the day's professional athletes, or even Kunkle, despite the guard's obvious lack of conditioning. Kunkle might have been robust like these fishermen had he lived then, while the most likely situation at sea that Dylan could imagine for himself was as a coxswain for an Ivy League sculling crew. Except, the sun would have destroyed his fair Gaelic skin.

The Homer was greatness, he nodded, but he shifted back to the Eakins where his heart lived. Maybe if he could put on a genuine show with real art, he could bring that Surrealist snob down here so she could see about these so-called realists, social or otherwise.

In a pig's eye, he sighed, heading for his office. Behind his desk, which was out of view of the door leading to the front counter, he studied the day's schedule. A group of high school students would be here at nine, which meant that he would have to alert Kunkle to watch the counter while Mary Beth, his intern, took them on the tour. That about said it for the day's activities.

Phone messages. He listened to one from Dottie Schaeffer, wanting to meet in the afternoon about the Avant-Garde show. She'd suggested two o'clock, late enough for him to be able to meet Ben for lunch, maybe. He called home, then remembered that Ben was tuning an upright in Ritzerstown, a good half-day's drive away. Oh well, he thought, listening to the next message.

"Hello, Mr. Mackenzie, this is Frank Kealy calling from the National Gallery of Art. I understand that you are the curator for the Williamstown Art Museum . . .? I'm working on an exhibit of Winslow Homer's work and I'd like to talk to you about it if I may. Could you please call me at area code 202-516-5489? If I'm not there, please ask for my colleague Nicolai Sikorsky—we're working on this project together. Okay, thanks, I hope to hear from you soon, and I'll call you back myself, too. Okay, bye, and thank you very much."

Dylan stayed absolutely still for a moment. He rewound the tape, listened impatiently to Dottie Schaeffer again, then concentrated on the message from Frank Kealy.

The National Gallery was mounting a Homer exhibit. It would be huge, thought Dylan, definitive, and the only reason Kealy was calling him was to get his hands on "The Day's Catch." Why else would he call?

Dylan stood up, walked away from the desk, returned, and sat down. He rewound the cassette and listened. The National Gallery wanted to borrow the Williamstown Art Museum's Homer. My God, he thought, what an opportunity. Just to have it there . . ..

He put his hands in the shape of a prayer over the bridge of his nose. If they wanted to borrow the Homer—they couldn't just borrow the Homer, it was really one of the few good attractions that Williamstown owned. No, they couldn't possibly just borrow it, they would have to compensate us, give us something in return, an exchange.

Dylan stood up, sat down again and punched the phone furiously, then slapped the receiver down; Ben was in Ritzerstown. He breathed in quickly, exhaled slowly. Okay, what needed to be done? Call Kealy, but first, think what needed to be thought first.

An exchange, but of what? He searched through the Museum catalog in his mind, dismissed Whistler, insufficient support by the Museum's own pieces. Beaux was out, not popular enough with the public. Sargent, no point; the Museum didn't possess even one Sargent, so how could he plan a show around one, or even two, God help him if he could persuade them to give him two? Besides, there had been a major traveling show of Sargent just five years ago.

Finally, his mind arrived where he really wanted to be in the first place: Thomas Eakins. He would trade for Eakins, two of them, the Homer was worth two, so little did they know. The Smithsonian had some good Eakins works, but the best were in Philadelphia. The City of Brotherly Love tossed Eakins out of the Academy, breaking his heart. Yet, those cretins now had his best in their galleries.

Philly had some good Winslow Homers, too, and Dylan weighed the likelihood of somehow working a three-way exchange Perhaps he could offer Cecelia Beaux to Philadelphia where she'd been born. The National Gallery had some Beaux's, and he would lend Williamstown's to Philadelphia in return for the Eakins. So, which ones?

He bustled to break free from his reverie. This was fantastic, he thought, a fantastic idea, but he had to approach it carefully, he had to suggest it to Kelay carefully. Dottie Schaeffer would have to okay the exchange, but she'd be thrilled. Kealy might have to be sold on it, however. He might think that the Williamstown Museum should be happy simply to take part in such a landmark show as a complete retrospective of Homer. And it would be extravagant, just like all of Mr. J. Carter Brown's monstrous megashows. But a freebie for a feeble "Courtesy of" plaque wouldn't cut it, Dylan determined. He would be quiet, slow, Southernly, feel the man out. But ultimately, he would be adamant and unmoving. Two Eakins for Homer, that was the deal, the B.L.

He rubbed his hands together and picked up the phone.

Tanya sat cross-legged on a high stool, naked, while Hitchcock stood slouching at work over a canvas opposite about fifteen feet distant. Music played in the background, Taj Mahal, which caused Hitchcock to gyrate now and then as he planned his next stroke.

Bored, Tanya rolled her eyes to look around the familiar room, part of a row house laid out like railroad cars, one room after another next to a long hallway running down one side. Hitchcock had knocked down the wall between the kitchen and the living room to enlarge his studio, which pleased the landlord to no end, Tanya imagined. It also meant that she posed as dramatically as possible in front of a sink full of dishes, the dirty stove, and a refrigerator with wooden panel cabinets encircling overhead. From her vantage point, she could take her pick of past work by Hitchcock, which demonstrated a stunning array of techniques and media, from life-size plaster dogs and even larger cats wearing thrift-shop suits and ties, to origami humans joined at odd angles by what was clearly their genitalia, to heavy abstracts sagging with layers of darkening acrylic paint. On one small wall he had pinned copies of artists he liked, among them some of Leonard Dufresne's chunky cartoonish characters from "A Streetcar Named Desire," thick, yet smooth-limbed, like two-dimensional Claymation figures. She saw a few of Henry Darger's exquisitely weird stories featuring little girls in some shockingly violent episodes, like some delicately rendered stories incongruously in a Fan K'uan landscape.

As she spied around, she noted the one departure from his catalog of the outlandish, a charcoal taped to a wall of stylized rust-brown bison with black manes stampeding across a dark gray wall, apparently inspired by the Lascaux cave paintings. Leaping ahead and above them was a black bull with a red mane, leading the charge of the anxious herd from one side to the other, from abyss to abyss. Closer examination on other occasions had revealed that these vivacious, snorting beasts were in fact all the same animal, traced from a template, then colored in. The relentless gray wall, too, had shades of gold underneath, as though a faint intimation of grassy plains had been attempted. When she asked Hitchcock about the drawing, though, he merely said it was his take on the beginning of art.

"Tanya," he said without looking at her, "I want you to know that my brush is my tongue coursing over your body, flicking your earlobes like drops of dew, working my way down one narrow of your neck into the hollow where the spear slew Hector, down over your clavicle to the slope of your perfect breasts. I pause for color, and now I'm using the tip of my tongue to trace the infinite crevices of one of your nipples, lapping the top to feel that mother milk-giving fissure, I hope, then back to licking the larger whole—surprising how hard a nipple really can be, you know—stroking forward and back, back and forth; brush technique is everything, wouldn't you say?"

He'd caught her eye wandering and this was his way of bringing her concentration back. She knew what he was doing and was even more annoyed with him because her nipples were getting hard.

"John," she said irritably, "what are you doing?"

"I'm doing you," he said.

"You wish," she said. They'd had a quick thing when she'd first arrived in Williamstown, but familiarity had taken over, revealing their strange struggle. Daily sightings drew them together, but different perspectives pushed them apart every day, too.

"You know, if you don't like the way I'm sitting, why don't you hire a professional model?"

"Ah, but I do like the way you sit, much better than a pro. Lucian Freud said that when professional models are naked, they are, in a sense, clothed. Besides, who can afford them?"

"That's great. And I suppose I'm going to look just like his stuff? Might as well paint a corpse in a morgue or someone in an asylum."

"Yeah, well, I'm interested in the plasticity of flesh but nothing so literal."

"Yeah, I'll bet. And, while we're at it, answer me this: How come out of all the different works on display around here I haven't seen one single nude?"

"Oh, I keep those tucked away in my bedroom closet for special inspiration."

"Unhuh, I can imagine.

At that moment, the kitchen timer sounded a raucous buzzing.

"Time," Tanya said, uncrossing her legs and stretching with a yawn.

"Damn," said Hitchcock. "I was just starting to get a feel for the line."

"Too bad." She moved over to another stool where her clothes were piled and began dressing. Hitchcock draped a cloth over his canvas and started for the stool, dropping his clothes as he went. Leaning on one hand, he stood three-quarters turned from Tanya, who had switched her tripod and paints with his. She paused and lifted the edge of the cloth over Hitchcock's painting for a peek.

As she looked, she remembered reading a description of Gillmore's collage murals in a Sunday Times magazine. The article described how he clipped words out of bridal catalogs and self-help manuals. He then placed them every which way on his canvas. Sliding back and forth between image and information, the article suggested, the technique caused an effect at once highly worked and crude, abstract and representational. At least Gillmore used real words to make his point, Tanya thought, unlike Hitchcock's striking confusions.

"Well, John," she said absently, "you're certainly out there, very original . . . startling . . . but accessible is not your middle name."

He turned his head to her and said, "Hey! You're not supposed to be looking at that."

"All right, all right," she said, dropping the cloth. "No need to go crazy."

"And what do you mean it's not accessible? It's very accessible."

She picked up some tubes of paint, squirted dabs on a makeshift palette, and began to whip colors together with a stick. "Well, to the hoi polloi, maybe not."

"Listen, that little number is going to knock people out. It'll generate a hell of a lot more gut checks than most of the fru-fru shit showing up around here."

"Yeah, well," she said, "the good news is that nobody will recognize me in it."

"Oh, really? And, since yours is so literal, I should be grateful that you have me facing away?"

"Well, your ass is better looking than your face."

He shrugged the dig off, "But what you're doing is meant to be literal, is it not?"

"I guess. More or less," she said, beginning to apply fresh paint in carefully controlled increments, almost stingily.

"Well, of course, mine is not. That is, not in a linear sense. Go ahead, take another look. Go on. Okay, now, in it think of yourself not as body but as thought or words. Think of calligraphy, of words as object not metaphor. That's what you see, aesthetic expression, body as language, proof of abstract thinking."

She gazed skeptically, mumbling, "If you say so."

"What do you mean 'If I say so'? It's obvious, self-evident!" he said sharply.

"Yeah," Tanya said, going back to her canvas, "maybe so, but it still really isn't all that easy to see, you know? Don't get me wrong, I love your work, but it calls for more than what the average Joe or Jane brings to it, you know?"

"Well, what the hell do you know about it, anyway? I mean, you're in fucking Williamstown, too, Ms. Here-from-New-York. If you're so on top of the cresting wave, what's your uber-objective, huh? You tell me!"

Stunned and flustered at his outburst, she glanced at her own work and grimaced. Finally, she stuttered, "To make something beautiful."

Silence followed.

"I see," Hitchcock then said coldly. "And here you are. That's how barrier-breaking your work is. Beautiful breakthroughs. Congratulations on cornering the market."

She frowned as she glanced back and forth, still trying to work. "Oh, come on, John."

"Right, who the hell knows what beauty in art is anyway?" Hitchcock pronounced in a quiet roar, "Yeah, like 'I don't know art,' the asshole said, 'but I'm told what I like.'"

"Jesus Christ, Johnny, just shut up, will you?"

"Sure, don't listen to me! I have my own views, just like you. Let's ask Joe and Jane Q. Public, as you so quaintly put it. Let's find out whose work does appeal to the great unwashed."

"They all wash nowadays."

"Okay, whatever."

"How're we supposed to do this?"

"The Avant-Garde show at the museum. We'll enter these paintings, the closest we have to corresponding work, and see how they do."

"What if neither of them get anything? Besides, mine might not be considered avant-garde. It's too literal, remember?"

"Ah, but so beautiful."

She squinted at her painting, hating the self-indulgence of it, hating talking about anything she did—anyway, more and more she found herself imagining grand installations, but here, in Williamstown, Pennsylvania? Simmering, she said, "You can be such a prick, John, you know that?"

"Only when provoked."

"Oh, like by the sun and the moon and the stars?"

"Hilarious. Say, why don't we bag this and go to the airport for breakfast? United has a complimentary station with buns and Starbuck's."

"No way, the timer's still ticking." She glanced at him squirming and arching his back. She frowned, then smiled. "John, my brush is my tongue, licking down your side to the curve of your hip, over the mound of your ass cheek, slowly toward the hollows at the base of your spine."

She grinned as she watched him stiffen.

"Well, Dylan," Dottie Schaeffer said, "do you see anything that strikes your fancy right off?"

They stood in the vestibule of the Museum watching the artists bring in their work. The lobby had been cleared of its usual accoutrements to make room for a variety of spaces and stands for the temporary exhibit.

Dylan glanced at her nervously, not knowing exactly how to answer her question. She was short with a midsection round like a small ball and with no bust to speak of, standing on slender, slightly bowed but muscular legs. He noted that her brilliant clothing clashed brilliantly.

"Of course," he told Ben, "in theory all color schemes exist because some people somewhere developed them and preferred them. But I never knew anyone in real life who, when faced with the either/or taste in color, actually chose the worst for the best—until I met Dottie Schaeffer, that is."

"Shocking," Ben mumbled, squinting at tiny pliers held up to the light, "pink?"

"True, through and through. I've been to her house."

He sipped his morning coffee at the butcher's block they used as the kitchen table. He watched Ben's long length coil over his oversize doctor's bag, checking to be sure he had all of his tools. One time he'd traveled all the way to Wilkes-Barre only to find that he'd left a critical, middle range fork in the basement. He beat his car's console all the way home and back, cursing nonstop all that night right through dinner.

"She must have been cute as a young girl, I suppose," Dylan said, moving his coffee mug back and forth through the ether as though weighing the notion. "Luther must have thought so back in 1965 when he wooed her from behind that lingerie counter to be his second wife. She looks pretty ordinary now," he said, "a so-so complexion and her hair is kind of a dullish brown, most likely from time plus coloring it. I would say that her appearance suggests an indifferent approach to cosmetic care."

"I believe I have everything," Ben said. He straightened up. As tall and slender as he was, with his dark hair slipping away and his black gambler's goatee, many friends said he looked like Mick Fleetwood. But he was of much greater substance, Dylan asserted. Sam Elliot, yes.

"Her girlish prettiness must have waned," Dylan went on, "into that plainness common to many women whose beauty peaks in their youth. You know, youth is an important promotional byproduct of nubility. Is nubility a word, do you think?"

"Don't hold dinner," Ben said, "I anticipate a late one."

Ben hated these long trips to the boondocks, but Williamstown offered only one small Catholic college for volume work, which meant that he had to wander far and wide to make a living, one piano at a time. There wasn't much of a market locally for pianofortes, either, complicating the sale of the one he had been building downstairs for the past two years. His exquisite artisanship, especially his marketeering, would sell it no question, thought Dylan. But it would take more time, just as it was taking longer to finish because he was away so many days in other parts of Eastern Pennsylvania tuning one piano or another.

"Word has it that Luther's ardor was fading, too," Dylan went on, "before he died. Later, for the sake of the children, he and Dottie had lived parallel lives; still together, but no touching."

Ben said, "See ya'all later. Good luck with hanging the avant-garde, today. They all deserve it, right?"

"Oh, indeed."

Ben leaned over and kissed him, "And, really good luck with those National Gallery boys."

A sudden chill of reality enveloped Dylan. Absently, he hurriedly called to Ben's back, "You be careful, too, on the highway of life." But he was already out the door, which left Dylan alone to contemplate the gravity of the day ahead.

"It's hard to see anything at this point," Dylan explained to Dottie, "with all their moving around, putting up their things."

"Well, then let's go to them," she said brusquely, starting to head toward the chaotic scene.

Dylan didn't move. "Yes. You know, Dottie, I'm expecting the arrival any minute now . . .."

She pulled up. "Oh. Those fellows from Washington who want our Homer."

"Yes, that's right."

"And you really think it's a good idea, to give them our best picture?"

"Lend, not give. We will get it back."

"In the same good shape? They won't ruin it?"

"Certainly not. They handle masterpieces all the time, from around the world. We'll have a placard in the National Gallery saying that it is on loan from the Williamstown Art Museum, promotional value that you just cannot buy. And we may receive in exchange one or, if we're fortunate, two works as the anchors of a major exhibition of our own."

"But that's not for sure."

"Well, no, it's not, but it is the accepted practice."

"I hope you're right. And this could take a year or more?"

"Why, yes."

"Unhuh. Meanwhile, we have a really important art show going on. You know, I think we should pay attention to it right now, until the guys from Washington get here to talk about some dream show."

"Why, absolutely, Dottie," Dylan said, drawling his words just a hint, "let's go on over there and take a preliminary gander."

Of course, she'd known beforehand all of the answers to her questions from their other discussions about lending out the Homer. Luther had hired him, and Dylan had liked the no-nonsense, wry approach of the Schaeffer patriarch. After Luther's death, Dottie had taken over, feigning as though she'd come out from under the shade of a sun-blotting tree. In exchange, Dylan felt he'd been moved underneath the same darkening arbor. He never knew how to respond to her comments or questions and now he had to wonder if she felt threatened by this development with the Homer.

They began to stroll among the busy artists, some chattering back and forth as they worked on their display, others wearing funereal expressions marking the seriousness of the event. Sixty openings had been announced for artists who qualified as residents—a loudly bitter contingent from outside Philadelphia already had been turned away—and who had gotten their applications in first. Each had been assigned a limited amount of space at random to set up a display. On the first night, awards would be presented for the best works, first place being a spot for the piece in the Museum for a year. Then, to milk the most out of the event, the show would be open to the public during the next two weeks.

Dylan didn't expect to see much, mainly because anyone doing good work most likely had left Williamstown a long time ago for New York or some other art Mecca. Maybe they'd see something nice from a gifted high school kid ready to take off for art school, but that was about it.

They stopped now and then as they wandered, and as soon as they did, conversation in the immediate area would hit a lull. Everyone there knew who they were.

A young man in his twenties smiled at them as they slowed at his station. His piece was a figure cast in plaster on a slightly heroic scale, a man, naked, straining against invisible chains, wearing a stressed expression on his taut face. He was entirely covered with what looked like Rorschach inkblots splashed in cruel colors, fresh bruise blues, yellowing purples, dried rusts, wet reds, and shiny blacks. Dylan saw something and stepped closer to discover darker colored silhouettes beneath the screening blots, a few of ordinary people in dull domestic scenes, but other images of helicopters suspended above scrambling troops, stark bodies hanging by their necks from wires, and babies playing with syringes under a Christmas tree. Dylan glanced at the young artist, a short, soft man with eyes sincere like a dog's, who was placing a card in front of his statue: *Homo Ego, Ergo Id-iot.*

"Segal skips his Prozac?" whispered Dottie in his ear. Dylan twisted his head at her in surprise as they continued walking.

One young woman, tiny and birdlike, with hair like a spray of golden grass, had set up green faux pods with big, orange plastic fish grinning big toothy cartoon smiles emerging from the blossoms. Shyly, she looked at Dottie and Dylan expectantly. They both nodded noncommittally and passed by.

"What did you think of that?" Dottie breathed, barely suppressing a smile. Dylan refused to react, annoyed. Instead, he moved ahead, then suddenly thought to swing his eyes back to the front door as he went.

In the corner next to the reception desk, he noticed a striking woman in black jeans and a black tank top folding up the simple brown wrapper that had encased her work, a painting of a nude man standing next to a stool, leaning on it with one hand. She had used the colors of cold meat to evince his flesh, blues, reds, and grays plied in long vertical strokes. When she saw the two officiaries, the woman straightened up from her task and leaned back against the desk, almost resentfully resigned, Dylan thought. He couldn't help himself; he glanced back at the front entrance again.

"And this?" Dottie said.

They were there, two men silhouetted against the glass doors, one of average height, the other a bit shorter.

"Yeah," Dylan said, needing to leave now, "nice."

"What about the figure? Very athletic, almost like an Eakins rower or that El Greco knight, do you think?"

"Eakins. Unhuh," he said, knowing she knew that he adored Eakins. "Listen, Dottie, they're here, the gentlemen from the National Gallery. We should go see them now."

"Oh, I see. Dylan, why don't you take care of them? Really, you're the expert. I'd just get in the way."

"No, Dottie, not at all. Please come meet them."

"No, go on. I'm happier this way. Go ahead."

"Are you sure?"

"Sure," she said, and he beamed, relieved. "And good luck!" she said heartily as he turned away, which actually surprised him.

"Mr. Kealy?" Dylan said to the shorter man, who was older, with gray hair and a mustache, dressed in a blue striped seersucker suit.

"Nick Sikovsky," he said, "this is Frank Kealy here. He called you, I believe, about your Homer."

"Oh, yes," said Dylan, turning to the taller, younger man, who had a short, dark beard and glasses, and wore a dark suit with suspenders. He reached his hand out to Dylan and said, "Nice to meet you in person, Mr. Mackenzie."

"Please, Dylan," he said, "and the pleasure is all mine."

"Great. Listen, I hate to be so direct, but we're on a very tight schedule, tearing all over the place. Could we go look at yours right now?"

"Why, of course."

"And" Kealy continued, "if you don't mind, I'd like to take some Polaroids?"

Dylan winced, "Sure, though I have to warn you, the lighting isn't the best in the world."

He led them left to the Traditional American Arts Gallery, smiling warmly at Dottie as he passed on the way.

"Did you ever see any of Robert Hickey's work? He's done these amazing miniature houses."

Hitchcock and Tanya lay on her bed in the single boardinghouse room. She rented it when she first arrived in Williamstown, thinking to see how she liked the town before committing to an apartment lease, cheap as they were notwithstanding. They'd grabbed a late meal at Denny's, after which he had driven her home where they collapsed, worn out from staying up all night for no good reason.

"No, he's in New York, right? You saw him when you were there?"

"Yeah. He's good and getting some good ripples."

He turned to her and propped his head up in his palm. "You weren't getting any ripples? That's why you left New York?"

"Nah," she said, "I was making some headway. I showed at the Gramercy. And once in one of Kenny Schachter's show, you know, Death of Death themes. Joe Amrhein still has a few things of mine in his flat files," Tanya said. "But it was expensive, and I wanted to do larger installations. So, I came here." She laughed again, "And look at the size of this place. Rodney Dangerfield: It's so small, you gotta say 'pintsiz; there's no room for the e.'"

"Hah," Hitchcock grunted. He rolled over to lay flat on his back again.

She turned to him, and said, "What about you? How come you

didn't leave Williamstown?"

He twisted his lips, "I'm from here. At least, since I was eleven. I thought I was close enough for New York to come to me. That was a while ago," he said sardonically.

Or was it wistfully? she wondered. He stared at the ceiling until she punched him in the shoulder.

"So, whose stuff do you like?"

"Who do I like? Old or new?"

She shrugged, "You're old. Start at old."

"Okay. Cupules discovered in the Bhimbetka Rock Shelters in India date back to 290,000 B.C.E., though many archaeologists think they could go back 700,000 years. Australian Aborigines in Jinmium carved wall art shaped like kangaroos 75,000 years ago that threw strict theorists on the origin of abstract art into consternation."

She punched him again, hard.

"So nice to see you again, Mr. Mackenzie."

"The pleasure is all mine I'm sure, Mr. Mission," Dylan said, shaking Ben's hand with his right while lightly touching his own breast with his left.

"Maybe now, but not necessarily later," Ben murmured, wiggling his middle finger against Dylan's palm as they clasped.

"Shhh. You'll disrupt the awards announcements with such carrying on."

"When will that happen?"

"Soon, I think. They like to get the ceremonial stuff over quickly so that they can move right into socializing."

Ben glanced at his watch, "Well, six o'clock ought to be early enough. And who's going to win?"

"I haven't a clue. Dottie Schaeffer was adamant about keeping me out of the loop. You know, she spreads all that manure around about me being the sole arbiter of fine taste in Williamstown with, as she says, all my schooling and experience. But then she goes ahead and declares my influence to be too undue in what is supposed to be a community competition."

"Sure, it makes sense. Amateur critics for amateur art."

"Oh, you know, it's how she rationalizes doing what she wants when she wants. The Board judged, which of course means that she judged. And she's been very close-mouthed about her pickings."

The vestibule of the Williamstown Art Museum was beginning to fill up with people, the hopeful artists hovering close to their creations. The Museum Board members assembled up near the reception desk, which had been turned into a makeshift dais with Dottie Schaeffer standing just beside the podium. A mass of Williamstown's citizens, all decked out, art aficionados and curious alike intermingled at one of the big occasions of the year for the small city-town. Even Kunkle looked like he and his deputy security guard had taken their uniforms to the dry cleaners.

A five-piece band positioned in the contemporary gallery played soft jazz, a departure from the usual string quartet. Dottie thought of jazz as more appropriate for an avant-garde event. The music was hard to hear though because the room was awash in low level noise from the conversation of the crowd.

"So, have you heard from the National Gallery?" Ben asked.

Dylan brightened immediately, "Not yet. But things look promising. I called the Gardner in Boston about a possible exchange, and their main curator, a fellow named Goldfarb, sounded interested, no, almost guardedly excited. He mentioned that Sikovsky and Kealy had been there and that they'd remarked on having seen 'The Day's Catch' in Williamstown."

Ben smiled, "Why, that sounds terrific."

"I know, it could be fantastic!" beamed Dylan, grateful to Ben for being happy for him.

"When do you think they might call?" asked Ben.

"I don't know, but I'm ready at any time," Dylan said, pulling out a cell phone from the breast pocket of his jacket.

Ben shrugged, "Maybe you could call them."

"No, no, I don't want to be too eager, it could compromise my position in asking—in requiring—a trade."

"Ladies and gentlemen," Dottie Schaeffer called from the podium, "if you all could please gather around, we will delay no more in announcing the winners of the Williamstown Art Museum's First Annual Avant-Garde of the Area exhibit. I hope I'm correct in calling it the first annual exhibit—am I, Dylan?" she asked coyly.

Surprised, Dylan smiled and nodded his head slightly, hoping it appeared to be more of an acknowledgment rather than agreement. He was aware of the swarm of eyes upon him at that instant, particularly the artists. Some seemed to stand in defense of their work, others grouped together close to the front, as though hearing better might improve their chances. Dylan noted a few of the artists he'd seen setting up that fateful day last week, the childlike woman and the attractive dark-haired one with the cool demeanor. She stood next to a tall, lean, older-looking man with a short gray beard and ponytail. He recognized him then, John Hitchcock, a long-time local artist known for extremely outré work in all sorts of media. They all turned back to Dottie as she began speaking again.

"Just before we begin, however," and she smiled at the mild laughter that followed, "and I will make this quick, I would like to introduce and thank the persons most responsible for this wonderful show. Let's start with our great curator, Mr. Dylan Mackenzie. Without his remarkable insights, his intuition, and his background, none of us could possibly have gained the knowledge, the artistic ken if you will, or the confidence to propose a show like the Area Artists of the Avant-Garde. He was instrumental in choosing the excellent art and artists that will be recognized tonight. Thank you, Dylan."

Everyone stared back at him again and applauded lightly, as he tried to control his expression.

"My God!" he whispered to Ben out of the side of his mouth, "she's laid the entire thing off on me. I can't believe it!"

She continued by introducing the judges one by one, then paused. "Okay, no more thank-yous. To the first ever award winners: Third place, Amy Fenstimaker for her whimsical sculpture 'Blooming Fish Flowers,' showing that art on the edge can be flighty and fun, too."

He gazed in amazement as the young woman, embarrassed and giggling, stepped up to accept her prize.

"What's wrong?" asked Ben.

"Our second award goes to Mr. William Schneck for his remarkable multimedia work 'Homo Ego, Ergo Id-iot,' a post-modern, apocalyptic rendering of the modern human condition. Come up here, William!"

Dylan watched in slack-jawed astonishment as the soft-featured young man, grinning broadly, marched up to the podium.

"Dyl, what is it?" Ben said with urgency.

"She picked—" Dylan started, but stopped when Dottie Schaeffer spoke again.

"Finally, the first place award winner in the Williamstown Art Museum's first annual Area Artists of the Avant-Garde goes to," she hesitated and Dylan inhaled, holding his breath until she finished, "Tanya Scott for her neo-realist rendition, 'Male Nude,' a superbly subtle painting that both evokes admirably, yet with gentle parody, the style of our own Thomas Eakins and his classic figure studies. Congratulations, Tanya," Dottie said heartily, turning to favor her with a brilliant smile.

Dylan's sight was already on her, the attractive brunette. She was red-faced, now, and still. But Dylan's attention had been captured by an even more astonishing hue of red that flushed coursing up the face of John Hitchcock. The applause of the audience drew attention away from Dylan's program hitting the floor. Tanya tried to grab Hitchcock's arm, but he shrugged her off. As she reluctantly moved toward the front, glancing back now and then as she went, Dylan watched the tall man turn briskly around, stride to his station, remove his painting, and walk out the Museum's front door.

"Now that wasn't very sporting," Ben said. When Dylan turned his head to him, he said, "What just happened here?"

Dylan blew out a sigh and said, "Dottie Schaeffer just announced as the award winners the very same artists we passed on a quick tour together when they were all setting up."

"Yeah? So?"

"So, she selected the only three artists that she knew I'd seen. She was asking me about them the whole time, and I wasn't paying one bit of attention. That was the day the National Gallery fellows came to see the Homer. I was thoroughly distracted, yet somehow Dottie got it into her head that I liked those three and made them the winners."

"And what's so terrible about that? It shows that she does value your opinion after all."

"Oh, bullshit. She was just covering her ass."

"What do you mean, none of them deserved to win?"

"Lord no!" roared Dylan under his breath. He grimaced, "Oh, maybe the beat-up statue of mankind is weird enough to be avant-garde. But the goofy fish sculpture, no way. And that nude shows good technique, but it's completely conventional. Now everyone thinks I'm the one who chose them. You saw Hitchcock storm out of here, didn't you? He's furious, for good reason, maybe, and it won't take him long to focus his anger on me!"

"Who, the lanky guy? So, why do you care what he thinks?"

"I don't know why," Dylan said, his frown almost a pout, "but I do, I guess."

"Well," Ben said, "I guess I don't understand. I think Dottie Schaeffer made quite a statement today in your favor."

"Yeah, well I do not."

"Oh." Ben paused, then said, "Okay." He gazed around the room for a second, watching the crowd milling, breaking up into smaller groups of artists, patrons, and mixes of both. Some headed for drinks and food. The jazz band smoothly slipped into a quiet piece that barely accented the murmur of warm conversation floating through the Museum.

"Well, I'm for heading home. You'll need to circulate, I imagine?"

"I suppose so," Dylan said, observing Dottie in animated chatter with some of the other judges.

"Okay," Ben said. "Should I hold dinner for you?"

"No."

"Well, then, okay. See you back at the farm."

"Yes."

Ben left, and Dylan chided himself for treating him so badly. He goaded himself for stewing about what by all indices was a very small matter. Yet he couldn't stop. This was exactly the kind of dog and pony show he'd hoped to avoid, even though he knew perfectly well beforehand that it had been inevitable, ineluctable.

He spied a joyous Dottie Schaeffer wending her way toward him, which reminded him of the spiraling despair in which she had cast him, a void that seemed to deepen every time he was required to deal with her. For the bottom line was clear, she was determined to shape the Museum into her legacy in the world, even though she had come to it late. He was wondering how he would be able to face her now, or ever again, when the phone in his breast jacket began to ring. Startled, he yanked it out to answer.

"Yes? I can hardly hear you, I'm on a cell phone in the middle of a reception. Do you mind holding while I go to my office? Excellent, Mr. Kealy, one moment."

He waved the phone to get Dottie's attention, pointed at it, pushed his lower lip out in a pantomime of dismay and apology, then left quickly for his office.

John Hitchcock returned to the Museum long after the last guests had left, and almost after the cleanup crew had finished. Without hesitation, he trooped purposefully past the exhibit of the Avant-Garde, carrying a rolled piece of tan paper bound with a rubber band beneath his arm. No one paid any attention to him as he headed into the Traditional American Arts gallery.

Alone in the room, he propped the wound paper cylinder against the wall, then pulled a roll of two-inch wide masking tape from the pocket of his jeans. He tore off two long strips, and lightly pressed the ends of each to the wall. He then worked the rubber band carefully off the roll and unfurled the paper. He leaned it against the foot of the wall, stepping away, then back again to steady it when it started to fall.

He straightened up and took a step back. Reaching out his arms, Hitchcock grabbed both sides of Thomas Eakin's "Subject of Anatomy Class" and with a small, firm tug, lifted it free. The klaxon of the alarm sounded throughout the building as he quickly put the painting down against the wall. In fluid movements, he picked up his paper, unrolled it, and spread it across the wall, holding it still with one forearm while using his free hand to tape one side, then the other. He stepped back to study his work for a moment.

"You assholes want conventional realism," he muttered, "now you got it."

He started walking calmly toward the entranceway only to see a flock of faces staring at him. Gradually, he recognized three or four sets of Latino features, the cleaners, and a couple of Dutchies in uniform, Kunkle and Mitch.

"What?" Hitchcock said defiantly.

When he heard the clamor of the alarm, Dylan still sat with his eyes fixed on the phone where he'd laid it on his desk, hours before. What could it be? he asked himself absently.

As if he cared, he thought.

"I wanted to call you personally, Mr. Mackenzie, to let you know of our decision and to thank you sincerely for your hospitality."

Hospitality. Of course, Southern hospitality, y'all, a speciality in the South where he was from. Where he most likely was soon to go, to return. Hotter than hell in the South.

"I hope we haven't inconvenienced you too much, especially since you phoned."

Of course he had called, right after speaking to Goldfarb at the Gardner no matter what he'd told Ben. Ben personally saw all of his other weaknesses, why should he know about this one, too? Except, Ben had probably figured out that he had called those National Gallery boys.

"You understand how difficult it is to make these choices. Winslow, God bless him, he did a lot of paintings, a thousand or more."

Ben was Ben, God bless him.

"'The Day's Catch' is a marvelous work, seminal Winslow Homer. But when it came right down to it, Nick and I just felt that we needed to show the deeper, symbolic essence of his work. That meant that we needed to limit certain types of studies. We went with 'The Undertow' from the Clark."

From Williamstown, of course, the one in Massachusetts, Dylan noted.

"The good news," Kealy said, "is that you'll have to keep your Homer right there on display." He ended with a false conspiratorial laugh and Dylan joined in with him, Ha ha.

He sighed and lifted his head. Why was that alarm going on so? Did someone trip it by accident?

Kunkle stuck his head in. "You hear the alarm?"

Dylan stared at him deliberately, without indulgence.

"Someone grabbed the Eakins."

Dylan jerked straight up. "What? When? Under cover of the show?"

Kunkle smiled slyly, satisfied. "No, no. No reason to get excited. We got the guy, and the Eakins is safe and sound. Needs some dusting on top of the frame, though."

"Oh," said Dylan.

"Yeah, I don't think it was a theft attempt. The guy put the painting on the floor and taped some other picture up in its place. I think it was more like a protest."

"I see," Dylan said quietly, almost sorry that the distraction was gone. "Who was it, do you know?"

"Sure. John Hitchcock."

Dylan raised his eyes again. "Really? Hitchcock?"

"Yup. I asked him why he did it, and he said 'just exercising my artistic temperament.' So I said, 'Ha-ha. When does the artistic part show up?'"

Kunkle laughed, and Dylan said, "Yes, that's good, pretty good." He paused, then said, "So, is he going to jail?"

"For the night. He's not a bad guy, he bused my kids to school for years. He takes my grandkids now."

"Oh?"

"Yeah. He's harmless," Kunkle said, "unless, maybe you think we should press charges. You know, to discourage this sort of thing."

Dylan said, "Well, if it's all the same to you, Charlie, I'd rather not. I'd just as soon forget the whole affair."

Kunkle smiled, again in that knowing way of his, which always made Dylan wonder what in the world he possibly could know.

"Okay. I'll just run him downtown for the night to cool his heels."

"All right, if you think that's necessary."

"That much I do," Kunkle said firmly.

The Museum was utterly quiet. Dylan stalked the route of his usual morning tour, though at this hour, he couldn't see much. He preferred not to, wishing instead to enjoy the memory of what he saw daily rather than the distorted view that artificial lighting would show, even in the old upstairs wing.

He stroked St. Bartholomew's termite-scarred visage before descending the stairs to the American wing. He ignored the other paintings and went straight to the Eakins.

It was fine, he decided, without a sign of ever having been

disturbed. The Homer looked the same, too.

As he was about to leave, he noticed the tan paper on the floor leaning against the wall, with the masking tape still on its sides. Dylan stooped over, picked it up and held it out in front of him. A charcoal drawing of ancient bison pounding across a rocky plain. He rolled it up, tucked it under his arm, and left.

Tanya stood at the front doors waiting for the Museum to open for the morning. She wore a black pullover, hot for the season, and a dark-plaid skirt and tights, the closest thing she had to formal clothing. When the door was unlocked, she asked to see Mr. Mackenzie. The young woman behind the front desk called Dylan, then ushered Tanya to his office.

Dylan worked over a drafting table, fixing the matte board to the drawing. He was just about finished when Tanya entered.

"Mr. Mackenzie?"

"Yes, hello." Dylan swung his head around and said in surprise, "Why, it's First Place in the Avant-Garde exhibit."

Tanya said tightly, "You should know, you gave me the damn thing."

"As a matter of fact," Dylan said, "I had nothing to do with it. That was Mrs. Schaeffer's show all the way, and I have no idea why she invoked my name for any part of it."

"Well, whoever made the decision, it was ludicrous. I shouldn't have won, I had no intention of winning. You ought to know that."

"You're a good artist."

"Sure, but not with that piece. That was an indulgence of mine, a way to relax. It's hardly revolutionary. Why was it chosen?"

Dylan said, "I told you, I don't know why. I didn't do the choosing. Anyway, why not your work? If not you, who else? And what difference could it possibly make anyway in this tiny little town?"

Tanya hesitated. "John Hitchcock."

Dylan leaned back on his stool, resting against the edge of the table.

"John Hitchcock. You're not here for yourself, then."

"No," said Tanya.

"You know what happened last night after the reception?"

"Yes," she said. "Mitch, the security guard, he's a friend. He told me. That's why I'm here. I came to ask you not to file a criminal charge against John. You need to know, he's a gifted artist and he's frustrated after all these years of getting nowhere. He was particularly frustrated after yesterday's farce."

Dylan returned to his matte work. "Most artists are frustrated. Most die that way. Most people, for that matter."

"Yes, but John's never really had a chance before, and if he has to go to prison now, he won't get one. We're—"

She drew closer as Dylan turned the drawing right side up.

Tanya stopped in mid-sentence. "I recognize that drawing. That's Hitchcock's."

"Yes," Dylan said, studying his handiwork, "this is what he taped up in place of the Eakins. An early work, look at the date."

He flipped it over and pointed to a rude signature that he'd found on the back when he was measuring it: John Hitchcock, 10-3, 4/4/66.

"The beginning of art," she said. Then, "You liked it. You like John's work."

Dylan replied, "His early stuff. After all, I am the curator of a traditional museum. At least, right now I am."

"Still, you mounted it."

"As a gift to him," he said, "an apology for last night's . . . farce." He handed it to her. "Tell him to get if framed. It's good enough for that, anyway."

"And the criminal thing?" she asked.

He smirked, "No one's going to charge him. He's a home-grown artist, for heaven's sake."

"Not for long. Those were the plans I was talking about, you know? We're going to be going to New York."

"Oh, really?" Dylan said.

"Yeah," she said. "He's excited."

Dylan nodded, and said, "You're committed to Hitchcock, then?"

Anguished, Tanya said, "I don't know. He's so God-damn difficult."

Dylan smiled sadly, waving a hand, "Exercising his artistic temperament."

She frowned, "I guess so."

"What about your work? Will it suffer?"

"No," she said, "I don't think so. I hope not anyway. I need another change. Williamstown's gotten too comfortable for me."

"I can imagine. Well, good luck."

"Yeah, thanks."

Tanya turned to go, when he said, "Wait."

Dylan quickly wheeled around to the table and scribbled something on a pad of paper. He ripped off the sheet and gave it to her. "That's an address in North Carolina where I believe you will find me in a short amount of time. My partner and I have plans to open a gallery in Greensboro, with a website, too, of course. When you get settled in New York, and you have something to show, send me some slides. I'd love to see your work, maybe show it."

Thanks," Tanya said, warmly, surprised. "I will."

"Good."

"And John? Can he send you his work, too?"

Dylan laughed, "Of course."

"Why, thank you very much, Mr. Mackenzie. Really, I really appreciate it."

"You're most welcome. Really."

Marveling at the turn of events, Tanya, smiling, left.

Dylan gazed unseeing at the empty doorway for a moment, then began to straighten up the table.

The Catch

The ball spiraled up into the sun, eclipsing one small, moving area, just under three inches in diameter, that couldn't be watched for fear of blindness until it had cleared the greater ball of energy and fire. Woody did his own awkward, churning dance below, shading his eyes with his glove trying to pick up the ball as it started its looming descent. In the background he could hear the other kids yelling, screaming for him to catch it, miss it, catch it, swelling incoherently as the ball came down like a satellite in free fall. He moved left, right, turned around, seeing the threads even as its closing weight created a greater gravity within his heart. The ball hit his glove's webbing and bounced to the ground.

The opposing players shrieked as their base runners joyously pranced home to score and win, while his own teammates howled their scathing disappointment.

His best friend Jimmy Reese trotted over to him from center field and said, "Woody, you dork, that was an easy catch."

Woody quit the Fogelsville Little Big Leaguers right after that, barely the start of the 1993 season. They wouldn't miss him.

But he still loved the game. He loved baseball even though he wouldn't play.

"You could still play if you want," his dad had said as they walked home that evening. "There's a place for everyone. Every dog has his day, believe me."

He looked up at his dad, big to him but not bigger than a lot of other kids' dads. Everyone called him Badger because of how strong he was and how he never gave up. His dad's strength awed Woody, scaring him a little when he got mad. But his dad never did anything to him, and whenever the Badger grabbed Woody's mom from behind in his tan, hairy arms ripply with muscles, wrapping her up so gently like a tall silver flower, Woody relaxed. His dad did it pretty often and his mom seemed to enjoy it. Secretly, though, Woody wondered how she ever had come to like Dad since he looked more friendly than he did handsome, while his mom was just completely beautiful.

His dad had told him a lot about playing baseball when he'd been a kid. He went on about what guys like Carl Yastremski had meant to him, and how he'd tried to copy Yaz's game. When the Badger realized that he was more of an infielder than a hitter, he'd switched to Rico Petrocelli. He told Woody that he hadn't been that good, really, but that he'd kept trying, working, concentrating, learning. Most of the time he didn't play much. But now and then he'd get in because someone was hurt, or there was a family thing, something. Then, he would try his damnedest, even on the school's raggedy-ass, sub-500 team. Because, the Badger said, nothing mattered more than doing your best, and the game.

"So, wouldn't you know," his dad would tell him, "I'm put in against our archrivals, Notre Dame High, a team just as lousy as we were, but we wanted to beat them bad anyway. Timmy Ott, the starting second baseman, was out with the flu and his backup Joey Francke had been pulled for a pinch hitter, which didn't work. So, there I was, leading off in the bottom of the ninth, nothing-nothing tie. I could hear the Italian guys on our team yelling to me as I stood at the plate, 'Come on, Badger, knock the be Jesus out of the ball,' just to jerk the Notre Dame kids around, you know. Most of them were Irish kids, which made me even more nervous. I mean, win the game, maybe, but the fight afterward? Anyway, I swallowed, then swung hard, keeping it level, at the first pitch and whacked it right over the second base bag. I ran as fast as my short legs could go, straight to first, safe. I didn't try to steal or anything like that, I just took a short lead to get a good break on any potential double-play ball.

"Well, then Petri slaps a ball on the ground between first and second—I had to hop over it to avoid being hit. I run like hell, ready to take out the second baseman, but the play goes to first, one out.

"Jack Roth hits a long ball, so now I have to tag up before I can run and I don't run fast, remember, though my heart beat like a rabbit, believe me. I dove face first into third just under the throw. The other guys are screaming, 'Badger, Badger!'

"Two outs, Ruben's up. He hits a deep bounder to third base, a routine play in any other situation, but this was the bottom of the ninth, two outs. I run on contact, pumping as fast as I could, knowing that a throw to first would be too late; the only play was at home. I leap into the air and slide in with both feet on the plate as the ball whizzes above me, right past my head.

"The other guys mob me, lift me up, shouting at me, and I start to cry. They let me down and Ruben comes up to me, laughing a little in a friendly way, and he says, 'Badger, my man, why are you crying?'

"So, why were you?" Woody asked. "You just won the big game."

"That's what Ruben was thinking, but he never knew what it was like, he was regularly hitting the hell out of the ball, scoring runs. Even if he could figure it out, he still probably never felt like that himself no matter how many game-winners he hit. You see, I had that moment," his dad would say, "I never had another like it, but I had that one."

The Badger told the story whenever he thought Woody needed a lift, until he saw him drop the ball at the last game. Afterward, he came over and grabbed Woody to him with his arm around his shoulder, saying, "Everybody has things like this happen, Woody. Billy Buckner was blamed for losing the World Series when he muffed a grounder. Went right between his legs. He had to leave town. But it wasn't Billy Buck's fault, it was that dumb-ass manager McNamara for putting Schiraldi in to close. Guy was petrified, threw nothing but fast balls right down the pike. Rally city for the Mets and McNamara wouldn't let Roger the Rocket pitch relief in the seventh game. Wouldn't let him pitch in the big game," he said, shaking his head. "Went with Schiraldi again in the seventh game, and that was it. I sure hated the Mets winning. But Buckner had a couple more seasons with different teams, and he came back to Boston to a standing ovation a few years later. The Sox had a nice run, too, that year, though they pooped out at the end, of course, just like always."

But Woody felt too bad to listen. He moped around the house forever afterward, wounded to the soul. After a few days of this, his mom came up to him and tried to catch hold of his dark green eyes with her own matching set, but he wouldn't have any of that. Instead, he pretended to study the third button down on his polo shirt.

She grabbed his chin. "Woody, Woodrow, let's see it, the Woodman, the Wood-meister, the Wooden one," she said jokingly, mimicking some old show she seemed to like watching on the Comedy Channel. He pulled away.

She brushed the curved blade of hair away from her cheek as she always did. Her hair was blond, burnished bright where the sun had touched it, that and from the highlighting caused by a few gray hairs. Woody had her eyes, but his skin was nutty colored like the Badger's, not like hers, crystal clear showing the bluest of veins.

"Woody, look at me," she said in a soft, solemn tone.

"No," Woody said.

"Honey," she said, "don't let this get to you so. You'll do better next time. If you ask your dad, I'm sure he'd love to help you practice."

"I don't want to," he said, fiddling with the edge of his shirt. "It doesn't matter anyway, I'm not playing anymore."

"But you love it," she said.

"Not anymore," he said. "Just leave me alone, will you? You're always butting in."

She straightened up, and he hated himself more for the way she looked at him.

"Okay, tough guy. Wash your hands for dinner."

When his dad came home, he watched her bend to whisper in his ear. His dad stood there, facing Woody as he listened, his gray work shirt radiating a dried aura of perspiration from his neck to his chest. As she went on, his dad's face drew down, more and more somber, and Woody began to feel nervous about how mean he'd been to his mom, the only thing that really set the Badger off.

His dad shook his head after she finished. He pushed his half-rolled sleeves up over his biceps as he walked by Woody to the hall bathroom, saying as he passed, "You ought to be nicer to your mother."

Woody could hear the water running, changing timbre as his father ran his forearms beneath the flow. For no reason, he felt close to tears, until he felt the pressure of his mom's arms around him.

"Don't feel bad, Woody, you're a great guy. You're just going through a bad patch."

After dinner, he sat in front of the TV half-watching *Top Cat* on Nickelodeon. Suddenly, his dad appeared and nudged Woody's legs off the Ottoman to sit facing him, holding a shoe box. Before Woody could complain, he said, "Playing ball isn't the only way to enjoy it, Woody. There are all sorts of different ways to have fun—fantasy baseball, watching on TV, or just going out to the park to see a game once in a while. Minor league ball is becoming real popular again, too. I told you, I was no great shakes at playing myself."

"Oh yeah? What about beating Notre Dame?"

His dad wrinkled his nose, "That was the only highlight, believe me. I didn't tell you about the millions of times I fanned, or flubbed grounders. One time I ran to second on a fly ball without tagging up first, ran right into a double play. I didn't know the rule. Man, did I ever hear it from the guys that time."

"Yeah, well, I'm not going to hear it from them ever again. I refuse," Woody said in a pouting tone.

"Yeah, sure, okay, that's fine. But it's still a great game. I always loved it no matter what, even when I rode the bench for most of four years."

"You sat on the bench for four years?" Woody asked, and when his dad nodded yes, he said almost contemptuously, "Why? If you were no good, why didn't you quit?"

The Badger's features tightened, "Because I made the team." He took a breath, "I got some bubblegum cards when I was a kid, a couple of them my favorite players, too. It's another way to have fun. Here, you can have them, if you want." He handed Woody the box and stood up to head for the kitchen. "Who knows? Some of them might even be worth a couple of bucks."

In his bedroom, Woody fingered through them, not recognizing any of the players—Tony Canigliaro, Horace Clarke, Tony Kubek, Brooks Robinson, Dick McAuliffe, Ritchie Allen. Some were old football cards, Norm Snead, Washington Redskins. Dick Kazmaier, Heisman Trophy Winner. He tossed them back into the box, then tossed the box onto the windowsill above his desk, where it lay for the better part of the summer.

He stood behind the closed screen door not saying a word, still an imposing figure after all of the years, though hard to make out through the rusted metal mesh.

The young man on the porch shaded his eyes, trying to peer past the screen, but there seemed to be no light on inside.

"Mr. Paul? Is that you, sir?" No answer. He'd heard that the guy was utterly intractable, which was why he had assumed the severely deferential tone. "I'm Stephens Brinert from *S.I.*"

The dark shape made no sound.

"You know, *Sports Illustrated*?" Brinert said, as though not sure himself.

"I know what *S.I.* stands for," a craggy voice said with no effort to hide disdain.

"Yes, well, I was sent to ask if you would submit to an interview for an article about the past great days of the game. You know, memories running from Ruth to DiMaggio?"

"No."

The door behind the screen swung slowly shut.

"Son of a bitch," breathed Brinert to the closed door.

After Woody quit, his dad never pushed him about playing. But he did insist that they regularly go to Sox games, usually on Sunday afternoons, seats in the bleachers.

"Whether you play or not, or follow the game, it's still a great afternoon out," the Badger said during the first game.

Woody wouldn't answer, slouching instead like the forced grump he felt himself to be with his parents penning him in on either side.

"Come on, lighten up," his mom said, roughly mussing his hair.

"Mom!" he protested.

"Yeah, loosen up," his dad said. "Man, it's hot!"

The Badger pulled his t-shirt over his head to sit bare-chested in the sun. His hairy breast glistened with perspiration. He used the t-shirt to wipe his brow, then fashioned it into a Bedouin's headdress, with the hair from the crown of his head sticking out of the collar.

"Hey, that looks comfortable," his mom said, and she crossed her arms to lift up her shirt.

"Mom!" cried Woody, grabbing her arms.

"But I'm hot too," his mom lamented.

"It's not decent!" Woody said.

"Sure, it's okay for your dad," she pouted.

"No it isn't either," said Woody. "He looks goofy."

The Badger grinned silently.

In spite of himself, Woody began to get caught up in the game. The green of the grass warmed him differently from the sun, though its rays felt good as long as he could sip on his cold coke, then suck on the ice. By rote, he ate peanuts offered by his dad, the first one exploding a range of flavors in his mouth, the rest just salty and feeling good to crunch. His dad complained about the price of food, "Here, have a solid gold hotdog," and his mom fidgeted as the lead swung back and forth, "C'mon, get a hit, get a hit!"

The big right-fielder stepped to the plate, swung on the first pitch and sent the ball careering low twisting toward the stands, toward them.

"Hey-hey," the Badger said, rising from his seat with the trajectory of the ball. Without thinking, Woody rose too, excitement thrilling through him as he lifted halfway out of his seat. The ball continued to loop into the stands, curling downward four rows below and to the right. It thudded off the concrete base, shot high in the air, and bounded back and forth between some empty metal seats. A cluster of fans dove toward the ball, heads banging together trying to grab it. One of them popped up, teeth gleaming, and thrust the ball high in his fist.

The crowd roared as the hitter padded around the bases.

"Man, that was close!" shouted Woody, "We almost got that one!"

"Yeah, it was close," said the Badger, "a great shot."

"A terrific shot!" his mom said, clapping her hands once, then holding them together. "Why, he just stroked the Hel-sinki out of that ball!"

After the third or fourth game, Woody had to admit to himself that he was having a wonderful time. The Bosox were making a run at first place, and that was exciting. But he also found other things just as interesting. Alphons Johnson was the name of the right-fielder, a switch-hitter who batted .290 lefty and .260 righty. Woody had found it on a card from some bubblegum that he'd bought to take to a game. He took the card home and put it in the box with the others. By summer's end, he had added fifty more cards to the box, eight of them Red Sox.

Brinert stood with one foot still on the porch and the other on the second step. Puzzled, perplexed, and a little fearful, he called out, "Mr. Paul? Can we talk a little bit about this? I didn't mean to offend you, if I did," and under his breath, "you old fart." He raised his voice even more, "Mr. Paul, you are a national treasure, you know? Your fans would like to know how you are, they want to know what it was like to play head to head with the great ones, you know? I mean, to be a great one?"

Nothing moved but a short breath of hot Missouri air that whispered by his ear, then died immediately. "Shit," Brinert said, this time fully audible. He turned to go, then looked around at the farmhouse, its peeling paint, and the curling shingles of the roof. As they disintegrated, they formed a pile of grainy, diamond and black glistening particles radiating two feet out around the basement wall.

Brinert paused, then said, "Mr. Paul, you should know, too, that I wouldn't think of taking up any of your valuable time without offering you some proper compensation for it. In a remunerative sense, that is."

The screen door snapped open and the tall dark shape from before emerged as a tall thin man with piano wire muscles and a face full of hollows.

"How much?"

When school started again, Woody brought some of his favorite cards in to show to his friends. Jimmy Reese said, "Nice cards, but the Sox are going nowhere this year. That one of Martinez is worth something, though. He's a sure bet for the Hall."

"Yeah, well, I keep my best at home," Woody said.

"Oh really? I'd like to see them," said Jimmy. "Can I come over after school?"

Woody hid a quick frown. "I don't know, my mom doesn't like me to have kids over when no one else is at home."

"Oh, come on, man, what's the problem? I just want to look at your really good cards. Or maybe they aren't that cool?"

Woody's face tightened. For being his best friend, Jimmy could really get to him sometimes. It didn't help that he was all that Woody wanted to be, tall, fast, and good at every sport. Whenever they got together, they had a great time. But he never knew when Jimmy would tease him about something. If Woody let on that it bothered him at all, Jimmy wouldn't let up until Woody wanted to kill him. Which of course, he couldn't do since Jimmy was so much stronger. Jimmy didn't seem to care, either. After Woody dropped the ball, he hadn't seen much of Jimmy for the rest of the summer. True, after dropping the ball, he hadn't wanted to see anyone himself. But even before then, Jimmy always seemed to show up when he didn't appear to have anything else better to do.

Woody sighed, though, and said, "Yeah, all right, come on over."

When Woody opened the front door, he was surprised to see Jimmy standing on the stoop holding three thick binders in his arms.

"I thought I'd show you some real cards, man."

Woody had to admit that Jimmy's collection was impressive. He liked the way he had them arranged in the binders, each card in its own clear plastic slot. All-Stars came first, then regular players next to others on their teams, and finally a few team shots in the back.

"It's hard to figure out what to do when they trade a guy," Jimmy said, "I mean, should I move him to the other team, even though the card I have has him in his old uniform? When it happens, I try to get a new card fast with him in his new colors. But they don't do a new card in mid-season and nowadays there are so many trades."

"Yeah," said Jimmy, looking at the array of All-Stars; Barry Bonds, Randy Johnson, Pedro, too, and almost all the other guys.

"I didn't know you were into cards," Woody said.

"Oh, yeah, for years. But, you know, it's something I did by myself. Some guys think it's kid's stuff."

"Unhuh."

"After you've done it for a while, though, you get a lot of cards you don't need, like dups. I have dups of all the All-Stars for example."

"No kidding!"

"Yeah. I don't really want them, but they're worth something, so I just keep them in a box like yours."

"Wow. You have another of each of these?"

"Oh, yeah. I have old-timers, too, like I have Yaz, and Jim Rice, and a bunch of others. I even have one of Ted Williams, though it's not in the best of shape."

"Wow!"

"Yeah, it's missing a corner. I have one of Rod Carew that's pretty nice."

"Rod Carew?"

"Yup."

"Wow," Woody said softly, not really sure who Rod Carew was.

"Okay, man, let's see yours."

He sat on the bed while Jimmy worked his way through the box.

"You call these great cards? Yeah, this Billy Ripken is worth a ton, just like Cal's," he said, laughing. "But what I really like are these football cards." He flipped one over and read, "'Frank Budd, World's Fastest Human.' Wow! What a star! Look at that uniform, will you? You think Randall Cunningham would wear something like that? How about this one, 'Tommy McDonald, receiver half of the famous combination Jurgenson to McDonald.' Who the heck are they?" he laughed, "And look at his helmet. No wonder his nose is crooked. He looks more like a hockey player," he roared.

Woody lunged for the box, "You don't have to look at them if you don't like them."

Jimmy pulled the box back, cradling it to his shoulder, "No, no, they're great. A treasure chest," he giggled, starting to look again. "Sure," he said, "some of these baseball cards are worth a couple of bucks." He lifted one out, "Roger Maris. That's worth something."

He looked at it more closely. "Yeah," then put it back and picked out another. "Carl Yastremski. This is a good one, too. No, really, Woody, you have a couple of nice old ones here. I like the new guys better, but these are okay."

"Yeah?" Woody said suspiciously.

"Sure. Come on, man, let's have some real fun. Let's trade!"

They had a blast after that, pouring over each other's cards. Jimmy kidded him endlessly, offering to trade Mario Lemieux for Tommy McDonald, "Come on, Woody, I know he must've played hockey. Look at that nose!"

They could barely sit up from laughing, and his mom smiled at them when she came in from work. "Dinner will be ready soon, guys. Do you want to stay, Jimmy?"

Jimmy pouted, "You know I would, Mrs. McCormick, but I need to give my mom more notice."

His mom smiled in a funny way and said, "Sure, Jimmy, I understand."

After she left, Jimmy said, "I really got to go or I'm toast. My mom doesn't even know I'm here."

"Oh, man, Jimmy!" Woody said, awed.

"Yeah, well, it's no big thing. But I better go. I'll see you tomorrow in school."

He gathered up his binders and the cards from his trade and headed for the door and home.

"You remember that book by that guy, that pitcher, a knuckleballer . . . ."

"Phil Niekro?" Brinet said, "He wrote a book?"

"God, no, not him. Or maybe he did, but not that book. No, the guy who tried a comeback in his forties, some slick wise-ass that nobody liked after he wrote his book, Bunting, Browning, ..."

Brinert shook his head, the old crank definitely wasn't connecting all his circuitry. "Jim Bunning?" he said.

Paul looked at him with loathing that made him cringe inside.

"Well, who then?" Brinert said, almost ready to cash in on this hopeless interview. The guy was too ancient to give him anything he could use.

"Why did they send you?" said Paul. "No, not Bunning, Jim Bouton."

Jim Bouton, thought Brinert, *Ball Four.* Son of a bitch.

"Remember? He trashed Mickey Mantle, the whole Yankee pantheon? Everyone hated him for it, remember? Except for the publishing gang, they loved it, made him slick back his hair, put him on TV. You remember?"

"Well," said Brinert, "no."

Ray Paul leveled him again with a withering expression of disdain. "How old are you, son?" he said, not attempting to temper his acrid tone.

Automatically, Brinert said, "Thirty-four."

"Well, let me tell you something, youngblood. If you want to do something, you got to do your homework. Even if Bouton's book came out when you were still crapping in your tidies, you should've read it. Not that it's a great book, mind you, this isn't Willy Shakespeare we're talking about, here, or even Willy the Spook. But it don't matter. You need to do your spade work so you know what the hell you're talking about."

Brinert wanted to poke his own eyes out. This has got to be the absolute worst, the award-winning Interview from Hell.

"Your point being, Mr. Paul?" Paul gazed at him pitilessly and he quickly said, "I mean about the book."

The old man waited a beat. "What Bouton said about the Mighty Mantle and the rest of them?" he said. "It was true."

Brinert screwed up his face in utter confusion and Paul went on. "You'll understand after you read the book, Shorty. They were all assholes, all of them. Almost everyone I knew, anyway, including me."

Woody couldn't stop talking about the fun he'd had that afternoon with Jimmy and his cool cards. He gushed on, repeating the joke about Tommy McDonald's crooked nose and his helmet as if he'd made it up, then showed off the new cards he'd gotten from Jimmy. Studying the Red Sox team card again and again, he missed his mother whispering into the Badger's ear, who grimaced, frowned, then nodded okay.

In the evening, just before dinner, Woody's mom sat him down at the table. She went into the living room and returned with a book marked in the middle by a receipt. She spread it open at the marked page in front of Woody. Grouped around a few photographs of ball players were lists of names, years, and dollar amounts in very tiny lettering.

"What's this, Mom?"

"It's a book about sports cards, Honey. It tells you how much the cards are worth to people who collect them."

"Yeah?"

She pointed her finger at a card in the lower right corner of the page. Roger Maris gazed back at him with a small, stiff smile forced over the haft of a bat held just off his shoulder. Yankee pinstripes ran down his shirt, though, weirdly, he wore a red Cardinals cap on his head. A short sentence ran below the photo, "Topps 1966 Roger Maris rarity worth $300.00 in mint condition."

Woody swallowed as he read the number, $300.00, then looked again at the familiar picture in the book.

"He was traded to the Cardinals at the beginning of the season," his mom said softly, "so the photographer had to hurry. He took the shot with the cap on Maris without him changing his uniform. Later, they did another one after he put on a St. Louis uniform, which is why this one is so rare."

Woody stared at the book, refusing to lift his eyes to his mom's.

"Woody," she said.

He turned the page.

"Woody, look at me."

"Why? This is a neat book."

She cupped his chin and gently forced his head up. "Jimmy took advantage of you."

Woody shook his head free and returned to the book. "No, he didn't." He continued to gaze at the book, flipping the pages too fast to see them. "We made a trade."

"Woody, he did. He knew how much that card was worth. He probably has this book. When he traded for the card, he wasn't being fair to you, he wasn't honest."

"He was too! So, I made a dumb trade. A trade's a trade. Anyway, I'm happy, I got the Red Sox team card."

"Woody," she said, patting his hand.

"Leave me alone, will you?" he said, starting to cry. "Why don't you just leave me alone!"

He ran out of the kitchen into his room. He slammed the door and flopped face down on the bed, sobbing. When his mom came to the door, he wouldn't let her come in.

The loud voices in the kitchen woke him up.

"Well, he's right when he said he made a dumb trade, but it is a trade," he heard the Badger call out.

He could hear his mom's voice, but too low to make out what she was saying.

"Look, Jen," the Badger moaned, "why do I have to get into this? Boys have to learn this stuff on their own. They have to be able to deal with it for the rest of their lives."

Again, the even murmur of his mother's voice barely left the kitchen.

"All right, all right," the Badger said, his voice growing louder as he approached Woody's door, "but let me tell you, you're lucky I love you. Both of you."

The door swung open with the Badger's hand resting high on it.

"Come on, Woody, gather up those cards you got from Jimmy. Let's go see what we can do about it."

"But Dad!"

"I know, I know, but your mother insists. Who knows? Maybe she has a point."

Clutching the cards in both hands, Woody made his way out and headed toward the station wagon.

"No, come on, we'll go in the truck," his dad said. "I'm too dirty to get in the car."

On the short trip to Jimmy's house, Woody glanced at his father, who sighed as he drove, his arm resting across the top of the steering wheel. His blue work shirt was sweat streaked as usual, and slow to dry because of the midsummer heat and humidity.

"What do you say, we head off to a bar instead?" the Badger said.

Woody blinked, surprised. His dad almost never ever went to a bar. Then he said quickly, "Okay."

"Naw, no. Duty calls. I guess."

Mr. Reese answered the door and the Badger explained why they were there. Mr. Reese was tall with skinny legs and arms Woody knew from seeing him work in his yard. He was a little fat in the stomach, too. But wearing his suit pants and suspenders with his white shirt and his tie now, he looked more serious, like the assistant principal at school. Woody could see Jimmy staring out behind him, his mouth wide open.

Mr. Reese shook his head, "What can I tell you, the kids made a trade."

"Yeah, I know," the Badger said agreeably, "but they're kids and they're friends. If they could just undo this, it might be good, you know, a nice thing for each of them."

Mr. Reese seemed to weigh the possibility in his mind, then slowly shook his head again, "I don't think so. No, it's a better lesson for them to learn to be aware of the worth of things. And anyway, your son does have the team card, which is valuable." He turned to his son, "How much does it bring, Jimmy?"

"Fifteen."

"There," he said, returning his sight to the Badger. "Obviously, it's not in the league of the Maris card, but personal feelings count, too. I understand that your son is quite a Red Sox fan."

The Badger moved closer, which made Woody nervous.

"Look, I'm not saying that your kid cheated my kid," he said in a low voice, "and it's not the money. Friends don't do this to friends."

"Well, I can't help that. Friends do enter into agreements and in these instances, the usual rules of business apply." He chuckled a little as he said, "You know, 'caveat emptor.'"

The Badger raised his hands, "These are kids!"

Mr. Reese half-stepped back. "Yes, but they're growing up and they need to be able to handle themselves in an adult world."

The Badger stood still, speechless, and Mr. Reese took his glasses off and began to wipe them clean with a handkerchief pulled from his pants pocket.

"So, you won't let them trade back the cards?"

"I'm afraid not."

The Badger hissed and said, "Man, that is total—"

"Listen," Mr. Reese said, pointing one arm of his glasses at them, "I think this conversation is at an end. Now, if you're still unhappy with the outcome, we can meet in court. But I'm not going to stand here for anymore of this kind of abuse. And if you show up here again, I'll have a peace bond slapped on you in a second for harassment."

"Harassment?" Badger breathed. His eyes still fixed on Reese, he shook his head slowly. "Let's go, Woody."

As soon as they were in the truck, the Badger struck the steering wheel with his fist. "Man! What a—," he bit off the word. "Remind me to get your mom some flowers, will you? Damn!"

They drove silently home. Before Woody could get out of the car, his dad put his arm around his shoulder. "I'm sorry you had to see that, Woody. I'm sorry I lost my temper. Listen, when we go in, you go straight to the bathroom to wash up for dinner. I'll tell your mom what happened, okay?"

"Sure, Dad."

"Okay, Buddy. I love you," he said, giving him a squeeze before he could leave.

Brinert scratched his head, wondering where to go now, and wishing that he hadn't paid the guy first. But Paul had insisted. Tentatively, he tried again.

"So, Mr. Paul, you were that rarity back in those days who completed school, went to college and graduated, right?"

"Yeah," Paul said, "so what? You went to college, right?"

Brinert nodded.

"I rest my case."

Brinert shrank a little more into his chair.

"Listen, are you through yet? Do you have any more questions?"

Brinert tried to gather himself to focus. But he couldn't think of anything, though he was sure that there was more he wanted to know, more questions to ask. Hell, he still needed to ask all of them. But he found that he couldn't.

"No," he said, "I guess not."

"Well okay. My soap starts in five minutes. See you."

"Yeah," Brinert said, turning back on the way out, "I would like to see you again," but the screen door closed in his face.

October, and it was a nice birthday. Woody beamed as the Badger and his mom sang to him over the soft, warm glow of the candles, more light this year than last and more to come, he thought. The presents were cool, too, not too many clothes and not too many misses. But the special one, the one he really liked, was the card. It was like no other in his collection, like none he'd ever seen before. The photo was old, weird-colored, of a young player wearing an old-fashioned uniform. His face was pale with funny rosy cheeks and a lick of brown hair peeking out from under an odd cap. He had dark gray eyes and instead of holding a bat, he just stared straight out as if he could see Woody looking at him. Next to the picture was the player's name, followed by a bunch of stats, "Bats/Throws" under different columns marked left and right. Woody read the name.

Raymond G. Paul, Fielder

He continued reading, Boston Red Sox, Batting Average .277. The back of the card told him to collect all 32 and return them for prizes. A spattering of diamond-shaped holes zigzagged across the bottom.

He fingered them as he turned the card over and back, mesmerized, while the Badger went on about it, saying something about where it came from.

"They're not a lot of these around. The guy at the shop said it's one of a set printed in 1933 by the George C. Miller Company out of Boston. Because they didn't print so many in the first place, they're worth a couple of bucks. This one's in pretty good condition, although it's not worth as much because of the holes. The guy said the holes mean that someone turned it in for a prize. They'd get a prize and the card back, too, but with the holes punched in so that no one could try to cash in twice."

What kind of prize did they get in 1933, Woody wondered. What did they have to give away way back then?

"I remember Ray Paul," said the Badger. Seeing Woody's incredulous look, he went on, "Oh, I don't mean I saw him play. I'm not that old, Pal. But he did some coaching in the Bigs when I was a kid, for the Yankees of all teams, can you imagine it? A former Red Sox? This photo must've been taken close to his rookie year. I think he's still alive, matter of fact."

Woody's head shot up from the card. "Alive? He must be a hundred!"

"Well, more like eighty-something."

"Good math work, Woody," his mom said, sitting at the table thumbing through his baseball card book, another present.

"Hey, Mom, it's my birthday, okay?"

Without looking up, she murmured, "Right, how old are you? Sure you can count that high? Remember, you have to leave your shoes on."

Woody pouted, "Very funny." But he couldn't work up much anger, he felt so good.

"So," the Badger said coyly, "how do you like it?"

Woody felt like grabbing him in a bear hug. Instead, he smiled and said, "A lot, Dad, really a lot."

The Badger grinned, then engulfed him in his arms, "That's good,

Kiddo, I'm glad."

He was showing it around to the other guys, explaining why it looked so strange and what it was worth. The book said $100.00. One hundred bucks! His dad had spent a hundred bucks on just one card for him, not to mention all the other cool stuff he'd gotten.

As he crowed, out of the corner of his eye he noticed Jimmy leaning against the corner of the cafeteria door. Quickly, Woody turned back to the others. But he felt strange, not quite as elated after noticing Jimmy. Irritated, he tried to reclaim his mood.

"My dad told me that Ray Paul is still alive, too, you know? I mean, he's really ancient, but he's still walking I guess, unless he's in an old folks home or something. So, I'm thinking of getting his autograph on the card, you know? It'd really be worth something then."

"Oh, yeah, I'm sure," Jimmy said, strolling over. "How the heck do you think you'll do that?"

"I don't know, uh, maybe I'll go see him," Woody said, stuttering, which really made him angry.

"Right. Do you even know where he is?"

"Yeah, Missouri. There was an article that talked about him in *Sports Illustrated.* He lives in Kansas City, Missouri."

"Oh, so what are you going to do, hitchhike? Or ride your bike? Hey, maybe your dad will take off from work to drive you," Jimmy said.

"Yeah, maybe he will! Or maybe I'll mail it. Did you ever think of that Mr. Einstein? I'll even send return postage so he can send it back the same day."

The other boys craned to see how Jimmy would answer. Jimmy blinked, then turned to go, saying in concert with the bell, "Yeah, or he might just use it to mail a check for his phone bill."

Jimmy swaggered off, and Woody said under his breath, "We'll see, smartass."

He wasn't sure he could do it. The article in *S.I.* had been brief, but the writer had called Paul "irascible," which scared Woody after he looked it up in the dictionary. But he found himself gripped by Ray Paul, by the old picture of him as a young guy only ten years or so older than he was now, and already two years in the Majors. He'd collected other cards showing Paul later in his career, piecing together what he'd done first with the Red Sox, then with the Boston Braves. Finally, Woody took himself to the library to discover who Ray G. Paul really was.

"Ray Paul, utility fielder, 1931 – 40, Boston Red Sox; 1941, Boston Braves; 1946 – 1952 NY Yankees; retired 1953; fielding coach, NY Yankees, 1953 – 56; lifetime batting average .283."

He'd finished with the Yankees! The Badger hadn't mentioned that, which explained why Paul had been a coach for New York. A good hitter, a really good fielder, but not in the Hall of Fame. Not enough at-bats, maybe, Woody thought.

Ray Paul, Born 1910, St. Louis, Missouri. He'd love to know more about him. Maybe if he sent him the card, he would write back. Maybe they would become pen pals. That would be so great, thought Woody.

But if he sent the card and didn't get it back, and his mom found out, he would be toast. Worse, it would kill the Badger. But, Woody thought, gazing fervently at the blankness of his bedroom ceiling, it would be so great.

He read the first line of the article and laughed, causing a morass of mucous to brim in his throat. Damn cigarettes, he thought. He slipped the butt between his lips and turned the page. All that crap for this crap, he thought. He went back to the beginning of the column and started laughing again.

"The ever-irascible old-timer Ray Paul read this reporter out up and down for daring to interrupt him in the middle of watching his favorite daytime soap opera."

Bending over to try and catch the lit butt fired out of his mouth by another fit of coughing, he cackled, saying to himself the stupid idiot really thinks I watch soap operas.

Woody was stunned to see Jimmy standing at the front door. He stood there after school, before Woody's mom had arrived home.

"Hey," Jimmy said.

"Hey," Woody replied singsongingly, wary but cool.

They stared at each other for a time, wordless. For once, Woody felt completely relaxed around Jimmy, as though his ex-friend could do nothing more to him.

"So, what's up?" Jimmy said.

"Nothing," Woody said, again in a neutral voice that didn't give anything away. An expression of anguish flashed across Jimmy's face.

"Listen, I think this is dumb, you and me being mad at each other. I mean, I wish I'd never seen the stupid Roger Maris card, you know? We're friends, aren't we? I mean, we were before."

Woody felt as though his brain had flipped over in his head. He hesitated, "Well, yeah, we were, sort of, I guess."

"Yeah," Jimmy said, abashed, "I wasn't the best of friends."

"No, you weren't."

Jimmy stuck his hands in the pockets of his jeans. "Well, anyway, if I could give you back the Maris card, I would. But, you know, my dad . . .."

"Yup."

Jimmy waited, then said, "Well, anyway."

But he didn't leave. Instead, he rocked, back and forth.

"That is a cool new card you got, really."

"Thanks," said Woody.

"Yeah," Jimmy said, then "Do you think I could see it? I mean, no trades or anything like that. I just want to see it."

Woody's mind raced in debate. He stood unmoving in the door trying to decide. Then he saw the sad, disappointed look on Jimmy's face, who seemed to shift toward the sidewalk.

"I sent it to him," Woody blurted.

"Huh?"

"I sent it to Kansas City," he said, "to Ray Paul."

"What?" Jimmy cried almost as though he'd been wounded himself. "I don't believe you, how could you be so dumb? A card like that?"

"I'm not dumb."

"No, I know, but, Woody, man, what were you thinking?"

"I sent it with a letter asking him to please sign it."

"Woody, these guys sign cards and things for money! He's not going to sign it, he'll probably sell it."

"No way!"

"I'm telling you, Woody."

"No, he's not like that. I read about him, Jimmy, he was a great all-around ballplayer. He had near Hall of Fame numbers. If he hadn't had the bad luck to play for the Sox when they sucked, and then with the Yankees when they had DiMaggio and those guys, he would have made it."

"He's a cranky pain in the ass, Woody. You read that *Sports Illustrated* article, didn't you? The reporter paid him for the information!"

"Oh, that's just a story. Believe me, Jimmy, he'll do it."

"Woody," Jimmy said, then trailed off, shaking his head. After a moment, he said, "Okay. He signs it and sends it back. What'll you do with it then, sell it?"

Woody shook his head, "No. Of course not. I'm going to keep it forever."

Jimmy laughed, "You're nuts, Woody."

"Yeah," Woody laughed.

They stood smiling at each other silently.

Jimmy said, "So, does the Badger know you sent it?"

Woody paled, "Gosh, no. And neither does Mom. Man, if they find out, I'm over."

"Uh-oh."

"Yeah. Listen, you got to go before Mom comes home. I'll see you at school, okay?"

"Sure, man. Bring your cards. We'll trade."

"Yeah, dream on, Reese."

Jimmy flashed an evil grin over his shoulder as he ran for home.

He opened the letter wondering if it was money. Hoping it was money, he realized, low as he was on butts and booze. But no check fell out of the envelope, even though he shook it high above his head, blew into it, and stared inside. No telltale pale green, scallop-edged wafer offering a promise of soon-to-be good times. Hell.

He leveled his eyes on the white sheet on the floor and the bit of cardboard next to it. He picked up the paper and unfolded it.

> Dear Mr. Paul,
>
> You don't know me, but I'm an eleven-year-old boy named Woodrow Woodson, called Woody. I'm a big fan of yours even though I'm way to young ever to see you play. But I have lots of bubblegum cards with your picture, and that includes the one I sent you when you were almost a rookie for the Red Sox in 1933. It's a George C. Miller card and it's pretty valuable, and I was wondering

What? He folded the letter and bent over to look for the card. After a short time, he spotted it, face down on the floor. He picked it up and stared at himself at twenty-three, two years out of Northwestern, two years with the Sox batting .277, not too shoddy for a punk kid who didn't know a dugout from an outhouse. He always could hit though, and field. He could do it, he could run and throw, he could play. And he had for all those years, tirelessly, timelessly, taking his chops, getting machine-like with his system, raising that average day by day. All those years with the Dead Sox, then the Braves, from bad to worse, he thought. Then the war, and finally the World

Champion Yankees, hooray, at a time when his eye was rusty, when he'd lost a step, his skills were stale, then gone. He'd feel sorry for himself if he thought he had the worst of it, but he put in twenty-two years playing and a few more coaching. And it was like sex, you never got tired of it. Hell, he'd gotten tired of sex.

He'd seen the good guys, too, Joe DiMaggio and Dom, and even Ruth. Boys, most of them, and he was one of them except for his big-deal college degree. There they'd be in the locker room, Rudy Davis leading the rest against him, Twenty Questions. Just to show that Paul the snot-nosed college kid really didn't know shit. And he didn't.

On the field, though, they had to give him his due. Most of them remembered the homer he got off Feller that won the game 1-0, throwing Cleveland into a tie with Detroit. Detroit won the pennant and for years afterward fans came up to him about it. Big career highlight, making a basement team the spoiler. He could hit, even now he could feel the stroke, stroke after stroke, until the swing felt as natural to him as tossing a newspaper on a lawn.

That hit off Feller, he recalled it, he could see it, feel it, but it wasn't the thrill of a lifetime for him, not the memory of the game that stuck with him. It wasn't seeing Ruth play, who was about done anyway. It wasn't trying to hit Lefty Grove when he owned the mound, hell, the whole damn ballpark. Or watching Judy Johnson deck Bill McGonagle in the locker room for calling him a Black bastard during an exhibition game. Not one other white guy moved, not even the other rednecks, that's how much they didn't love old Billy Mack. Or the time he himself popped Mickey Mantle for making a pass at his second wife. It cost him his coaching job, any chance at the Hall, and the second wife. All that was there in his mind, but it was all bullshit, too, twenty-five years of it. None of that mattered, none of it counted.

In left field, the grass was high, higher than you'd expect, but there'd been a lot of rain. The sky was still gray, no striations, just a solid wall on a cool August day. The game was close in the seventh, and Ted Williams came up. Williams cracked that high liner, and he was on his bicycle, running flat out backwards for the fence, fast as he could, looking over his shoulder, raising his glove above him facing backwards, and snagging the ball. Williams stomped, robbed of extra bases. He breathed, throwing the ball leisurely back to the infield.

Ninth inning, Williams came up and hit the same shot. Again, running full sprint, fading, seeing the ball in the same place, raising the glove over his head, having the ball in the web, almost in the pocket, then watching it pop out. The same hit, the same play, he thought, but the ball came out and the game was over. The Sox went to the Series, the Yankees finished third.

The grass stayed as green and as long in his mind, the sky as solid gray as that day. He caught it, then lost it. Why? Was there that much of a difference between the first hit and the second, the velocity, the vector, when he turned to run, maybe a mini-second later? Or had he lost heart? I can make one spectacular catch like that, but not two. Is that what he told himself running back for that ball? He would never know.

Nineteen forty-six, the beginning of his second career, this time with a winner, and midway through that first season, he knew it was over. Even though he hung on for another six years by his wits alone, when it's over, it's over.

He looked at the letter again, and the picture and threw them on the couch. Thanks for the memories, kid.

Nothing showed up in the mail. Woody checked the mailbox every day after school, but nothing. During the first few weeks he grew more and more depressed watching, hoping, then finding only the usual coupons and bills for his parents. The Badger had asked him about the card during the first few weeks and he'd sidestepped the question. It was in his locker at school so that he could show it off to the other guys. His mom had warned him to be very careful not to lose it or damage it. But the Badger called her off.

"It's his card, Jen, let him do what he wants."

"The card is worth more than the price of some bubblegum."

"Yeah, but it's his. So, leave him alone. He'll take good care of it, won't you Woodhead?" he said, rubbing Woody's scalp hard.

Woody grinned sickly.

After a while, his folks forgot about the card. But Woody couldn't. He was so sure that Ray would send it back, he was positive. The guy had played all those years on such lousy teams. Then, when he finally made it on to a good team, a great team, he sat on the bench. He must have loved the game to do that for so long. Even though the *Sports Illustrated* guy had written that Ray Paul was a pain, the near Hall-of-Famer had talked to him, even if it was for money.

The last thought sent Woody tail spinning into a darker mood. Jimmy was right, probably. Paul probably sold the card. And, I am stupid, he thought. The thought filled his mind, yet he still went out to the mailbox every day, to find nothing.

When spring came around, his dad dropped hints that little league would be starting in a couple of months. If Woody maybe was thinking about it, now would be the time to shag some flies. As soon as he saw Woody start to pull into himself, he'd quickly switch to plans for opening day.

Woody tried to act disinterested, but as he watched some of the spring training games from Florida on ESPN, he felt something growing in him. The green grass began to get to him, the blue skies, the sunshine, and the ball flying all over the field. The click of the bat. The Red Sox looked strong on paper again, and they were winning everything in spring training. Woody didn't want to admit it, but he was getting excited.

Jimmy egged him on to try playing again this year, but Woody wouldn't buy it. They still fought a lot, especially when Jimmy rode him about the terrific Ray Paul card that he didn't have anymore. Woody would become furious, swearing that the card would come. But the weeks passed by and the mailbox remained empty to him.

He wondered if writing to Mr. Paul again would make a difference. Maybe he didn't understand how Woody felt about him and his career. If he knew that Woody loved the game as much as he did, maybe he would send the card back. But he'd said those things already in his first letter.

He sighed. But he refused to give up. He would wait.

He was running out of stuff to sell. All of the bats were gone, and the uniforms, hell, they were the first to go. But he had a lot of crap up in the attic, he laughed to himself. After twenty-five years you collect a lot of crap.

He had the shoes, a couple of backup gloves, and one bat. Not the bat, that one he'd sold in the sixties for nearly a grand. He wondered what it would fetch now in the age of big bucks. Well, hell, who could've figured on this happening? Not only that, not too many people remembered him anymore, only the hard core. His things didn't bring in much anyway.

Where did this bat come from? Then, he remembered. The Kid had bought it for him from the Yankees as a memento. Dead now for three years, cancer at the age of sixty-one. Not a young man, but not old, either, like himself. Even so, he'd always called him "the Kid" to other people until the day he died. Damn cigarettes.

He searched his front pocket and pulled out the last one in the pack. He'd never been that close to the Kid since his mother had walked out. His last living kin, too. When they'd both been drinking one night, he'd asked him why he'd never had any of his own?

"What," the Kid laughed, "and risk being a father like you?"

He crumpled up the empty pack, tossed it in the air and whacked it with the bat. The crumpled pack crossed the loft and bounced hard off a wooden stud in the wall.

Nice heft, he thought. It could have been one of my old bats. The Kid thought so, anyway. Funny how his son cared more about that kind of stuff. Trying to make up for lost time, maybe. Too bad. It could be one of his old bats, he thought, swinging it again. Could be.

"Well," he said, sitting down gingerly and placing the bat across his lap, "it is now."

He yanked a grease pen out of his back pocket and proceeded to write his name with a flourish on the barrel. Then he grabbed the box where the gloves rested and pulled them out. He signed one and put it next to the bat. He pulled out the other and paused.

"Hmm," he thought, pulling it over his hand. A bit stiff, but familiar just the same. A bit roomy, actually, since his hand had grown so skinny. Should he?

"Ah, what the hell, we'll save this one for a different rainy day."

He threw it back in the box where he spied a white piece of paper. He plucked it out of the box and flipped open the top part.

That kid's letter about the card. Where had that gotten to? He searched around in the box but couldn't find it. Fingering the letter, he noticed some thickness in the middle and he remembered. He unfolded it and saw the card paper clipped to the bottom flap. Windfall, he thought.

He gently slipped it free from its spot covering the last paragraph.

> I love baseball, Mr. Paul, although I don't play much. I'm not very good at it. But my dad and mom take me to see the Red Sox, your old team, and I watch them whenever I can on TV. I know you were a Brave and a Yankee, too. I try to know as much as I can about you. You are my favorite old player. If you would sign your card, it would mean so much to me !

I'll bet it'd mean a lot to you, you mercenary little bastard. A couple hundred bucks would be my guess, more when I croak. But, who's it good for right now, kid? He rubbed the bristle on his face, then flipped the card back into the box. There are a lot more rainy days ahead.

He grabbed the autographed glove, pushed himself upright with the bat, and disappeared in slow stages down the attic stairway.

Woody lay on his front lawn next to his bike, debating whether or not to ride over to Jimmy's or just stay where he was. The grass, already long and deeply green, smelled good on this warm day, the first real whiff of summer, he imagined. He had just about reached a decision weighed by the worry that the Badger would come out and tell him to cut the grass when Jimmy rode up on his bike.

"Avoiding cutting the grass, Jimmy? Maybe we both should cut out for the park."

Jimmy didn't answer. He looked serious, almost mad, or sad. He climbed off his bike and let it drop on the ground. Amazing, thought Woody, that he would treat that cool mountain bike like so much junk.

Jimmy sat next to him cross-legged. He reached into his breast pocket and handed Woody a small package, "Here."

"What's this?" Woody said as he started to unwrap it.

"The Roger Maris card."

"What?" Woody finished opening the cellophane and, sure enough, Roger smiled uneasily at him again beneath that red cap, holding that heavy bat.

"What are you doing? Why're you giving me this? It's yours."

Jimmy shook his head emphatically from side to side, "You take it."

"Man, your dad will kill you!"

"I don't care, I tricked you out of it. You should have it."

"You're crazy, Jimmy. No way. Anyway, why are you doing this?"

Jimmy clenched his mouth shut, looking more fearful than Woody had seen him ever before.

"You didn't hear, then?" Jimmy said, his voice quivering slightly. "Ray Paul died, Woody. He died yesterday in his house."

Woody took one look at Jimmy, dropped the card, and ran howling into his house.

His mother intercepted him, holding him close while he sobbed out what had happened to him, Ray Paul was dead.

"Oh, Sweetheart, that's too bad, that's so sad," she said hugging him to her, pulling him back to kiss him, then hugging tight again. "It's so sad. But, you know, Woody, he was a very old man, you know? And when people grow old, then they die. He was a very lucky man to live for so long."

Woody swung his head, inconsolable.

"It's true, Woody," she went on. "It's something that will happen to all of us. But you still have him, in your heart, your mind. You can remember him with your cards, and you have the special one, best of all."

Woody hiccoughed, "No, no, no," between heaving sobs. Finally, he shouted it out, "I sent him the card, Mom. I wanted him to sign it, but he never sent it back."

His mother relaxed her arms slightly.

"You sent it to him?"

Woody suddenly felt scared instead of sad. He stuttered, "Yeah. I thought it would be great to have it autographed. Now he's dead and my card is lost."

"Oh, Woody," she sighed in timeworn fashion.

"I know, Mom, it was stupid. But I never thought he wouldn't send it back. He was so great."

"Yes," she said, renewing her hug, "He was. Well, it's gone. I guess that's a lesson learned. But I'm not sure how your father's going to take it."

"Mom, do we have to tell him?"

"Woody," she said, holding him at arm's length, "you know better than that."

"Yeah. I guess."

"My God, Jen!" shouted the Badger, "It cost me a hundred bucks! And he sent it in the mail, a hundred-dollar card mailed to Missouri in an envelope stuck with a thirty-seven-cent stamp? What the heck is wrong with that boy?"

Woody again couldn't hear his mother's defense, she talked so low. She was good, she usually won him over, but the Badger sounded angry, really mad! This might be the one time that she couldn't save him.

The kitchen grew quiet and Woody grew even more nervous.

The door burst open and the Badger strode through past him, saying, "You're a stupid kid sometimes, you know that? Come here."

He held Woody's shoulders in his hands, gave him a hard shake, then threw his arms around him. "I'm going to kill you, Woody," he said, kissing him on the cheek, "but not today, you lucky son of a bitch!"

"Hey!" his mom yelled from the kitchen, and the Badger quickly shouted, "Bastard, son of a bastard!"

Woody laughed out loud through his tears.

Almost a year ago since he dropped the ball. Soon, school would be out, Little League teams were holding their tryouts, and the Badger was still hinting. Jimmy was out front about it.

"C'mon, man," he said, tossing the ball.

"I don't know."

"Look, it's a new year. You can do it. You've grown bigger, your catching is a lot better, thanks to practice with me. "

"Oh, yeah, thanks a lot," Woody smirked.

"It was nothing," Jimmy said, not missing a beat. "You can make the team, you'll probably play more this year, more than you think. I almost promise it, that's how much better you are."

"I don't believe you, Jimmy. I still suck."

"No you do not." Jimmy trotted over to him, brandishing the ball in his face, "You are better. Remember who's talking to you, bud. I'm the one who said you stunk last year, remember? Well, now you don't stink so much."

"Thanks a lot."

"You know what I mean." He dropped the ball to his waist. "Look, it'll be fun. Even if you do play as bad as last year, we'll still have fun. I'll have more fun because you're on the team."

But Woody still said, "I don't know."

And Jimmy hit him on the arm with the ball, "Come on, man."

Woody smiled shyly, and said, "Okay. Maybe."

He couldn't sleep the night before, he was so nervous. And excited. Jimmy was going to ride over on his bike, then they would ride over to the park together. The Badger wanted to go too, but Woody insisted no, and his mom backed him up. The Badger looked more like a disappointed little brother than his dad, but that was too bad. Woody thought that he'd wouldn't have a chance with the Badger watching him. If he screwed up now, at least he could be ruined alone. He was out on the front lawn throwing the ball high in the air, then running around underneath trying to catch it. He missed a lot. Maybe it would be three innings and the bench again, he sighed.

"Woody!" his mom shouted, "Come on in for a minute, will you."

"Aw, Mom! I'm practicing and it's almost time to go!"

"Woody, just for a moment."

"Aw." He stalked into the house.

"A package for you. UPS gave it to Mrs. Powell to hold for us."

"A package?"

Puzzled, he went over to his mother holding a small cardboard box. He took it from her and looked at the label: St. Louis, Missouri.

"Here, here're scissors."

Woody cut the tape and opened the box flaps. He slowly pulled out wads of tissue paper to reveal something dark. He lifted it out of the box, a glove, old, cracked in some places, but otherwise in pretty good shape. He slipped it on his hand; it was too big, but it felt good.

"Wow," his mom said.

"Yeah. Who's it from? Is there a letter?"

He looked in the box and found an unsealed envelope with the flap tucked inside. He put the glove in his armpit, opened the envelope, and took out the letter. It was blank but clipped to the middle was a card. Woody gazed at it, and twenty-three-year-old, rosy cheeked Ray

Paul looked straight out at him, gray eyes and all.

"Mom, it's my card! My card! I've got my card back!"

He erupted, yelling and shrieking with his mother, jumping up and down together.

"I can't believe it! Wait 'til Dad hears about this! This is so cool!"

"It's wonderful, Woody! He sent it back! See if he signed it."

Woody examined the card, front and back, and front again.

"No," he said, "he didn't sign it. He sent it back, but he didn't sign it. Why?"

"I don't know."

"And, what about the glove?" Woody stooped down to pick it up from where he'd dropped it. "Why'd he send this?"

"I don't know, Woody. Are you sure he sent it?"

"Well, he must've, he had the card."

"Yes," his mom said gently, "but he died Woody. It could be that someone else found it with your letter and sent it back. Look, the package is from St. Louis, not Kansas City."

"No!" Woody shouted. "Ray Paul sent me my card back. Ray sent me my card and his glove. That's Ray Paul's glove, Mom, I know it. He knew I love baseball, even if I don't play very well. He loved the game, too. And he proved it by sending me my card back and his very own glove."

"But he didn't sign the card, Woody."

"I don't care. He sent me his glove. That means a lot more to me than the card. I have Ray Paul's baseball glove! He sent me his glove!"

His mom smiled. "Yeah," she said, "I guess he did."

Jimmy yelled from the front yard, and Woody said, "I gotta go, Mom, it's time. Here, put the card in a safe place, will you? I have to run."

"What about the glove? You're not going to take that with you, are you?"

"You bet! Ray Paul's glove? I'm in, man!"

He stood out there, in the field, with the sun an hour away from setting, waiting for his turn at a fly. The Badger stood hiding behind a corner of the bleacher, but Woody had picked him out right away. Jimmy stood to his right yelling, "Batter, batter, swing batter." The glove was too big on Woody's hand, he'd had to stuff a sock inside to make it tight, but it felt good, really good. "Swing, batter," and sure enough, the batter swung, the bat sounded the familiar click, and the ball flew high above into the setting sun, spiraling toward Woody. Woody lifted the glove above his brow to shade his eyes, forced to smile by the sunlight as the ball came spinning down.

The Road Long Traveled

Low lights barely glimmered beneath the shelves running the length of the dark bus, offering sojourners rapped knees and bumped elbows on the way back to the pissoir in the rear. But, most of the seats had emptied at this point, though their high backs hid occupants from sight even when the bus was full. Next stop, end.of the line. His stop, Dennis sighed.

The road long traveled isn't something one can grab hold of in any qualitative way, he thought. Quantitative, yes. He'd been at the mercy of public transportation for so long now, he was beginning to feel existential. Returning nonstop from "Down Under" had turned his world upside down and himself inside out. Missing the express hadn't much dispelled the illusion. After two months away from home, though, including continuous motion for the past five days, how could an added hour matter so much? But it did.

"You headed for Williamstown?"

Dennis bobbed up out of his reverie to hear the question, surprisingly addressed to him. Round, Hispanic features, cherubic and brown, peered at him out of an Afro-coif from the next row front.

"Yes, I am," he said, passing by the fact that Williamstown was the last stop.

"Me too. Gonna be working there."

"Unhuh."

"For my main man Enrique. He owns a place there, says I can live with him, make a few bucks while I go to school. He and me, we're close, man. He's my cousin."

"Oh. That's good, great. Make some money while you go to school, it's a good idea."

"Right, man, and I can make good, good bucks at Enrique's, good bucks." He nodded his head assertively to himself.

"Well, terrific."

"Yeah. I been there before, just to visit for a weekend, you know. But this time I'll probably be staying for a while."

"Unhuh." Boy, this kid is serious, he thought.

"Only thing is, I have to leave my chick back in the city."

"Oh. Yeah, that's too bad."

"Right, man, I feel bad about it. I'm going to miss her. But, you know, that's the way it is, they come and they go. You come and you go, you know? That's life."

"Unhuh," he said, oddly wondering as he peered into the youth's smooth brown face if in the new order of things, Marie had turned fair and blond. "So, what'll you be doing for your cousin? What kind of work?"

"I don't know, man, busing or dishes. He's got a club, you see. Ever heard of the Copykat Club?"

"I'm not sure."

"You from Williamstown?"

"Yes I am. Just getting back from a long trip."

"Oh yeah? Well, the CopyKat is on 8th and Liberty. You think I can walk there from the bus station?"

"I don't know. It's a pretty long walk."

"Yeah, maybe I'll call up Enrique. He'll come get me. Or maybe I'll walk."

"You could take a cab."

"Yeah. I could do that."

For some reason he realized that the last didn't ring true. This kid would never take a cab, he'd walk. Maybe he ought to give him a lift, he thought. Marie'd get a kick out of him, she loved Third World types. But that would just make it later.

"My name is George Morales," the kid said, reaching back a hand. They power handshook.

"Dennis McConaghy."

"Nice to meet you. Hey, this must be the station."

"Yup," he said, stretching on an instant's impulse to try to see out the bus's windshield.

"Well, I guess this is it, man. Listen, c'mon down to the 'Kat and ask for me. We'll take real good care of you, man. It's a great place, great to meet chicks, too."

"Okay, George," he said, shaking his hand again, conventionally this time. "Good luck in school."

"Thanks, man. Maybe I'll see you at the 'Kat."

Their farewell had taken them down the corridor and off the bus, Dennis absently viewing the tight white stitching around the rear pockets of the slim youth's designer jeans, fitted like denim-print wrapping paper. Once down on the sidewalk, they turned away from each other immediately. Dennis slung the straps of his bags over his shoulders and circled to the front of the bus, where all thought of introducing George to Marie flew away when he spotted her at the end of the terminal, standing under the last streetlight.

Her long, straight black hair possessed that fresh-washed quality, a displacing of the glisten of oil for the sake of an airy beauty. Its dry sheen seemed to float in freefall, a fine match for her wholesome, dark tanned skin and the neatness of her clothes, simple shirt and maroon pants. When he stepped eagerly over to her, their "Hi's" passed out into the night, old-familiar, followed by a dry kiss.

"How was your trip?"

How was his trip, 25,000 miles long? Complicated to answer a question like that; he said, "Fine, great! So, how're you?"

"I'm good," the sound of it trailing off in an unfinished timbre. They walked to the car, his arm comfortably around her waist. The passenger door on the old Hornet creaked its way to three different levels upon opening. As he slid in, he inventoried the rust cancer along the running board further compromising the car's yellowing cream paint job. She climbed in behind the wheel and he noticed again how the seat on the driver's side dipped low at the corner. She had to hike herself up and fasten her seatbelt tight to keep from slipping down.

"How's your hip?"

"Better," she said. "It still bothers me when I run."

She pulled out onto the quiet street up to the red light.

"Unhuh. Can you stretch it out at all?"

"That's when it hurts the most."

"Right. It must still bother you, then, when you drive, because of the seat."

"No, it doesn't much."

"Well, it's got to be uncomfortable anyway, with that spring broken. You could take it to the guy where I got mine redone. He's good and cheap, and I'm sure he does that kind of work."

"It doesn't bother me."

"Man, it'd drive me nuts. If I had to drive it, I'd get the seat fixed immediately. I could follow you over—"

"Look, you don't have to drive it. It's okay, okay? It doesn't bother me."

"All right, okay." Twenty-five thousand miles later, two months later, and this is it? He rolled his head to the side window and exhaled thickly through his nose. She glanced at him out of the corner of her eye.

She made the left turn at the second light and ran up to the next one at Seventh Street, which was red. Ahead on the left, he could see the backsides of the town's commercial institutions. Berman's concrete parking ramp looped heavily to the ground, looking like some structure of Social Realism. Next to it the flat face of the Power Company annex with its egg-white slabs barely adorned by dental teeth cut-outs oddly suggested a misplaced Moroccan desert fortress. Up on the right a turn-of-the-century cemetery and its companion, West Park, contrasted daintily with the newer Center City buildings. Beyond these, though out of sight now, they'd pass the spired towers of the old houses put up in the 20's and 30's, neo-Victorians he'd once dubbed them, or neo-neo-Gothics, take your pick. Old impressions of old landmarks, they usually registered unconsciously unless some perturbation changed the pattern. So far, though, everything looked pretty much the same.

The light turned green and he said, "So, what's new? What's happening at the ranch?"

"Nothing much. The same old crap. Harry's driving me crazy. He's so picky."

"Unhuh," he said, keeping to himself awareness of the need for closer attention to detail in their kind of work, one of her exasperations. Her boss Harry stipulated like a stickler.

"I might as well tell you now that Pete has been in a state of depression for the past month, over Jill."

"What?"

"Yup. He took her to the airport, to go to the Bahamas—"

"Right, he did that before I left."

"Yeah, well he picked her up, too. About then, so he said, he decided that he really did love her—"

"Oh, no."

"Yes, so he went over there the next weekend to tell her. When he got there, she was with another guy she'd met down in the islands."

"No! Uh-oh."

"Yeah, so Pete really freaked. Jill was surprised herself, to say the least, but she introduced Carlos to Pete and all. But Pete just fumed, he just stood there shaking. I mean, he left almost immediately."

"My God."

"Well, the next night he went over there and threw himself on his knees, saying how much he loved her and how he had made a mistake and wanted to marry her."

"This is amazing! I'm amazed!"

"She said that she couldn't handle this, that she'd worked all this time to get her feelings for him straightened out so that she could function, and that she didn't feel she could trust him. So, for the past month or so he's been a complete wreck. He hasn't been able to sleep, to do anything at work, oh, and he didn't quite finish your new bathroom."

"Great."

"He's been too beside himself to do anything. He had his mother in there last night to clean it up for you, that's how bad he's been. He's talked to me about it a lot, crying and everything."

"Pete?"

"Yup," she nodded, "he really looks terrible."

"Oh, for . . . I cannot believe this! This after he broke up with her for, what, the third time? He's always been so casual about it. You know, 'Hey, Babe, if you can't handle the way I am, then we better call it a day.'"

"Yeah, well, he's been over there a number of times asking her why she doesn't love him, that he has so much to give her, and he can't understand why she doesn't take him up on it."

"Terrific." Brought down, he thought, this friend proximate rather than close. The same for whom he'd once categorized sarcasm and humor; sarcasm exists as a mean subcategory of humor. High school sophomores taking their initial, faltering steps toward adult sophistication most often begin with sarcasm. Oh? Pete had smiled good-naturedly, then what is your idea of adult, sophisticated humor? Any solely at one's own expense, Dennis replied, unless of course it's self-sarcasm. He shook his head, thinking, Pete's a nice guy except for this emotional hole, like being what they used to call an idiot savant only in reverse. He wasn't going to be much fun to be around now, not for a long time.

"So, who's Carlos, where's he from?"

"Venezuela, I think, but he goes to New York a lot. She met him down in Nassau and they spent a weekend together later in New York."

"You've talked to her, I take it."

"I don't know why Pete has to carry on like this," she continued, "he's acting so stupid. Jill isn't serious about Carlos, the guy lives in

Venezuela!"

"Yeah, but as soon as Pete saw him, knew about him, well, there you are. Who can blame Jill, for Christsake? The guy dumps her six months ago, and as soon as she shows up with another guy, he professes his undying love. I'd tell him to shove off if I were her."

"Yeah," she said.

She was about to make the final left turn, which would put them only two blocks from his apartment. As usual, everything had shut down at nine-thirty, and except for the teen rockers hanging out at the AM-PM, everybody had gone home to the suburbs. The town slept, almost as dormant as the places where he'd been. The closed shops and the half-mall, empty of traffic rendered Hokitika or Timaru to him again, under the autumn Southern Cross. But, no, the bars in Williamstown didn't close at eleven. An occasional lone figure stood out on the sidewalk, maybe taking a step one way or another, but aimless, really. A town straggler, a straggler of society, he lyricized silently, caught undecided forever in the frozen amber light of a middle America summer night.

She pulled into a space in front of the building, a straight up-and-down structure that showcased old green awnings with yellow stripes over the front windows on the upper two floors, his floors. He worked his bags out of the back seat and they headed for the front landing. As they took to the steps, she said, "Be prepared. He looks bad."

"Okay, but let's make it quick. I'm tired and it's been a long trip, right?"

As they entered the hallway, the door to Pete's apartment flew open and he filled the door frame bearlike, almost eagerly. He hesitated, though, and exhaled lightly.

"Why, it's the landlord," Dennis murmured, smiling. "How are you, Pete?"

"Oh, you know. Okay."

"Unhuh." He did look bad, pasty and wild in the eyes. His black hair, always a full shock, a mane in which he showed pride, fell over his brow more unruly than usual. And he looked tired, wiped.

"So, how was your trip?"

"Great, wonderful," one of Pete's favorite words, Dennis remembered after saying it. "I'll tell you all about it."

"Good."

"Yeah. But, I'm glad to be back," he said as he started up the stairs. Marie picked up on his move and followed after him.

"Well, fine," said Pete. "It's good to see you. I look forward to hearing about it."

"Right."

"Good night."

"Yeah, take it easy, Pete."

They reached the second floor, and after Dennis closed the door behind them, he said, "God! He looks terrible!"

"I told you."

"Yeah, well," he shuddered. "I guess I'll have to go down and talk to him sometime."

"Yeah."

"Tomorrow."

He dumped his bags on the landing and peered around at the cramped space. He unconsciously ducked his head into his shoulders and said, "Huh, the missing bathroom makes this place small, like a tenement."

Drywall faced him where the door to his old bathroom had been. A loose piece of wooden molding lay on the floor next to the new wall, allowing light to shine from beneath the edge left uncovered. A sign, he thought, his old bathroom now the landlord's new one adjoined to his bedroom. Small comfort to him now, Dennis imagined.

He grabbed up his luggage again and said, "Well, let's go see my new one." He peeked into the kitchen and then the living room as he passed back through the hallway to the next flight. Nothing had changed, an odd familiarity after so much time and space had passed by him. Upstairs, he inspected the new bathroom.

"Lord, Marie, it's tiny. The shower's ridiculous."

"Yeah," she said softly.

"It's got one of those stingy little water-saving showerheads, too. I hate them."

"Unhuh."

"Damn it, I wish he'd waited."

They headed into the bedroom. He slung the bags down and cruised around the usual clutter of books, papers, and mementos. The stereo had been stacked in its boxes on the steam radiator next to his desk, which was covered with mail. Carny colors easily marked great piles of the stuff as junk, though the stiff white covers of a few formal envelopes peeked out, too, prompting a fleeting grimace. Over in the wall next to the queen-size bed, a new doorway opened into a dark room. White plaster dust coated the floor in front of the door in weakening waves.

"Shit, what a mess," he said. He strode over to the door and looked in. Groping around, he found a light switch, flicked it on, and started to laugh.

"Marie, look at this place. What in the hell did he have in mind?"

The room was perhaps nine feet by nine, made smaller by the space taken up by the closet left over from the old floor plan. Marie leaned in next to him and began to laugh, too.

"Now, what am I supposed to do with this? Look, he left the closet in, for God's sake. What is the rest supposed to be, a guest room?" They laughed together and he said, "I'm going to call it the Franz Kafka room. Not even a window!"

"Or Proust Place," she giggled, "He was supposed to put a window in—well, you know."

"Yeah, he isn't putting one in now. No more renovations."

He stood in the doorway propped up by one outstretched arm, gazing in amazement. She stepped away to the foot of the bed.

"So, tell me about your trip. How was Australia?"

"Oh." He flopped onto the bed. "Australia. Rainy, lots of it. I almost killed Joe a hundred times. We'd be going out the door, he first. I'd close the door and he'd say, 'Did you lock it?' While I was saying, 'Yeah, I did,' he'd test the knob." He shook his head, then smirked, "Of course, I was sweet myself sometimes." Looking at her, "You know, like Richard Pryor said, I'm no day at the beach."

"Unhuh."

"But I suppose the long friendship of the lads will survive. Anyway, we had a good time, mostly. Once we were walking in the Domain Park in Sydney, right, a big town green sort of, with manicured grass, flower beds, palm trees and coconut trees. So, we're walking through on our way back to our hotel and we pass by this bench under a coconut tree with these two guys, winos I guess, sitting there. Well, while we're walking by, we hear this scraping noise up at the top of the tree. We look up and we hear more scrabbling above. Then something falls out. We thought it was a coconut at first, you know, a regional hazard. But as it fell, we could see that it was some kind of animal."

"Oh my God!" she said.

"Yeah, it turned in the air and we could see its tail. Anyway, it hit the ground with a thump, bounced once, and then lay still spread-eagled. It must have fallen fifty or sixty feet."

"Wow!"

"So, it's lying there flat out, and Joe and I look at each other, amazed. Then, I walk over to see it, you know; is it dead, is it injured, what is it? Suddenly, it jumps up and runs around the tree!"

"What? You're kidding!"

"No, it was alive! Just stunned. Well, Joe and I crack up and so do the guys on the bench. I walked to the other side of the tree, and this thing has climbed halfway up and hangs there, looking right at me. So, I shout, 'What happened?' At that, it chattered nasty stuff at me and ran back up to the top of the tree.

"Now Joe and I and the guys on the bench are in hysterics. They made some kind of comment, and we couldn't understand a word with their accents, but we were dying anyway. Joe said it must've been stunned, lying there for so long, but I said, 'No, no, it was embarrassed. It was lying there saying to itself, 'If I just stay still, no one will notice.' I mean it was hilarious, the funniest thing that happened on the trip." As he recalled it, he couldn't keep the laughter out of his voice. "All we had to do was just start to bring it up again, and both of us would die helplessly laughing."

Laughing herself, she said, "What was it, do you think?"

"We decided at that moment that it had to be a wombat to look so stupid. But as it turned out, it was a Common Brushtail Possum, or Brushtail, whatever. We saw it in the Natural Museum later on."

"Oh." By this time, she had taken a seat on the edge of the bed. "So, what were the islands like? How was Fiji?"

"Ah, the Fijis! Tahiti! They were great. But you can read about them in my journals. I'll give you your souvenirs now, though."

He jumped up and knelt down next to the bags. Rifling through one, he pulled out several packages, tightly wrapped, some in colorful paper, others in simple brown wrappers. He took one small brown one and handed it to Marie.

"From the Fijis."

She opened it to find a long length of batiked material, mauve with a gold pattern. "Oh, it's lovely!"

She turned it over, examining it with her hands as he spoke, "See, half the people in the Fijis are East Indian, brought in by the Brits to raise sugar cane. The native Fijiians wouldn't do it. It's designed for you to be able to cut it into a dress, sort of a muu-muu, I guess."

She glanced up at him, "No way, this is to hang, to show."

"Oh. Okay, here's your present from Tahiti."

With characteristic insouciance, she quickly tore apart the pastel wrapper, like a Matisse print, he remembered thinking when he'd first seen it. Just two days before coming home he and Joe had shown off to each other their souvenirs and gifts for the girls, carefully prying off the scotch tape so that they could close them up the same way again.

"Oh, this is nice," she said, without the enthusiasm she'd shown for the batik. She held up another bolt of cloth, cotton this time, egg-white with large black orchids printed all over. Joe had warned him that it might not be colorful enough. But he'd pictured her glorious, dark-tanned skin against the white material and the shimmer of her hair falling below like a long waterfall over black sand banked by the exotic ebony flowers.

"This'd make a nice cover for something."

"Hell no, that's for you to wear. It's a pāreu. You wrap it around yourself like a sarong. Go ahead, try it."

She stood up and cinched it above her breasts, silently critiquing the look as she spun this way and that in front of the mirror. Wearing it while fully clothed beneath, the effect on her wasn't what he'd thought it'd be.

"Eh, I knew you'd like the batik better. It's purple. You always go for purple. "

She grinned mischievously and came over to hug him, "Thanks," and kissed him.

"Oh, well," he said, kissing her back. "Yum, yum," he said, murmuring through their pressed lips. He tumbled her back onto the bed, not believing it after all this time and all that distance. Unbelievable.

"Is that light bothering you?" A corner streetlamp stood exactly at window height, shining a shaft of ersatz moonlight into the eyes of the bed's right-side occupant.

"No," she said, her head turned away into her pillow.

"Are you sure? I can block it off."

"No. I'm fine."

It hadn't been the greatest lovemaking he'd ever known. Then again, neither had his first time, two thousand years ago. It stemmed from the same problem, outsized anticipation. Outrageous anticipation. Too, Marie had been stiff at first, probably sensing his hurry. Well, patience is hard work, he thought, especially after two months.

He jumped out of bed and started to feel around the desk.

"What are you doing?"

"Looking for something to block off that light."

"But it doesn't bother me."

"It bothers me. It bothers me that it could be bothering you."

He found a cardboard rectangle, RT. 80 on one side, PENN STATE crayoned in on the other. He propped it in the window, then said, "How's that?"

"Fine."

"Good." He vaulted back into bed, leaned over her for a moment, then jumped back out. "Not quite."

He adjusted the sign, then slipped under the covers. "There," he said, settling in on his side.

"You're not real sleepy, are you."

"No. Though, I'm really tired. Jetlag, I guess. Are you?"

"Mmm."

He thought she'd drifted off when she spoke again, a surprise in the dark.

"What are you going to do tomorrow?"

"I don't know, sleep I bet. Set up the stereo, look through my mail, read the sympathy cards."

"Are you going to look for a job?"

"I expect I'll get around to it eventually. Give me a break, I just got in the door."

He stared at the blackness above where he knew that somewhere the ceiling lurked. "I suppose I'll have to talk to Pete at some point."

"Yeah, that would be good. He's really a wreck."

"I'm not looking forward to it. So, what are you going to do?"

"I have tap dance after work. I'll come over, then."

"Okay."

Another pause, and Marie said, "I'm falling asleep. I'm going, I'm going . . .."

"Good night," he said, leaning over her, searching around for her mouth. They kissed good night.

"I'm gone."

"Hi, Dennis."

"Pete, how's it going?" The big man ushered Dennis into his apartment, a long narrow string of rooms, brick along one wall, separated by glass doors between the living room and the dining area. Artwork of fine-lined illustrations hung in simple frames. An elaborate reel-to-reel stereo tape deck took up one side next to a cast-iron wood-burning stove.

If anything, Pete looked worse than before. He sat on the edge of a couch with his shoulders slumped and his hands dangling between his knees. His hair showed the mussing of fingers pressed to the forehead countless times, and the rims of his eyes appeared layered with red, new on top of old.

"I suppose Marie told you about me and Jill."

"Yeah. She said you were feeling pretty bad."

"Oh, I can't do anything, I can't sleep. I think about her all the time." He dropped his eyes to his feet.

"I can imagine."

"Thank God work isn't too busy, lately." He looked up, "I have so much to give her, I mean it's right here for her. I can't understand why she won't . . .," his voice quavered.

Dennis shifted in his chair. "Well, you know, Pete. She's been burned before."

"Yeah, and now I'm offering her what she always said she wanted, it's all here for her, a commitment. I'm ready to marry her, I tell her. And she says she can't trust me, that she worked too hard to put me out of her feelings to start it all over again."

He stared in pain at Dennis, silently imploring with raised hands jerking in a gesture of helplessness. Dennis sighed, grimaced with tight lips, then lifted his eyebrows in a sympathetic shrug.

"She's blocking her feelings for me on purpose! I ask her if she feels anything for me at all anymore and she says she won't let herself. Jesus!"

"Hold it. She said she won't let herself feel for you, but she didn't actually say that she doesn't have any feelings for you anymore?"

"She said that later."

"Oh. Okay, but did you press her on it?"

"Yeah. I guess I did."

"Well, all right. You pressed her and she drew back instinctively. Listen, every time you push her, she's going to push back, like a reflex. She probably doesn't even know how she feels about you. I mean, you did drop quite a load on her all of a sudden. She probably was in a state of shock."

"Yeah," he said glumly, again looking into his hands.

"Look, Pete, you've got to face it, too, that you really did a number on her. You two have broken it off, what is it, three times now? And the last time was your turn, am I right? Man, she's been hurt."

"Yeah, yeah," Pete muttered. "Just a few months ago she couldn't walk past me down a hall at work without breaking into tears. Now she won't even talk to me about us."

"Sure, she just got over her crying jags and now she feels she can be in the same room with you without folding up. Then you lay all this on her. Think of how she sees it; you take her to the airport for her trip, one she's taking by herself. You pick her up and seem only mildly interested in hearing what she has to say about Grand Bahama. Then, not long after, you find her with another guy and suddenly you're back in love with her again."

"I wanted to wait until she came back so that she wouldn't have to think about it on her vacation. I'd made up my mind before she left, but I wanted to wait for her sake. I told her all about what I was thinking."

Dennis screwed his face up, skeptical. "Yeah, I heard. But it doesn't really sound all that believable. Whatever, right now she's not buying anything you have to sell after the last few times around the block. You know, 'Fool me once, shame on you; fool me twice, shame on me.' Let's face it, your track record is not good."

As a reply, Pete blew out his breath in an audible huff.

"And this 'Why won't you marry me?' routine is no good, either. You can't hound her like that, you come off looking like you're nuts. You have to present yourself in such a way that those qualities which originally attracted her to you are out there for her to see again. You've got to be normal again."

"I've tried to. But then, whenever I try to talk about us, she throws up a stone wall."

"You tried to! When did you ever try to, and for how long? Two weeks, then you were all over her again? This is the love of your life we're talking about here. You have to be patient if you really want her back. And that means treating her like a friend, an independent friend, for as long as it takes."

Dennis raised his hands to hold off Pete's response. "Allow me to share with you the wealth of my romantic knowledge. Now, I'm not claiming to be any kind of Lothario, but I've had some experience. I've split about fifty-fifty as both the dumper and the dumpee. Shit, one time I told this woman—on our first date, right? And I'd had two quick scotches. I told her that she'd never had to make a comeback. You know, it was a joke; I can't remember the context. Well, she said to me, 'Never had to make a comeback!' almost hissing it. Then she told me that her husband, the editor of a magazine she'd helped build up, he called her into his office one day and told her she was fired. Then he told her that he wanted a divorce so he could marry the new art director. Of course, when she told me all this, I felt like a real asshole. But we mended fences over dinner.

"So, I took her to the movies, and what did we see? *Kramer vs. Kramer*!' God, the courtroom scene comes on, and I look at her out of the corner of my eye, and she's weeping and sobbing . . .."

He shook his head, chuckling as he wiped pantomime sweat from his brow at the memory.

"So, when I took her back to her car we'd left from work because she lived somewhere way out in the country—so I took her back to her car and said, 'Uh, that was fun, let's do it again sometime.' And she said, 'Yeah, but not real soon.'"

He laughed broadly, but saw that Pete's expression remained the same, stricken. He leaned toward him, spreading the fingers of both hands wide open. "What I'm trying to say, Pete, is that anything can happen, and I'm convinced it does, it will, sooner or later. I mean, I was deflated after the disaster of our first date, I never thought I had a chance. And I didn't, but that was just bad chemistry; ours was not a match made in heaven. But we did go out again, several times, until she finally said to me one time, getting out of my car, 'I just want to be friends, okay?' There she was, leaning back into my car to tell me this, and the only thing I could think of saying was, 'You mean, you don't want to be the mother of my children?'"

He burst out laughing again, cutting it short at the sight of Pete's somber eyes, the glazed look about them. Wondering what good he was doing, he forged on.

"All right, that's lightweight stuff. Before I met Marie, I was going with Karen. You never met her. I wooed Karen for eight months, and it was a real French love affair; I loved her, and she permitted me to do so. This went on for eight months until the time that she and her sister went to Italy. Coming back, they got caught up in the air controller strike. So, instead of arriving at three in the afternoon, they came in at midnight. But I had called the airport ahead, so I didn't go out there until ten or so, to get there just before twelve. Well, the two of them came rushing out of Customs, and they're turning around, looking nervous, wondering what to do. See, I was watching them from an upstairs balcony. So, I walk over to the steps, casually stroll down, hands in my pockets, and they jump all over me, hugging me and kissing me with relief.

"I was a hero!" he exclaimed, barking out a laugh. "Their mother told me so later. Well, I figured this was my moment. I took Karen home to her apartment and all night long I talked to her, telling her about all the plans I had of things we could do together, you know, sailing, going to New Hope and Mystic, shows in New York. We were up until four a.m. I mean, man, I was ready!

"The next night she came over to my place and dumped me." He laughed ruefully, amazed about it again. "And, you know, instead of going crazy like I might've times before, I just kidded her about it. You know, I held one of my hands over a gas burner in the kitchen and said in a melodramatic voice, 'Karen, if don't love me, I shall burn myself.' Then I turned on the gas, and yelped, 'Youch! I almost burned my hand!' She laughed, but it was over.

"I felt terrible for a long time," Dennis nodded his head, "like you do. Eventually, I met someone else. This was eleven months later. So, as I was about to meet this new girl for a weekend in Mystic, I got a call from Karen. I mean, I'd literally just finished talking to this new interest, hung up, and the phone rang. Well, that was it. My ego couldn't turn her away, even though deep down I knew it was too late. The other new thing fizzled out pretty much on account of it, and between Karen and me, the roles reversed. I occupied the catbird seat this time around. Oh, it was great and everything, but I finally broke it off. You see, I never forgave her for dumping me in the first place.

"Anyway, what I'm telling you is that she came back after eleven months, not just two weeks. But I'd left the door open, see? I was terribly disappointed. I cried. But I didn't pressure her. I'd never talked to her in the entire eleven months. And I think it can happen with anyone. People's emotions move around, but I can't believe that a person can lose sight completely of a loved one's qualities that originally led to that love.

"But you have to defuse the awareness of the immediate situation," he said while hefting an invisible weight in his hands, "you have to regain her trust. Show her that charming side of you that attracted her before. Be funny, joke with her. Creep up on her."

Pete grabbed his head and said, "1 know, I know, but it's hard. It's so frustrating. I mean, it's all there for her, what she always complained about me before, a commitment. Now this broad won't even talk about it."

Dennis straightened slightly. He said, "That's something else, too, Pete. She may never come around again, and you're going to have to accept that in the long run. Remember what I said about Karen and it being too late. I never forgave her. Jill may never be able to forgive you. Really, maybe you ought to examine your own reasons for wanting her back a little more closely."

"I want her back because I love her," he said plaintively.

"Yeah, I know. But you weren't seeing anybody seriously up to now, and it's often the case that a person thinks of the last love when a new one hasn't appeared. The other thing is, you did find her with that other guy, and then you went nuts."

"Yeah, but that guy's just a joyride for her, a fling. He lives in Venezuela, for God's sake."

"Well, it's good to hear you say that. Regardless, you have to treat Jill a lot more lightly if you want to have any chance of getting her back, which may not happen, too. No matter what, this intensity of yours threatens her. Shit, it's almost like you're grabbing hold of her and shaking her, saying, 'Why won't you love me?'"

Pete glanced sharply up. Dennis felt a coolness creep up the nape of his neck, his hair tingling strand by strand. "You never did anything like that, right?"

Pete dipped his head. "I apologized to her and told her that it'd never happen again."

"Oh, brother."

"I thought you might have heard it from Marie, the way you brought it up. I know she's talked to Jill."

Man, Dennis exclaimed to himself. He shook his head, "Marie didn't tell me anything like that. But, that's bad stuff, man."

"I know, but I'm going crazy over this." He nearly leaped from the couch into midstride pacing in front of Dennis. "A couple of weeks ago, when I knew she was away visiting her parents, I snuck into her apartment and read her diary."

"Shit, Pete!"

"I know, I know, but I had to do it, this impulse to find out if she's seeing anybody else, not just Juan Valdez or whatever his fucking name is, but someone serious. I found out she isn't. I felt terrible afterwards."

"You should have. Pete, you can't do that kind of shit. It doesn't matter if she's seeing someone else. It's none of your business unless she tells you."

"I know." Pete dropped back onto the couch again.

Neither of them spoke for a time. Dennis finally said, "Maybe you ought to consider seeing somebody."

Pete peered up, squinting out of one eye. "A shrink? I don't think so, not right away. These two things happened a few weeks ago. I'm okay for now. I just don't sleep much. Your advice sounds good, like the only thing I can do. I really appreciate your talking to me about this, or letting me talk, anyway."

They heard the outer door to the vestibule opening, and Pete said, "Listen, I'd appreciate it if you didn't tell Marie about the last two matters."

Dennis grimaced, "Sure."

Marie knocked on Pete's door and peeked in timidly. "Hi."

Dennis stood up as Pete said, "Hello Marie."

"How you doing?"

"Oh, okay. Dennis has been patiently listening to my sad song and sharing his wisdom , for which I owe him a beer."

"Oh, good," she replied, smiling uneasily.

"You ready?" Dennis asked her.

"Yeah. See you, Pete."

She followed Dennis as he stalked upstairs, asking him, "So, how did it go?"

"The guy's nuts! He's really screwed the detail. I don't know why

I'm on his side. Maybe I'm not."

They proceeded around the second-floor landing through the narrow hallway to the next flight of stairs.

"But he's so miserable over it all," Marie said.

"Yeah, well, he's not doing anything to make it better with his approach. Distracted, they call it in the professional parlance, obsessive. Whacko, I say."

"Oh, poor Pete."

"Poor Pete? Why are you defending him, of all people? He's not exactly been a prince to Jill, you know."

"I know, but still . . .."

Dennis blew out his breath, rolling his eyes. "Okay, look. Let's forget it. How was your day?"

"Oh, the same as usual, rotten. Harry is driving me crazy with his nitpicking. He keeps returning my articles with criticisms about every itty-bitty little thing."

Dennis plopped down on the bed. "Well, you know, Marie, maybe you should go over your stuff more carefully before you give it to Harry."

"There's nothing wrong with my material. Harry feels like he has to criticize it just so he has something to do, a reason to be there. We do all the work; he doesn't do anything."

"Shit, Marie. I've seen your stuff. It needs editing. Everybody's stuff needs to be edited."

"That's why they have copyeditors!" she said heatedly.

"Yeah, yeah, yeah." He dropped back flat on the bed, rubbing his eyes with his fists. "You know, Marie," he said," I've been back all of twenty-four hours, and it discourages me to think that we've had two fights already in that short time."

"Yeah, well, I might as well tell you now; I've been seeing a counselor while you were away to try to get out of this relationship."

His eyes snapped open, and he sat up. "What?"

"Yeah," she nodded.

"I don't believe it. You're trying to get out of—when did you decide on this? Why didn't you tell me last night?"

"Well," she said, somewhat sheepishly, "it was your first night back. And, I haven't felt good about this for a long time. But every time I'd want to leave, something would happen. First, I got hurt, my leg, then you lost your job, then your dad died. There never seemed to be a good time."

"Oh, Jesus!" He sighed as he stood up. "This is great, just wonderful."

"Gosh, I'm surprised at your reaction. I thought you'd be glad. I mean, isn't that why you went to Australia?"

"Instead of our going to France together. Yeah, I know. And I know that I told you when I left that I'd be gone for two months, then I'd be looking for a new job that'd probably take me out of Williamstown, and that you ought to think about maybe finding a new horse. Yeah, I know what I said," he sighed heavily, mumbling, "But I've said a lot more than my prayers in my life."

She sat down on the edge of the bed, and he jumped up and began to pace in front of her, staring at his feet as he talked.

"Damn, Marie, I know we weren't doing too well before, but I thought a lot about us while I was away. I thought that we might try to work on something; we've been together for a long time."

"I know, but I hated it for a long time, too. I hated you. And I was happy being all by myself while you were gone."

Her tone was one of puzzlement rather than somber as she related these things. He sat dawn on the bed a few feet from her and expelled air. The last to know, of course, he thought, now seeing their fights and the lifeless lovemaking since his return in this light. The operative term was "relationship," the word substituted for love when love was gone. Though, he admitted to himself, what he felt for her wasn't love exactly, he found too much in her to criticize. That's what he decided in the Pacific after having suffered those months under Joe's cold eye, to live and let live with Marie. He realized that she couldn't love him undergoing such scrutiny. But they did comfort each other, truly. She'd called him her best friend many times. He'd entertained the hope that they could grow again into a solid union. Forlorn hope.

"I thought you'd be glad, too," she offered.

"Damn, Marie. Who the hell goes to a counselor to break off a relationship?"

She shifted uneasily, closer to him, then said, "We could go see her together?"

He frowned. Staring at her, he could see both ways up and down the road. The long memories of past times with her, and the fitful struggle to keep them going along in the future. He saw his hopes, then hurts from casual indifference, supplications, betrayals, absence, abject misery, resentment and bitterness, until the time finally would come when after all of it, he wouldn't be able to stand the sight of her.

She stared back at him, wide-eyed with different hopes. He sighed and said, "Aw, Marie," shaking his head back and forth in painful wonder.

Twenty

So why go? The letter lay at bedside, its folds a loose canopy of names, old names.

Ellie stretched, pulled free her twined nightgown, and arched.

Coffee.

Mary Moses, Cheryl Retarsky—Susie Wise, for God's sake. Whatever had become of them? As if she cared.

In her robe, she sliced and toasted a bagel, then hauled the paper in from the stoop, shielding her eyes from the noon sun.

She couldn't remember seeing them at their tenth. Of course, she had gone with Judy and they had hung out with Lanie. And she'd looked for Barry, but he never showed.

She flipped through the weekend glossies and wondered if he would be at this one.

"Yeah," she smiled, with his wife and the kiddoes. That summer had been pretty special, in the car, in the rain, under the covered bridge. She'd had better sex since, of course, but never a better time. Years later in Baltimore he'd spent lunch apologizing for dumping her for his now-wife Laurie. By then, Ellie hadn't cared. Their kids would be teens, now.

Anyway, college always had been her objective back then and the tenth had been no triumph, new body or not. Nothing had changed except for the people who had died—Buddy Miles, Cathy Sprantz. Sad news. Chilling news.

She propped her chin in her hand. Pat Johnson had been killed prom night. All the kids had cried. The Black girl Kelly Lewis died, kidney disease. She'd been in the school's madrigal chorus, so they sang at her funeral. So exotic, the congregation's wailing and singing, the clothes, the raising of hands up in the air to God.

Susie Wise left the pews, that's right! She walked down and hugged Kelly's mom and dad, the kids talked about it all day the next day. Huh! Completely forgotten.

Susie Wise. Cheryl Retarsky. Mary Moses. Would they all go?

Ellie went back her bedroom to get the letter.

Acknowledgments

Short stories seem straightforward enough—individuals deal with dilemmas that begin and end pretty quickly. Ideas for these stories often show up as stray thoughts, memories, or tiny "what-ifs" to be worked out like little puzzles or through deductive logic. Compared to novels, they seem simple, yet enforce the same demands on their writers. Like novels, short stories need to present compelling tales, characters, and denouements but on much tinier canvases. To succeed, these miniatures must move readers to wish for more at story's end rather than to wish it ended halfway through. Any hope of achieving good outcomes depends on engaging the best, honest editors and readers to critique every story before it leaves home. Those who have helped me through the past 50 years, for which I am deeply grateful, are listed below.

My brother George, to whom this collection is dedicated, has read them all, good, bad, and ugly. He has reviewed them for me with severe honesty, and I have followed his advice throughout. His credentials are impeccable, mostly because he is as smart as the Old Man.

My lovely wife Ivey, the most amazing and accomplished editor I have ever known, read the stories and offered suggestions whenever I asked. Her brilliance comes from knowing when to lay it on me and when to lay off.

Jim O'Donnell has read everything as well. My best friend and chosen brother, he never fails to support my efforts despite my spates of bad behavior.

Every one of my other family members read stories and encourage me: my brother Pat, world class musician and writer in his own right; Lucie, my pal with the biggest of hearts who with crystal clarity knows what is and isn't important; Anne, fine artist and all-in altruist who always lifts us up; Ellen, wicked smart, true believer, and our unfailing social justice bellwether. Finally, I offer my thanks and love to my daughter Molly and son Conor, who lead the way in progressive thinking, a great influence on their father.

About the Author

Dan Wallace worked in book publishing for 37 years, most of them at Gallaudet University Press. In 2014, he turned to writing full time. He has written five novels that include *Tribune of the People: A Novel of Ancient Rome* and *Run West: A Novel of the Civil War.* He has completed two other short story collections and also writes poetry and essays that can be read online at his writing exchange *In the Wallace Manner* (inthewallacemanner.com). He lives with his wife Ivey in the Washington, DC, area.

City Stories by Dan Wallace

Summoned to jury duty, a divorced carpenter finds himself neck-deep in a Philly mob case. In the high-stakes urban real estate trade, a young agent makes his move to join the heavy hitters. A housecleaner seeks a unique form of justice for her upscale clients only to run into unlikely speed bumps. Tired of his mundane work buying microchips, a computer tech road warrior stops in Las Vegas for twenty-four memorable hours.

These stories and their companions cast stark light on various characters striving to succeed in circumstances singular to life in urban settings. Far removed from the natural world, people are the game and currency is the currency. For many of those shaped by society's strictures, survival defines success. This collection reveals in striking fashion the means an assortment of individuals use to work out their own formulas for success in the city.

Jury of Peers
City Stories
By Dan Wallace
ISBN 978-1-7335725-0-3 pp trade pb.
ISBN 978-1-7335725-1-0 Kindle E-book
Wylisc Press, Silver Spring, MD
Available at Amazon.com

Novels by Dan Wallace

In the winter of 1861, East Tennessee mountain boy Billy McKinney finds himself marching with the Rebels to engage the Yankees at the Cumberland Gap. He never wanted to fight for the South because his preacher taught him that slavery was wrong. Mostly, though, Billy fears getting killed. In his first battle, he charges through a storm of gunfire and cannon shot amid a driving, icy rain. All around him his friends fall, their mouths bubbling bloody webs of agony. Terrified, Billy decides to run. In his mad dash, he meets up with four runaway slaves led by Bev Bowman. They take him along on their flight, though as prisoner or partner remains to be seen.

Run West is a compelling story of survival in a time of anguish and conflict that no one could escape.

***Run West:* A Novel of the Civil War**

By Dan Wallace

ISBN 978-1-7335725-2-1 trade paperback
ISBN 978-1-7335725-3-8 Kindle E-book
Wylisc Press, Silver Spring, MD

Available at Amazon.com

Publishers Weekly—Wallace's epic novel triumphs with a vivid historical account of ambitious elite Roman politicians and generals.
Library Journal— This thoroughly researched novel is as dramatic and gory as any swords-and-sandals epic and demonstrates how educational historical fiction can be. A wide cast of characters including soldiers, senators, slaves, mothers, and wives expand the reader's understanding of life in this time.
Midwest Book Review—A deftly constructed, exceptionally well written, and consistently compelling read from beginning to end, "Tribune of the People" is a truly impressive novel of the old Roman Empire by Dan Wallace. This is the stuff from which block-buster movies are made!
The US Review of Books: Professional Book Reviews for the People—Wallace's epic tale vividly depicts the opulence and grandeur of the ruling classes while simultaneously detailing the sights, sounds, smells, and squalor of those not born to wealth or position. His battle scenes pulse with excitement as he couples the weapons, tactics, and strategies of war with the carnage they wreak. No less compellingly does he describe the deceit and scheming in the porticos of power as well as the intrigue and hidden agendas in intricate familial relationships. RECOMMENDED.
The Historical Novel Society—A most timely novel; the characters are engaging and well-formed and the story well told. The novel gives you a feel for ancient Rome in the last years of the Republic.

Tribune of the People: A Novel of Ancient Rome

By Dan Wallace

ISBN 97917335725-0-7 trade paperback

ISBN 97817335725-1-4 Kindle E-Book

Wylisc Press, Silver Spring, MD

Available at Amazon.com

www.ingramcontent.com/pod-product-compliance
Lightning Source LLC
LaVergne TN
LVHW091136080826
845145LV00008B/2171

* 9 7 8 1 7 3 3 5 7 2 5 6 9 *